CONSEQUENCES OF SIN

CONSEQUENCES OF SIN

CLARE LANGLEY-HAWTHORNE

THORNDIKE
CHIVERS

FIC
LAN

This Large Print edition is published by Thorndike Press, Waterville, Maine, USA and by BBC Audiobooks Ltd, Bath, England.
Thorndike Press, a part of Gale, Cengage Learning.
Copyright © Clare Langley-Hawthorne, 2007.
The moral right of the author has been asserted.

The text of this Large Print edition is unabridged.
Other aspects of the book may vary from the original edition.
Set in 16 pt. Plantin.
Printed on permanent paper.

LIBRARY OF CONGRESS CATALOGING-IN-PUBLICATION DATA

Langley-Hawthorne, Clare.
  Consequences of sin / by Clare Langley-Hawthorne.
    p. cm. — (Thorndike Press large print mystery)
  "An Ursula Marlow mystery."
  ISBN-13: 978-1-4104-1452-6 (alk. paper)
  ISBN-10: 1-4104-1452-3 (alk. paper)
  1. London (England)—History—1800–1950—Fiction. 2. Large type books. I. Title.
PS3612.A584C66 2009
813'.6—dc22   2008053129

BRITISH LIBRARY CATALOGUING-IN-PUBLICATION DATA AVAILABLE

Published in 2009 in the U.S. by arrangement with Viking, a member of Penguin Group (USA) Inc.
Published in 2009 in the U.K. by arrangement with Viking, a member of Penguin Group (USA) Inc.

U.K. Hardcover: 978 1 408 44120 6 (Chivers Large Print)
U.K. Softcover: 978 1 408 44121 3 (Camden Large Print)

Printed in the United States of America
1 2 3 4 5 6 7 13 12 11 10 09

A12005286587

For Sam and Jasper

ACKNOWLEDGMENTS

I am grateful to a great many people who made this book possible. First and foremost I am indebted to my husband, Tim; my parents, Pat and Paul; and my mother-in-law, Marie, for not only providing me with valuable support and encouragement but also looking after my twin babies, Sam and Jasper, when I needed to make some much needed revisions. Thanks also to my agent, Randi Murray, and my editor, Brett Kelly, for their wise counsel and enthusiastic support. I would like to thank my nanna and grandad who worked their entire lives in the mills and factories of Rishton and through whom I learned much of what I know about the north of England. I would like to thank Peter and Lorena for organizing and sharing my visit to the Orinoco delta, which helped inspire this story in the first place. Finally, this novel would have never been written if it wasn't for the support of my personal cheerleading squad and writing group. To Pat, Gail, Melissa, Victoria, Eva, and Eileen: thank you for your unfailing belief that Ursula Marlow would one day make it into print.

ONE

London, October 1910

When the telephone rang downstairs so early that Saturday morning, Ursula Marlow knew it could only be bad news. Moments later she heard a soft, hesitant tread on the stairs and then a tentative knock at her bedroom door. It was still quite dark. Ursula rose quickly from the four-poster bed, slid her feet into a pair of ivory satin slippers, and grabbed the tawny cashmere shawl that lay furled on her bedroom chair and wrapped it tightly around her shoulders.

"It's all right, Biggs," she whispered through the bedroom door. "I'm awake. . . . I'll come downstairs."

The door opened slowly, Biggs handing her the lamp as she stepped through the doorway.

"Who is it?" she asked.

"Miss Stanford-Jones."

Really, Biggs could be so formal at times.

Ursula descended the stairs, Biggs trailing behind her, dutiful and silent.

She picked up the receiver in her left hand and leaned over the mouthpiece to answer.

"Winifred, is that you?" she asked.

"Sully — thank God. I had to call. Didn't know who else to turn to. . . . It's all frightfully shocking. I don't even know if I can tell you. It's just that there's somebody here — here in my room — and, Sully — I think she's dead."

Ursula was silent. The shawl around her shoulders slid noiselessly to the floor. Biggs, standing a respectful distance away, moved forward and picked it up. Ursula remained standing in the hallway in her white batiste nightgown. She realized that Winifred was right — who else could help her? Who else would have the connections to get this sorted — if "sorted" it could be? Who else but the daughter of one of the richest industrialists in England?

"Don't move. I'll be over as soon as I can." Ursula put down the receiver. "Biggs, run outside and get me a cab."

Biggs raised an eyebrow but complied.

Ursula raced upstairs to dress quickly, without waking Julia, her maid, to assist her. The bedroom was cold despite the coal fire in the grate that still glowed weakly. Not wishing to wake anyone further in the household, particularly not her father, Ursula left the main electric lights off and readied herself in the meager light from her bedside lamp, struggling to lace up the long, straight corset on her own. "Damn and blast!" she muttered under her breath while hastily buttoning up the taupe linen dress Julia had laid out for her the night before. The clock on the mantelpiece struck five. Ursula impatiently pulled on a pair of black gabardine-and-leather boots she found discarded under a chair, leaving the laces half untied as she hurried down the stairway in the semidarkness. Biggs was waiting for her at the foot of the stairs, umbrella in hand.

"Never mind about the brolly!" Ursula exclaimed. "Is the cab here?"

"Waiting outside," Biggs replied calmly. "And, miss, I expect you'll be needing this," he said, handing over her coat and Morocco leather purse.

Ursula held on tightly as the cab thundered its way down the dimly lit streets. A fine mist of rain was beginning to fall. The street lamps along Piccadilly Circus cast a luminous glow in the fog. A delivery cart made its way alongside them, its dark-coated driver hunched over in the cold.

After what seemed like hours, they turned on to Great Russell Street, past the imposing colonnades of the south front of the British Museum, and drove down Montague Street. The wheels grated against the pavement as they came to a halt outside a familiar white Georgian terrace house. The gas lamp on the street corner glowed hazily in the damp fog, but there were no lights on in the house. Ursula had come here many times for meetings of the Women's Social and Political Union, but only during the day. At night it all looked alien and strange.

Ursula met Winifred at one of the first WSPU meetings she attended, held in the Queen's Hall. Although she knew her by sight from Somerville College, their paths rarely crossed. By the time Ursula went up to Oxford, Winifred was already in her final year and her reputation as a radical was firmly established. As Ursula sat listening to Winifred lecture on the rise of the Women's Cooperative Guild, she had felt decidedly conspicuous in her fur-trimmed coat and hat. Her father's name was, after all, synonymous with "oppression of the workers," as Winifred so often put it.

She felt this same conspicuousness tonight as she alighted from the cab. Her world was about to collide with Winifred's, and she wasn't sure now that she was at all prepared for the consequences. She had forgotten her hat and her gloves. The late-autumn wind chilled her to the bone. No doubt she looked ridiculous standing there in the early hours of the morning — her hair still coiled in the loose plait she wore at night. Ursula had spent most of her childhood being cosseted against the weather out of fear she, too, might succumb to the consumption that had claimed her mother. It eventually became almost instinctive that she rebel against such protectiveness. She regretted that impulse now and shivered. What was she doing here?

"Are you goin' to be all right, luv?" the cabbie asked. "Don't look like no one's home, if you ask me."

"I'll be fine," Ursula replied with a smile, and reached into her purse to pay him.

The cabbie looked unconvinced.

"Truly," Ursula reassured him, handing him the coins.

He took them and tipped his cap, muttering something under his breath about "these modern women."

Ursula stepped back quickly from the curb as he drove off.

She walked up and tentatively rang the

13

doorbell, hearing its distinctive metallic clang echo through the seemingly deserted rooms. She wondered if Winifred was sitting upstairs waiting in the dark. Ursula had never been upstairs, but her imagination was quite capable of conjuring up a terrible and macabre scene. The hallway and living room, which she had seen many a time, remained silent and dark. There was no sound or movement. Ursula hesitated, then rang the bell again. Dark imaginings stirred within her — perhaps something far worse had occurred since that hurried phone call, which now seemed a lifetime ago.

The door opened suddenly, and Ursula quickly entered. Winifred stood holding a thick yellow candle. Wax dripped onto her hand, but she didn't seem to notice.

"It's upstairs . . ." she spoke hoarsely.

"Can you bear to tell me what happened?" Ursula whispered, putting her purse down on the hall stand.

"That's the most awful thing about it all," Winifred answered. "I don't know what to tell you. I don't know what happened. I don't . . . I don't remember anything."

"Can you show me, then?" Ursula asked, secretly terrified by the thought of what she might find.

Winifred's ashen face spoke of many horrors. Horrors that would have been inconceivable only a week before, as Ursula sat in this same parlor savoring afternoon tea. Ursula remembered how warm the room felt as the afternoon light streamed in through the windows, how the smell of freshly toasted teacakes and honey filled the room and the chatter of conversation reached a fever pitch over the fate of the Liberal government. As she followed Winifred along the hallway, these images swiftly retreated from her mind, like the sun disappearing below the horizon.

The scene upstairs was surreal and frightening. Everything was bathed in shadows and half-light. The coal fire was still smoldering, and the ebonized mirror above the mantelpiece caught the faint flickers of the dying candlelight. The bedclothes were all tangled about the body. Rough sheets. Heavy gold brocade bedcover. Vermilion-and-black Oriental cushions. It had the air of a sultan's harem, half discovered in the darkness. The window was ajar, and the curtains began to billow open with an unseen breeze, allowing the misty moonlight to enter the room. Ursula could just make out the angular limbs of a young girl. Naked, facedown on the bed. A dark stain beneath her, spreading out on the sheets.

Ursula knew that this was something too terrible for either of them to handle.

"Have you touched anything?" Ursula asked.

"No, I just . . . I just . . ."

"It's all right. Don't . . . don't say anything. We must get help."

Ursula carefully took the candle from Winifred's grasp and then led her out of the bedroom and back down the stairs. Ursula turned on the Rayo lamp that stood on a plain hallway table. Frantic thoughts coursed through her head, but none seemed to stop or make any sense. Her legs didn't seem able to support her weight, and as she gripped the side of the table, she felt the room spin.

She had to pull herself together.

Ursula took a deep breath.

"Why don't you wait in the parlor?" she asked.

Winifred remained standing at the foot of the stairs, a vacant look on her face.

"Freddie . . ."

Winifred showed no signs of having heard her.

"Freddie," Ursula repeated, "where is your telephone?" But there was still no response.

Ursula left Winifred standing at the foot

of the stairs as she walked back along the hallway toward the kitchen. Switching on the electric light, she soon saw the distinctive wooden box mounted on the wall. The shiny black earpiece was off the hook and dangling from a thin cord. Quickly, Ursula walked over and replaced it.

Ursula had never been in this section of the house before. She peered around the doorway from where the telephone was mounted and looked into the kitchen. She couldn't resist turning on the light, almost as a reassurance that nothing else nightmarish or strange resided in the house. The kitchen was comfortingly ordinary, with the cast-iron stove in the corner, the long wooden table in the center, and the rack of plates above the sink. It also looked recently cleaned — only a Huntley & Palmer biscuit tin lay out on the counter. The edge of a blue tea towel was visible in the sink. Ursula wondered (perhaps surprisingly for the first time) how Winifred could afford to live as she did. Clearly she had someone come in regularly to clean — perhaps a local girl — but it was obvious that no one lived in. Given the time, Ursula also realized that whoever the domestic help was, she was likely to arrive early.

"What are you doing?"

Winifred's voice from behind made her jump.

"Nothing . . . just looking for the telephone," Ursula replied cautiously as she turned her head to see Winifred standing in the hallway, her face illuminated by the glow of the kitchen light. Winifred was staring at her with a peculiar expression. It was an unnerving combination of wariness, fear, and anger, like a lioness, crouched down, ears back, deciding whether to attack or flee.

Winifred pointed to the telephone on the wall. "And you needn't worry," she called out, as if reading Ursula's mind. "Mary doesn't come on weekends. My aunt's generosity doesn't extend that far." Without any further word Ursula knew she must strike up all her nerve to face what had to be done.

She lifted the receiver, and the operator answered. Ursula then summoned her courage to ask to be connected to the one person in the world to whom she dreaded being in debt. Lord Oliver Wrotham. Thirty-nine Brook Street, Mayfair. King's Counsel and her father's most trusted adviser. The only man who could help her now.

The telephone call that followed was a blur. Ursula could recall only fragments of the conversation — disembodied voices, mostly her own. She couldn't remember his initial reaction, only a cool voice telling her to remain downstairs — not to return to the bedroom on any account — and then a faintly sarcastic tone that inquired whether her father was aware of her acquaintance with Miss Stanford-Jones. A rosy flush of shame crept up Ursula's face as she recalled her father's warning to her after his first introduction to Winifred: "Never trust a woman who wears brown wool trousers and smokes a Dunhill pipe."

Ursula and Winifred were in the front parlor with the curtains drawn when Lord Wrotham announced his arrival with a hard, sharp rap on the front door. Ursula grasped her friend's hand as they sat side by side on the buttoned-back sofa. Winifred remained seated, her eyes staring at the floor, as Ursula rose to her feet.

"I'll get it," she said.

She walked across the tiles, her footsteps echoing down the hallway. No sooner had she begun to open the door than a tall, dark shadow pushed roughly against her, closing the door almost as soon as it had been opened. In one quick movement, the shadow had removed his coat and hat and placed them on the hallway table.

He straightened up, eyed her with cool, appraising blue-gray eyes, and said, "You need to leave, now."

"What . . . ?"

This was not the greeting Ursula expected. Anger she could deal with. Arrogance she was used to. But this? The command, so calmly made, seemed a bit absurd.

"You must leave now. Did anyone see you enter?"

"I . . . I don't know. . . . Apart from the cabdriver, I don't think there was anyone. But what could that possibly have to do with —"

"You mustn't be seen here. Think of the scandal. Think of your father." Lord Wrotham picked up Ursula's purse and handed it to her.

Winifred came up behind them. "Lord Wrotham. Thank God." Tears started to run down her face. "Damn it all," she said, trying to brush them away with the back of her hand.

There was another knock at the door. This time quiet, soft, almost imperceptible.

"That will be Harrison," Lord Wrotham said. "Miss Stanford-Jones, if you would be so kind as to let him in. He's with the Metropolitan Police — owes me a favor. I told him to come straightaway to secure the scene. He knows you are my client. You are to say nothing to him, do you hear? Nothing. Just take him upstairs. Show him the room and then come immediately back down here to me. Do you understand?"

Winifred nodded wordlessly as she walked past them to open the door.

Lord Wrotham held Ursula's arm tightly. "You'll be leaving by the servants' entrance. I presume that's . . . down here — yes?" He didn't wait for a reply but led Ursula (rather roughly, she thought) along the hallway and into the darkened kitchen.

Ursula stumbled on the linoleum as she tried to wrench her arm free from his grasp.

"But —"

"I want you to leave now," he said with force. "Quietly. There is nothing more you can do here."

Ursula opened her mouth to speak, but something in his eyes made her hesitate. Lord Wrotham placed a finger to his lips silently. It was a slow, almost seductive gesture. His eyes locked in her gaze.

Ursula could hear the sound of firm footsteps on the creaking floorboards upstairs. There was a moment of stillness — no more than the holding of a breath — before she grabbed his hand and pushed him away.

"Don't worry," she said, hoping she sounded much calmer than she felt. "I'm going. But you will look after her, won't you? I only called you because . . . well, I told Freddie that you would be able to help. So you must promise me that you won't let anything happen to her."

"Have I ever let you or your family down?" Lord Wrotham asked grimly.

Ursula had no reply to that.

She opened the back door and looked out into the cold half-light. It was now approaching morning, and an early fog had settled between the railings. The sounds of London waking rose from the damp earth. The familiar grind of wheels along the cobblestones, the distinctive *clip-clop* of hooves as the delivery carts went by, all signals that morning had arrived again upon the city.

Ursula had taken only a couple of steps before Lord Wrotham reached and grabbed her arm again.

"Before you go . . ." he started to say.

Ursula turned around and looked at him querulously.

"Quickly — you didn't move or touch anything upstairs? Tell me you touched nothing."

"Oh, for heaven's sake," she replied, rubbing her arm gingerly. "You'd think I was a child. Of course I touched nothing up there."

With that, Lord Wrotham withdrew and the door closed. A halo of pale blue light spread above the houses to the east. Ursula knew she must hurry. Her father, always an early riser, would be up soon. Biggs would be able to cover her absence for only so long.

Colonel William Radcliffe sat at his mahogany desk staring at a piece of fine white paper and dreaming of Venezuela.

He was leaving the wide expanse of the Orinoco and starting the slow journey along its narrow tributaries. He watched as the oar dipped into the milky brown water and caught on a mass of snarled roots that lay submerged below the surface. He remembered that feeling, the knowledge he had suddenly felt, that death had come among them. Hovering in the heat and rising in his nostrils, its slow-encroaching decay was ever-present. Its eyes darted back and forth seeking him out, like the black jaguar that had been stalking them along the dark and muddy banks for days.

He crumpled the piece of paper in his hand, the shrill cry of the howler monkeys still ringing in his ears. He could hardly comprehend the news he had just received. How can a father bear to lose a daughter? It was a fresh wound, raw and burning, that brought the memory of every past wound back. How could he live with the conviction that her death was related to those terrible events over twenty years ago?

The images returned. It was as if an old fever had taken hold and refused to shake him from its grasp.

"Master!" a voice sprang out of the shadows behind him. "Look here — another one!" Glancing furtively behind him, he saw Bates in the other canoe sitting hunched and muttering over his books and plants. A hand reached out. There was a flash of white sunlight through the canopy and, suddenly, the sight of a brilliant red flower. Bates didn't move. After all these long months, he no longer bothered to look up. They were on a sightless journey now, a witless meandering through the streams and crosscurrents of their polluted minds. The fever was spreading among them. The Indians were drunk. There were rumors of an attack, of white men to be thrown in the river. Bates must be the first, he thought, if I am to survive. Before the darkness comes. Tonight. While Bates is sleeping, perhaps. A knife in the heart. A blow rearing up from behind. He was tormented by these images,

black blood, black night, shadows all around him. I must kill them all, he thought, before they kill me.

A single shot rang out in the study. The sound traveled quickly down the long picture gallery. It woke Fanny Radcliffe, who, unaware of her sister's death in London, was reclining in a wicker chair under the great elm. A bottle of laudanum rolled from her lap onto the soft green grass below. Ears and tails twitched as the two Afghan hounds who'd been asleep beside her raised their pale white heads in languid concern. Fanny stroked the tops of their heads and idly wondered whether her father had decided to accompany the gamekeeper on his rounds after all. Soon this thought dissipated, and Fanny leaned back against the pale yellow pillow and closed her eyes. A strange quiet then followed, and this, too, seemed to travel quickly, like the ominous silence that falls just before a thunderstorm.

Two

Winifred Stanford-Jones sat staring out into the rain. The steady pounding was soothing. At least it wasn't someone's voice asking her again to explain the events of that night. How could she explain what she didn't know? How could she make them understand that she simply had no recollection after falling asleep that night in her lover's arms?

She had met Laura Radcliffe three months earlier. It was a rainy Tuesday afternoon in mid-July, and they found themselves both standing in front of the same painting at the Royal Academy of Art — a Gustav Klimt that had recently come from the Exposition Universelle. *Pallas Athene.*

"It's her eyes, don't you think? She defies you with that stare," Laura had said.

But Winifred was mesmerized by something other than her eyes. It was the gold of the headdress, the gold of the scales of her armor, the staff that she held.

"It's about power. That's what draws you in," she replied.

Their eyes met in tacit understanding. They had then continued to wander through the hall, critically appraising each other as well as the art. There was a final Klimt on display that also caught Winifred's eye. *Silver Fishes.* It was the dark hair that drew her in. Just like Laura's, she thought, all dark and tangled.

A week later Winifred and Laura were lovers.

But how long ago this now seemed; it felt as if a lifetime had passed since their last evening together — although it was scarcely two days. The time since Laura's death had become a blur of questions.

Lord Wrotham had cross-examined her sharply about all the particulars — although her recollections were so hazy she could hardly give him any.

"Where did you dine?"

"I think it was Les Oiseux, the restaurant on —"

He had held up his hand. "I am well aware of it. And you dined there until?"

"About ten o'clock, I think."

"And then . . . ?"

"We attended a private salon, held . . .

well, I'm not supposed to —"

"Miss Stanford-Jones. This is getting extremely tedious. I must know everything."

"Well, at Madame Launois's. Are you familiar with . . . ?"

"I am aware of that establishment. I do not, of course, frequent it."

"No . . . of course you don't."

Winifred almost smiled. The conversation was becoming so stilted and formal — as if the real nature of the questioning that must occur was so distasteful it should be avoided until all common courtesies had been exhausted. She knew then she had to admit everything.

"Lord . . . I mean . . . well, Lord Wrotham, then — I have to tell you now that I remember nothing after that salon. Nothing at all. I remember the tableau — it was a Roman bacchanal feast scene. We drank loads of champagne. Cocktails, too. There was a lot of smoke and —"

"What about drugs?" Lord Wrotham interrupted her.

Winifred fiddled with the enamel box she had hanging about her neck on a fine gold chain. Lord Wrotham's eyes never left hers.

"I . . . I don't really . . ."

"I think we can dispense with the false naïveté, Miss Stanford-Jones. As I said, I am well aware of Madame Launois's reputation."

"Then you know that women only frequent the lower rooms. We aren't allowed upstairs, though I hear the bedrooms are most . . . luxurious."

Lord Wrotham sniffed with distaste.

"An opium den and brothel. So tell me then, what did you ladies indulge in on the ground floor? Opium? Morphine? Cocaine?"

"Whatever took our fancy," Winifred replied lightly, though her eyes flickered with annoyance at Lord Wrotham's tone.

"But that night I had only a little opium," Winifred continued. "Laura wasn't in the mood. She wanted champagne."

"So after you had the champagne . . ." Lord Wrotham prompted.

"Well, there were a lot of people," Winifred continued. "And Laura wasn't impressed. It was too much of a crush. So we left — probably about one in the morning — and Laura came back with me. We fell asleep and then . . . nothing. Honestly, I remember nothing until I awoke and saw her . . . just so still . . . next to me . . . and the blood, of course. The blood was . . . all over the sheets. And everything was so cold." Her chin quivered, and she tried to hold back her tears.

"What time was this? What time did you awaken?"

"It must have been about four o'clock," Winifred said, regaining herself.

"Did something wake you?"

"What do you mean?"

"Voices. An unusual sound. Anything."

"No. Although I think maybe I woke up because of the cold. The window was open. It was so cold. That was what woke me, I think. Yes. That was probably what did it."

"Was the window open when you went to sleep?"

"I can't recall."

"Think, girl — think! Do you realize that in the absence of any other plausible story, the police are going to assume it was you — even if it was in some opium-induced delirium or drunken stupor?"

Winifred flushed angrily.

"Is there anything else you can tell me?" Lord Wrotham demanded. "Any information at all that may help your case?"

Winifred shook her head and looked away.

Lord Wrotham's eyes narrowed before he spoke again. "The police will be going through all this with you in great detail, so are you quite sure there is nothing else you should add? Nothing else you should tell me that could affect the case at all?"

There was an uncomfortable silence. Winifred continued to avert her gaze.

After a moment Lord Wrotham sighed impatiently. "You must understand how this looks."

"I know. I know," Winifred muttered.

"Yes, but do you know who Laura's father is? For God's sake, girl, do you want to join your friends in Holloway Prison?"

Ursula could wait no longer. She'd paced the hallways for nearly a week since that dreadful night and not a word from Winifred or Lord Wrotham. She had been left to stew in ignorance long enough.

Indeed, Ursula Marlow was far more resourceful than some might perceive. It was over a year since she'd left Oxford, and all her plans to be a serious journalist had come to nothing. Just that morning she had received a note from *Ladies' Home Journal* saying they would be delighted if she would write a piece on the latest Parisian fashions. Despite studying political history, Ursula was merely a society girl to the magazines and journals she had approached. Her father now demanded that she find herself a husband, and even the mere mention of her undertaking any form of employment sent him into a rage. He had indulged her enough by allowing her to attend university. Nevertheless, Ursula continued to secretly apply for positions and send out query letters in vain. This morning's post plunged her into a deep depression, made all the worse for Winifred's lack of communication. Ursula restlessly prowled the house, driving Mrs. Stewart, the housekeeper, to distraction.

The Marlow family establishment was usually a model of efficiency. Ursula's father counted himself fortunate that he did not have the "domestic troubles" many of his friends and neighbors had. Apart from Mrs. Stewart and Biggs, the butler, there were only five other members on the domestic staff. There was Julia, Ursula's lady's maid; Cook (whom everyone, in awe, only ever called "Cook"); two housemaids (Bridget and Moira); and Samuels, the footman and driver. Mrs. Stewart and Biggs both prided themselves on the smooth running of the household. Ursula's behavior today, with her demands and counterdemands, fidgets and musings, upset the normal daily routine, causing considerable consternation belowstairs (and much relief when she finally left the house).

After a luncheon of gammon with parsley

sauce, Ursula settled on a course of action.

Once resolved, she hastened upstairs to get dressed.

She instructed Julia to dress her carefully, with the warning that today she needed to look particularly impressive. After many a silk tunic and gored skirt had been discarded and draped over the Japanese silk screen in Ursula's bedroom, Julia anxiously peered over Ursula's shoulder and surveyed the final results in the mirror.

"Well now, don't you look grand? Bonny as always, I'm sure."

Ursula scrutinized her reflection, ignoring Julia's chatter. While the white linen shirtwaist blouse with its square neck and flared sleeves pleased her, she wasn't entirely happy with the diamond butterfly brooch that Julia had pinned to the collar. It made her look young and naïve. Ursula tried to quell her nerves. She knew that getting information out of Lord Wrotham would be difficult. To help Winifred she had to appear to be calm and sophisticated. Ursula decided a plain bar brooch would be more appropriate. Julia scurried over to the rosewood dressing table to open Ursula's silver jewelry box while Ursula smoothed down her skirt, sucked in her waist, and continued to appraise herself in the mirror. Nervously, she drummed her fingertips on the heavy twill of her skirt. Julia stood by waiting for the assessment, holding a wide black satin sash in her hand. Ursula nodded, and Julia wrapped the sash around her, fastening it at the front with a large enamel pin. Ursula then chose a wide-brimmed black velvet hat which Julia secured by means of a large silver-and-amethyst hatpin. It was severe and plain. Ursula took a deep breath. She was satisfied.

"Tell Biggs to arrange to have the motor-car brought 'round."

"Miss, you're never going to drive —"

"No. No. Of course not. Tell Biggs that Samuels must drive me."

"Of course. Can I ask . . . whether . . . whether you might be visitin' his lordship in chambers?"

"And if I was, Julia?" Ursula responded, staring at Julia through the mirror's reflection.

"Nothin'. It's just . . ." Julia replied, her voice trailing off.

Ursula bit her lip. She had little time for Julia's trepidations, but privately she, too, felt uncomfortable. She didn't like feeling an obligation to any man, least of all a man like Wrotham.

Ursula walked slowly down the staircase,

lost in her thoughts. She had been only three years old when her mother had died, and at times she felt her absence acutely. Her father, Robert Marlow, was a self-made man. He believed in the power of commerce above all else. Any other faith he might have had was lost the moment tuberculosis claimed his vivacious wife. His latest indulgence, a new motorcar (a Silver Ghost Rolls-Royce, which Ursula had promptly christened "Bertie"), was designed to show the world just how far he had come, from the backstreets of Blackburn to the grand houses of Chester Square.

As Samuels brought Bertie around to the front of the house, Ursula felt a desperate urge to get behind the wheel. Everything seemed to be taking an absolute age — as if time had deliberately slowed just to thwart her.

Samuels sat in the front and Biggs came outside to open the rear door, a tartan blanket in one hand.

"Really, Biggs!" Ursula exclaimed. "You'd think I was a fifty-year-old invalid!"

Biggs had no need to reply.

She sighed and accepted the proffered blanket. Biggs gave her a pointed look. Ursula could almost read his mind. Although he would never dream of voicing his concern over the propriety of her visiting Lord Wrotham unannounced, he was clearly vexed. Robert Marlow may have pulled himself up by the bootstraps, but he was still aware of those in society who regarded him as nothing more than a "damnable upstart." Mindful of this, he demanded that his daughter maintain the standards of a proper lady. Ursula sighed again. No doubt the Marlow house would ring forth that night with yet another argument on the proprieties of womanhood, and no doubt Biggs would hear this with satisfaction, as he sat by the open fire in the kitchen reading the *Daily Mail.*

Ursula stepped into the back of the car and with a rueful smile tucked the blanket around her legs.

"What will you do when I finally land myself a husband?" she asked Biggs. "You can't follow me everywhere with blankets and pillows."

"When Miss Marlow does find herself a suitable husband, I'm sure we will think of something. . . . Just so you know — your father is due back from his trip up north at six o'clock. Dinner will be at the usual time."

Ursula laughed despite herself. "Right ho! Thanks for the warning. No need to worry, though, I'll be home well before then."

Biggs closed the car door and tapped on the roof, signaling Samuels it was time to depart.

Oxford had been Ursula's dream, a refuge from the profligacy and materialism of London. That she should marry well was not lost on her. Now that she was twenty-two, she was expected to attend all the modish parties, wear all the latest fashions, and make only polite conversation (neither too witty nor too indiscreet) at the frequent afternoon soirees held by her father's great friend and confidante Mrs. Eudora Pomfrey-Smith at her Chelsea home. Ursula was to be wooed and won, but, much to everyone's chagrin, she had so far refused to comply, preferring to dream of past debates in the Junior Common Room of Somerville College rather than winning the hand of one of the many chosen admirers who frequented Mrs. Pomfrey-Smith's parlor.

The London streets were crowded with cars and carriages. The roadworks in Piccadilly Circus filled the side lanes with acrid steam. Newspaper sellers carrying large posters shouted out the latest headlines, while a man with a sandwich board advertising Tomkins & Co. Gentlemen's Tailors paced up and down the pavement.

As they weaved their way through the city, trying to avoid pedestrians, horses, and bicycles, Ursula adjusted her hat and tucked back the stray hairs that insisted on coming loose. One of her chief vanities was her long auburn hair. She loved how, when loose, it tumbled down her back in seaweedy strands and curls. As a girl she'd imagined herself posing for a painting as the enchantress Morgan le Fay, head thrown back, casting her spells.

How silly those girlish dreams seemed now.

The car slowly wended its way toward the Embankment. They passed the WSPU duplicating office on the Strand, where Ursula volunteered one day a week. She and Winifred had spent many an hour standing behind a trestle table cranking out copies of handbills. The memory made her smile briefly until she remembered the look on Winifred's face the last time she saw her, stricken and pale among the dark shadows. Inevitably, the image of Lord Wrotham also intruded, and she tried to push it out of her mind as quickly as she could.

Ursula first met Lord Oliver Wrotham at one of Mrs. Pomfrey-Smith's soirees. She was only eighteen at the time and was immediately struck by his indifference to her. He clearly had not been invited as a potential suitor. She had heard of him, obviously, as her father spoke of his young legal adviser now and again (especially when trade-union matters were concerned — which was more and more often these days). Up until this time, however, the rare visit by Lord Wrotham to the Marlows' Belgravia home resulted in his being hastily ushered into her father's study or the library. Ursula would rush downstairs to catch a glimpse, but the most she had ever seen was the back of a tall, dark-haired man as he passed through the doorway.

This particular soiree had an Indian theme. Mrs. Eudora Pomfrey-Smith ("Dolly" to her close friends) was particularly fond of themes. She was also fascinated by transcendentalism and the possibility of communing with the dead. She had once suggested a séance for Ursula, to try to contact her dead mother, a proposition that had made Ursula's father promptly explode with anger, and it was never mentioned again. The themed parties now took a more subdued and less morbid tone. The servants were instructed to wear suitable costumes (the footmen in turbans, the serving girls with orange silk flowers in their caps), and guests were invited to "dress appropriately." For Ursula this meant she was allowed to wear a raw silk Fortuny dress of dark crimson with a matching garland of silk flowers in her braided upturned hair.

"Ursula, my dear." Mrs. Pomfrey-Smith swept before her. "I simply must introduce you to someone. Now then, tidy your hair — that's it — and for God's sake smile. You spend too much of your time with your nose buried in books, I daresay. Your eyes look positively squinty! Stop frowning and chin up — come on now!"

Ursula allowed Mrs. Pomfrey-Smith to lead her across the room to where a tall man, in his early thirties, stood talking to Ursula's father in hushed tones. As she approached, her father placed a hand on this man's arm, and their conversation ceased. Ursula was used to seeing a flushed face and a hesitant smile whenever she was introduced, so the cool, appraising gaze from this man's blue-gray eyes was unsettling.

"Lord Wrotham, my daughter, Ursula."

She returned his stare without a smile.

"Ursula, you'll have heard me speak of Lord Wrotham, I'm sure. Now you finally have the chance to meet."

Lord Wrotham inclined his head slightly. "It is indeed a pleasure." Yet his tone seemed to indicate something to the contrary.

Ursula smiled coolly. "I am always interested to meet Papa's business associates. Tell me, was it you who helped put those poor strikers out on the streets? One hundred men. With families. I hear most have not found other occupations, and their wives can be seen lining up outside the factory gates in Blackburn begging for food."

Ursula's father sighed.

Lord Wrotham replied, with a ghost of a smile, "I did indeed assist your father with his recent trade-union troubles. I am proud to say that the matter resolved itself entirely to our satisfaction. If we had met the unionists' demands, the Blackburn factory would have been forced to close as uneconomical. Then, my dear, all *three* hundred workers would be out on the streets."

The sound of Samuels switching off the car engine outside the Tudor Gate to the Inner Temple brought Ursula's thoughts abruptly back to the present. She caught sight of Tom Cumberland, the manager of her father's dockside warehouses and one of Mrs. Pomfrey-Smith's chosen suitors, heading toward Bouverie Street, his coat collar turned up against the wind. Ursula groaned and slid down in her seat. Tom ran frequent messages for his employer from the dock-yards, and Ursula did not wish to be seen. The thought of explaining her presence to him was too much. Besides, she generated far too much gossip belowstairs as it was.

Tom passed by quickly, and Ursula clumsily got out of the rear seat, declining Samuels's assistance and instructing him to "wait here for my return."

She smoothed her skirt, checked her hat, and then proceeded to walk into the quadrangle, conscious of the curious glances she was eliciting from the steady stream of black-suited men walking from room to room across the flagstones. Some were in wigs and gowns, others (clerks, she presumed) in single-breasted suits. Puffed-up and straight-backed, they passed by her with supercilious stares. Ursula returned their gaze and straightened herself up. She passed a gilt-edged sign bearing the names of the barristers by stairwell and floor. On the left was written LORD OLIVER WROTHAM, KC — ROOM ELEVEN. She hurried up the stairs.

Ursula squeezed past a crush of people outside room six, and headed up to the third floor, where she knocked sharply on the black-lacquered door with the number 11 emblazoned on it in gold leaf. A small man with a graying beard and a balding head answered. Lord Wrotham's clerk eyed Ursula warily.

"I'm afraid Lord Wrotham is not receiving visitors at this time. If you are a prospective client, you need to see your solicitor, and I must advise you that his lordship is currently much engaged. He is accepting no new cases at the moment —"

Ursula had to interrupt him. "I am Ursula Marlow. You must be" — she glanced quickly at the doorplate — "Mr. Hargreaves. Be so kind as to inform his lordship that I wish to see him immediately."

Mr. Hargreaves didn't move.

"You are no doubt aware of the valuable and lucrative relationship Lord Wrotham has with my father," Ursula continued. "So I feel confident that you will convey my message to Lord Wrotham with great . . . haste."

Mr. Hargreaves still made no move.

"I do not believe that his lordship is expecting any member of the Marlow family today," he said slowly.

Ursula was unimpressed. "Kindly inform him that, nonetheless, a member of the

Marlow family is here to see him — and that the matter is of some import."

"His lordship is currently engaged in very important pretrial matters."

"Mr. Hargreaves, are you deliberately trying to delay me?"

He eyed Ursula again. She felt a flush rise in her cheeks, but she met his gaze with a resolute stare.

"Please come in and wait," he said finally. "I will see if Lord Wrotham can meet with you."

"Thank you."

Ursula entered the doorway and was led down a narrow hall lined with bookshelves filled with leather-bound law reports.

"Please wait here." Hargreaves directed her to an armchair in the far corner of a room at the end of the hallway. Behind the armchair was a row of wooden filing cabinets, and on the clerk's table stood a tall stack of paper bundles, each tied with pink ribbon, in a wire tray.

Hargreaves knocked on a door to the right of the table and then exited silently, leaving Ursula to sit down and try to compose herself. She had rehearsed the conversation in her mind earlier in the day (all morning, to be exact), but now she couldn't recall how she intended to start or finish — not even the questions she had so carefully thought out. Her mind was blank.

She had fully expected Lord Wrotham to keep her waiting. Fully expected that he would refuse to discuss the case with her or would send a message to this effect via his clerk. Instead, however, he appeared in the doorway almost immediately. Ursula hadn't even time to check that her hat was still on straight. He seemed surprised. Perhaps a little unnerved. Vulnerable, even. It was as though she, suddenly trespassing on his domain, had caught him unawares.

"Miss Marlow," he said. "This is indeed a . . . well . . . unexpected, nevertheless."

"I am here to discuss the Stanford-Jones case. Has any progress been made?" Ursula heard herself speak quite clearly and forcefully, even though she felt her last shred of confidence waning under the guarded stare that met hers. She had always thought of Lord Wrotham as a tall and aristocratically thin man (all taut spine and stiff upper lip), but now he seemed arched and gaunt. His hair, normally combed back smoothly in place, was beginning to fall forward across his eyes. He had the look of someone who had just received a shock and was still recovering.

"Good heavens!" Ursula cried out involuntarily. "What on earth has happened?!"

Her mind leaped to all sorts of conclusions. Freddie dead in a gutter. . . . Her father murdered in his train compartment. . . . Her imagination needed very little encouragement to run away with itself.

Lord Wrotham raised his eyebrows. His composure was quickly returning. "Happened?"

"Have you had bad news? Has something happened to Freddie?"

"Freddie?"

"Winifred."

"Miss Stanford-Jones? . . . No, nothing else has happened to her as far as I'm aware."

"Then what?" Ursula asked. "You look as if you've received the most awful news."

Lord Wrotham ran his long fingers though his hair, smoothing it back into place.

"Please, Miss Marlow," he replied. "Spare me the dramatics and come inside."

Ursula followed Lord Wrotham into his richly furnished office. Above his leather-top desk hung a magnificent tapestry, like an Edward Burne-Jones painting, only intricately and beautifully woven. The scene depicted an ethereal-looking woman stepping forth from the shadows of a tower, the scales of justice precariously balanced in her hands. The tower was dark and covered in ivy, while the lady was bathed in a soft golden light as she emerged from an archway. Ursula had expected to find Lord Wrotham in a stark, austere room with nothing but a framed copy of his degree from Oxford's Balliol College on the wall.

She looked around further, trying to adjust herself to each new element she encountered. There was an antique terrestrial globe mounted on a pedestal, a stuffed blue-and-yellow bird encased in glass, and a display cabinet containing some kind of illuminated manuscript that was almost hidden in the corner. In her mind, with his streamlined and finely cut features, Lord Wrotham was like a machine in which every fragment, every muscle, seemed efficient and unyielding. That he should have chosen to surround himself with objects of such rich sensuality unsettled her.

In the center of the room were two leather armchairs for clients.

"Please take a seat," Lord Wrotham said.

Ursula removed her hat and gloves and sat down.

Lord Wrotham calmly walked over to the far side of the room, replacing a red and tan book on its shelf.

"Tea?" he asked, turning toward her.

Ursula shook her head. "I guess we must start with the usual pleasantries," she said. "But I feel that under the circumstances . . ."

Lord Wrotham walked in front of her and reached down to open a silver cigarette box on his desk.

Ursula was piqued but determined to remain calm. "I want an update on the Stanford-Jones case," she said. "As you refused to answer my letters and I had no response to my calls, I believed that a personal visit was in order."

"Indeed." Lord Wrotham lit the cigarette and sat down behind his desk.

Ursula noticed there was another doorway, almost obscured by the tapestry above Lord Wrotham's desk. The door opened a fraction and then shut quickly. Mr. Hargreaves, no doubt.

There was a long, cold pause. Lord Wrotham did not speak. Ursula smoothed her skirt, trying to control her anger.

The clock on the mantel struck half past two. Lord Wrotham reached into his waistcoat and pulled out a fob watch. He flicked open the case to double-check the time.

"You have an appointment?" Ursula asked, irritation growing in her voice.

"I am due back in court at three."

"But of course," she murmured, her jaw

starting to clench from the effort of having to remain civil. Impatience and frustration were starting to get the better of her. The door opened again, as if on cue, and the balding head of Mr. Hargreaves appeared. Hargreaves coughed, to which Lord Wrotham responded with a peremptory nod of his head.

Ursula caught a glimpse of the anteroom with its mirror, washbasin, and stand. Lord Wrotham's wig and gown were hanging on a coatrack. Hargreaves sighed and closed the door.

"My apologies," Lord Wrotham said calmly. "Mr. Hargreaves is not known for his subtlety."

"Nor his manners," Ursula responded dryly. "He certainly made it quite clear that I had no business being here." She shifted in her seat.

"Now then, about that tea . . ." Lord Wrotham began to say.

Ursula rose to her feet. She'd had just about enough of the small talk.

"Have you or the police questioned Miss Stanford-Jones about what happened?" she asked, her lace-up ankle boots making a *tap-tap* sound on the polished floor.

"Please sit down," he said more sternly.

"Pray remember," she replied tartly, "that

I am not one of your dogs. You do not need to wave your hand and command me to sit. I am quite capable of deciding whether to sit or stand on my own."

She cast him a defiant look, but Lord Wrotham, taking a slow draw on his cigarette, appeared not to notice.

She was still standing when he finally said, "Miss Marlow, naturally my colleagues at the Metropolitan Police have had a number of discussions with Miss Stanford-Jones. Unfortunately, I am not at liberty to disclose —"

"Then what *are* you at liberty to disclose?!" Ursula interrupted crossly.

"My dear," he began smoothly, "you must understand —"

Lord Wrotham stopped in midsentence. Deciding to take a different tack, Ursula had walked over to his desk, come around to his side, and sat down on the edge, less than a foot away from him. In her doing so, her skirt brushed lightly against the back of his left hand. Lord Wrotham sat stock-still. Ursula sensed the power in her trespass, and it was intoxicating. Lord Wrotham lifted the cigarette to his lips and let it hover for a moment in midair. He raised an eyebrow slightly. Ursula leaned forward.

"I was rather hoping that you would have

more information," she said with the merest hint of a smile.

"Really?"

"Yes — I felt sure that you would have had something for me." She stared at him, acutely aware of the narrow space between them — of the starched edge of his collar and smooth skin of his throat — so close. He smelled of tobacco and bergamot. A heady combination.

"I have nothing that can answer the real question you have," Lord Wrotham said, his voice dispelling the tension.

"And what question is that?"

"Whether she really murdered that girl."

Ursula rose quickly. She had trespassed too far.

"Lord Wrotham . . ." Ursula began, raising a hand to her throat to steady the indignation in her voice. "I can assure you that Miss Stanford-Jones is entirely innocent! I know her! There is no way she could ever be capable of such a thing!"

"Miss Marlow," Lord Wrotham replied, extinguishing his cigarette with a light rap on the edge of the silver ashtray, "I have seen dozens of cases where people have done the very thing no one thought them capable of. Prima facie, even you must admit, the evidence against Miss Stanford-

Jones doesn't look good."

"Looks can be deceiving," Ursula retorted.

"I suggest you leave that for the Metropolitan Police to decide," he responded dryly.

"Surely there must be something — anything — to mitigate the circumstances?"

"Well, attending Madame Launois's establishment certainly wasn't one of them."

"Madame Launois?" Ursula frowned. She felt as if she were suddenly under cross-examination.

Lord Wrotham's eyes bore into her.

"I have no idea what you're talking about," she answered frankly.

Lord Wrotham leaned back in his chair and clasped his hands. Ursula suspected he had been trying to draw her out and was irritated.

"What about this establishment?" Ursula demanded. "Could it be that someone there had a motive for murdering poor Laura?"

Lord Wrotham shrugged. His interest seemed to have waned as quickly as it had flared.

"Surely there must be something!"

With a quick glance at the clock on the mantel, Lord Wrotham rose to his feet.

Ursula tried to keep her frustration in check. Clearly, as far as Lord Wrotham was concerned, their interview was over. Ursula remained seated for a moment, tapping her fingers along the brim of her hat, before she got up from the chair.

Their gazes met. Lord Wrotham took a step closer. Ursula drew back slightly. Wary.

Lord Wrotham extended his hand to draw her toward the door.

"Mr. Hargreaves will show you out."

"I'm sure he will," Ursula replied tersely.

"Miss Marlow, you are far too young and inexperienced," Lord Wrotham said as he opened the door for her, "to be involved in such a sordid mess. I advise you to leave well enough alone."

Ursula's eyes narrowed. Lord Wrotham held the door open, and out of the corner of her eye she could see Mr. Hargreaves straightening his black waistcoat.

"I'm sure you must have plenty of other amusing diversions," Lord Wrotham continued with what was now unbridled condescension. "For your father's sake, why don't you just run along home and forget all about Miss Stanford-Jones."

Of all the things Lord Wrotham had expected in response from Ursula, the sharp slap to his face was not one of them.

THREE

After Ursula had stalked out the door, Lord Wrotham returned to his desk and sat down. He moved aside some papers to reveal a small and tattered suede-covered volume. It was lashed together with a separate strap that was so worn it had lost all pigment. He tapped his fingers on the cover of the book thoughtfully.

The book was a diary of sorts. Part actual travelogue, part travelogue of the mind. On the front page the words *The Radcliffe Expedition — A Journey Down the Orinoco* had been inscribed in fine calligraphy. A later handwritten note, cramped and spidery, had crossed out the last part and substituted the words *A Descent into Hell*. The early diary entries covered the expedition with a botanist's eye including beautifully detailed sketches of red mangroves, orchids, and bromeliads. Turning each page was like taking a step out into the light as the author passed from under a dense, dark canopy. As the entries continued, however, there was a progressive deterioration. The sketches became erratic and distorted, often featuring members of the expedition in gross and distended proportions. The last entry made was dated April 11, 1888, the day of the infamous massacre. No more entries followed, except for two roughly drawn sketches: caricatures that were almost faded from view on the inside back cover of the diary. One was of a white man, bound and gagged. His eyes, although open wide, were bleeding. The other image was of a grotesque figure in a mask, hunched over with all limbs touching the ground, rather like a monkey.

A small, black-edged card had been slipped between the first two pages of the diary. On it was written, *The consequences of sin cannot be denied. The child that is born to you shall die.*

The diary had arrived that morning by Royal Mail formally addressed to "The Right Honorable Lord Wrotham, KC." Mr. Robert Marlow, identified as the sender, had enclosed a handwritten note, penned with obvious urgency: *This arrived anonymously this morning, and I had to act quickly to keep it from Ursula's prying eyes. Arrange*

*a meeting for when I return, and do not yet
inform the others.*

Determined not to waste any more time,
Lord Wrotham called in his clerk and asked
him to schedule an appointment with Mr.
Robert Marlow as soon as possible.

The sun faded below the chimney tops, and
the chill of evening soon set in. True to his
word, Ursula's father arrived in Euston on
the six o'clock train. On account of Ursula,
Samuels had to hurry to be at the station to
meet him. As soon as she got home, she
went straight upstairs to change, refusing all
Julia's offers of assistance. There she had
remained, sitting on a silk-covered stool in
front of her dressing table staring at the mirror. As she often did when angry, she fixed
her gaze on her own reflection and tried to
force the "other self" she saw to regain some
self-control, while hot tears of frustration
streamed down her cheeks.

She hadn't felt this discomfited since the
day she met Alexei, and today's humiliation
in Lord Wrotham's chambers brought back
all those painful memories. Alexei was the
son of one of Winifred's old tutors at
Oxford, Anna Proznitz, who had fled Russia
in the wake of the Kishinev pogrom of
1903. Alexei had followed his mother to

London after the failure of the St. Petersburg Revolution in 1905. A fervent Leninist, he remained in London after the Third Congress of the Russian Social Democratic Party to help coordinate support for the Bolsheviks among Russian expatriates.

Even now Ursula could recall every detail of their short time together. How she and Winifred arrived at Anna's apartment in Fitzrovia to find him seated in the front parlor, his dark, angular face buried in a book, feet propped up on the desk under the window. He wore navy blue pants, scuffed leather boots, and a khaki shirt with the sleeves rolled up, suspenders showing. As Ursula entered the room he looked up, peered over the top of a pair of wire-rimmed spectacles, and laughed. Ursula had instantly felt self-conscious. Dressed as she was in a hand-embroidered silk pongee walking suit and wide-brimmed straw hat, she was the epitome of the bourgeoisie. Later that morning, angered by his snide comments about "rich heiresses playing at politics," Ursula stormed out of the apartment. Leaning from the third floor window, Alexei then shouted out a very public apology and tossed down a copy of Lenin's pamphlet *To the Village Poor* with an invitation to attend a public meeting of the

Bolsheviks. So began a heady, passionate, and tumultuous relationship that Ursula would now, nearly two years later, rather forget.

The front door opened, and she was jolted back to the present. She heard the familiar tread of her father's footsteps in the hall as he called out a greeting to Biggs and Mrs. Stewart. Ursula rose from her seat, hastily poured some cold water into the washbasin, and splashed it over her face. She then patted her pale skin dry with an Irish linen face towel and looked at her reflection again, wondering if she could make herself look sufficiently presentable to avoid any awkward questions from her father.

"Can I come in now, miss?" Julia asked through the bedroom door. "We need to get you dressed for dinner."

"No — don't worry. I'm going down now to meet Papa first."

Ursula put a dab of Floris's Rose Geranium perfume behind each ear, then walked over to the door and opened it.

Julia was still standing at the door in her apron and cap.

"I'll come back up and change before dinner," Ursula reassured her. "Why don't you lay out the lavender silk — it's Papa's favorite."

"Of course, miss." Julia bobbed a perfunctory curtsy and hurried off to iron said dress.

Ursula's father would be expecting his usual greeting — a shout from the top of the stairs and a wide smile as she came running down to meet him. Ursula would not disappoint him. She peered over the banister at the top of the stairs and saw her father standing below, looking weary from his time in the North.

"Papa!" she cried, and he glanced up with a smile.

Robert Marlow handed over a charcoal gray overcoat and felt hat to Biggs, as Samuels came in carrying a small traveling trunk. He had been away for two days visiting his Lancashire mills and factories, a visit prompted by a growing sense of unease. There were rumors of labor unrest and rising militancy among the trade unions. Although her father tried to keep most of his fears from her, Ursula knew there was already talk of the government introducing a minimum wage. Ursula had heard her father speak many times of the need to stand firm against the liberal threat. To give an inch, he said, would be to release the tide of socialism.

"Glad to be home?" she asked, kissing him

on the cheek.

"Aye, glad as always to be back."

Despite his words he looked tired and worn, prompting Ursula to feel a sudden pang of guilt.

He patted her hand. "Don't you go worryin' about me, lass — and no botherin' me neither." He rubbed the back of his neck and yawned. "Eigh up, I nearly forgot, Tom said he may be droppin' by. Wants to speak to me before we meet McClintock tomorrow." He yawned again.

Ursula groaned, but her father merely continued. "You might have to entertain him for a bit. I've a couple of telephone calls to make."

Just as Ursula started muttering excuses, the doorbell rang.

Her father kissed her forehead lightly. "Don't worry, I won't be long."

Ursula sighed.

"Biggs," her father called out as he walked into his study, "tell Cook we'll be ready for dinner at eight."

Biggs nodded and strode down the hallway to open the front door. Ursula forced a smile before turning to greet Tom Cumberland as he entered the house.

Tom handed over his hat and coat to Biggs and followed her into the front parlor.

"Please take a seat," she said politely as she sat down on the winged sofa. "Papa will be joining us shortly."

As Tom sat down opposite her in a leather armchair, Ursula noted that, as usual, Tom had used far too much hair oil. His flaxen hair glistened in the glow of the standard lamp beside him.

"Miss Marlow, you're looking as lovely as ever," he began before Ursula dismissed him with a wave of her hand.

"Spare me your compliments, Tom, really. They are quite unnecessary!"

Tom was the kind of man who grated on Ursula's nerves. A regular guest at Mrs. Pomfrey-Smith's soirees, he had sweet-talked all the girls of Ursula's acquaintance with his smooth charms. At thirty-five, he had spent most of his life at sea, as his tanned face and sun-bleached hair attested, and was full of stories of his adventures, designed to amuse "the ladies." Unfortunately, Ursula was not so easily won over. Despite her father's partiality (Tom had raised himself up from nothing, just as Robert Marlow had), she found his attentions exasperating.

Tom brushed his mustache lightly with his fingers.

"Your father's friendship is of supreme

importance to me. I only hope to repay his great kindness by honoring his daughter."

Ursula bit her lip and paused before replying. "Of course, Tom. You know that my father appreciates everything you do for him."

"Be assured I would likewise do anything, anything at all, to assist his most beautiful daughter."

Ursula stifled a laugh before scrutinizing Tom's face carefully. Maybe he could be of some use after all. She hesitated for a moment and then said, "Actually, there is something you may be able to help me with. You see, a chum of mine has got into a spot of bother, and I've been trying to help her." Ursula deliberately kept her tone light. "Only a lady's name keeps coming up, and, well . . . maybe someone more worldly than myself would know who she is. . . ." Her voice trailed off.

"Please go on," Tom urged her.

Ursula feigned embarrassment. "It's a tad awkward, you see, as I think the lady in question may not . . . may not be entirely respectable."

Tom leaned forward in the chair. "Rest assured, Miss Marlow, I am all discretion."

Ursula lowered her voice conspiratorially. "Have you heard of a Madame Launois?"

Tom instantly paled.

"I can see from your face that you have heard of her, and clearly she is not respectable," Ursula said hurriedly.

"Indeed she is not," Tom replied, color slowly returning to his face. "She runs an establishment that is nothing short of a den of iniquity . . . or so I hear."

Just as Ursula opened her mouth to speak, her father strode into the room.

"Tom! Glad you could make it. Need some advice on McClintock!" his voice boomed. Tom leaped to his feet and shook her father's hand eagerly. "Only too glad to be of service, sir!"

Marlow turned to Ursula. "Best go up and change for dinner, lass. No need to hang about listenin' to all our business prattle."

Ursula, piqued at her father's patronizing words but nonetheless eager to be rid of Tom, got to her feet.

Tom reached out and took her hand in his. "Miss Marlow, if I can be of any assistance in this matter — any at all — please do not hesitate to ask."

Robert Marlow raised an eyebrow.

"I only hope we can continue our most interesting conversation," Tom went on. "Another time?"

Ursula winced at his eagerness. She was

already beginning to regret giving him even the slightest excuse to interpret her behavior as a sign of encouragement. She extricated her hand with a murmured thank-you and, careful to avoid her father's gaze, quickly exited the room.

An hour later Tom departed, and Ursula joined her father in his study as they waited for Biggs to announce dinner. Robert Marlow stood beside his English oak desk, harrumphing as he opened various pieces of correspondence with a flick of his ivory-handled letter opener. Ursula smiled, reassured as always by her father's presence, and picked up the latest copy of the *Strand.*

Eager to put the day's humiliations behind her, she was already engrossed in the latest Arthur Conan Doyle story, "Through the Veil," when Biggs knocked, entered, and announced that dinner was served. Her father gave Ursula a quick prod to get her to move from the chair before they made their way into the dining room.

As always, they sat facing one another across the long mahogany table. Mrs. Stewart had arranged a beautiful centerpiece filled with Christmas lilies and had set out the silver service on the sideboard for after-dinner coffee. The copper-and-brass chandelier over the table shone brightly with the recently installed electric lights.

Ursula toyed with her soup spoon while her father sat reading over a letter as he ate. He seemed preoccupied, and there was an unusual silence as they proceeded from the soup to the ptarmigan pie.

"Papa — is something troubling you?" Ursula finally asked.

"Hmm?" Her father looked up from his plate and indicated to Bridget to take it away. Ursula saw Bridget's look of quiet dismay. Belowstairs, Cook would demand to know why her master's favorite dish remained only half eaten.

"*What* is the matter?!" Ursula asked, putting down her knife and fork in exasperation.

"Why do you think anything is the matter?"

"Because you've hardly eaten anything. You've hardly said anything. It's not like you. Was everything okay at Oldham?"

"Everything was fine."

"Then what?" Ursula was uneasy. "Did George say anything?" George was manager of the Oldham mill.

"Only that Shackleton should be shot."

David Shackleton was the local member of Parliament and a member of the Labour

Representation Committee. He and Robert Marlow had experienced their fair share of run-ins in the past.

Ursula fell silent again.

"Is it something to do with that letter? Have you received bad news?" she asked after a bit.

Her father hesitated.

Bridget entered the dining room carrying two plates of stewed plums and custard.

"I think we may wait till later. Thank you, Bridget," Ursula said.

"Let's go sit in the study," her father answered finally. "We can discuss it there."

Ursula rose to her feet. In the electric light that shone overhead, she suddenly noticed how old her father looked. How the graying of the hair at the temples seemed accentuated. How the lines around his eyes and mouth seemed deeper, more entrenched. It was as if old age had found a place to settle and had decided to stay.

She followed her father into his study, taking care to close the heavy wood-paneled door behind them. Once inside, she tossed off her shoes and curled up in the leather armchair in front of the roaring fire. In her father's presence, the turmoil that had followed the interview with Lord Wrotham seemed to fade away.

Her father sat down heavily in the chair opposite.

"I'm sorry, love," he said. "But I've a great deal on my mind at the moment."

Ursula shifted in the chair uncomfortably.

His gaze moved to the fire and then back to Ursula. He seemed to be reminded of something long forgotten.

"Your mother . . ." he started absently. "How you do remind me . . ." He gazed at the fire again and fell silent.

"Papa . . ." she prompted.

He sighed and sank back into the chair.

Ursula got up from her chair and knelt down in front of him. "Papa, please tell me. . . ."

This seemed to bring him back to the present.

"Laura Radcliffe," he said after a hesitation.

"Laura . . . Radcliffe?" Ursula replied warily.

"Don't play silly buggers with me, lass," her father replied sternly. "I know all about your visit to Miss Stanford-Jones's house. Wrotham told me everything."

"Oh." Ursula waited for her father's anger, but it never came. Instead he said, "I knew Colonel Radcliffe many years ago. . . . Laura was his eldest daughter."

Ursula frowned. She had never heard her father mention the name Radcliffe before.

"That letter was from his wife," he continued. "She writes to tell me that the colonel is dead. Took his own life." Her father sank back in his chair disappearing into the folds of shadow and firelight. "When he received the news about Laura, he shot himself."

"God, how awful!" Ursula cried. "Did you know him well? Did you know Laura?"

She wanted to bombard him with questions. Instead something in her father's eyes, something dark and enigmatic, made her halt. Normally she could interpret his moods and gauge his thoughts just by reading his eyes. Tonight, however, they were suddenly inscrutable.

"Oh, Papa, I'm sorry." She could think of nothing else to say.

Her father sighed, clasping his hands in front of him.

"We must tread carefully," he said slowly. "Very carefully."

Then, as if some terrible memory reemerged, he leaned forward and spoke with a frightening intensity.

"I couldn't bear to lose you like I lost your mother. I couldn't go on —"

"Dear Papa!" she cried, clutching his hand in hers. "Never speak of losing me!"

■ ■ ■ ■

Ursula was in bed reading H. G. Wells's *Ann Veronica* when she heard her father leave. She was used to his nocturnal wanderings (they had certainly ebbed and flowed over the years), but up till now she had never thought to question them. Although she guessed that Mrs. Pomfrey-Smith's house was his likely destination, she felt an unusual pang of concern. Her father had always seemed so strong and capable, but tonight he had shown a vulnerability that worried her. In spite of this, or maybe even because of it, she was determined to use his absence to undertake a few investigations of her own. Her father's relationship with Colonel Radcliffe intrigued and puzzled her. She had to know more.

Ursula climbed out of bed, wriggled into a shirtwaist and skirt, and pulled on a pair of woolen stockings. By now the fire in the study would be out, so she grabbed a cream knit cardigan from the chest of drawers and slipped her feet into a pair of soft leather shoes. She then leaned against the bedroom door and listened intently.

The grandfather clock struck midnight. Ursula quietly opened the door and crept out onto the landing.

The house was silent and dark downstairs. She did not doubt, however, that Biggs was awake. He was probably double-checking the wine cellar before turning in for the night. Mrs. Stewart for her part was a sound sleeper, and Ursula felt confident that she would not disturb her. Sure enough, Ursula could hear the distinctive grunt of her snores as she tiptoed past the stairs that led to the servants' rooms in the attic.

Ursula carefully made her way downstairs. It was a clear night, and the pale moonlight filtering through the top-floor windows helped guide her path. She entered her father's study, closing the door softly behind her. Ursula could hear the wind rattling the railings outside. Through the bay window, she could see the dark silhouette of oak trees waving and groaning against the sky. She closed the curtains and turned on the leaded glass reading lamp on her father's desk.

The day's correspondence still lay scattered on top of the desk. A bill from her father's tailor. A request for additional deliveries from a New York garment manufacturer. A summary of bank-account details in Geneva. Ursula perused these letters quickly, looking for the letter from Colonel

Radcliffe's wife. It lay in the middle of the pile, handwritten on thick ivory paper.

Robert,
I couldn't bring myself to call with such bad news. No doubt you have heard the reports of Laura's death. It seems I now must bear the loss of a husband as well as a daughter. William took his own life three days ago. You know he has never fully recovered from what happened in South America, and I fear that Laura's death precipitated another one of his melancholic bouts. I should have seen it was coming. Should have spoken to you earlier. You were the only one who could ever reach him when he was in those deep black moods. I feel I failed him in not seeking your advice sooner. That dreadful expedition was much on his mind. I wish I had sent for you before it was too late. Robert, it is too much for me too bear.

Please tell me this is not the start of all that we feared.

Ursula leaned back in the chair and frowned. The final line of the letter made her shudder. What was it that they feared? What was her father's connection with

71

Colonel Radcliffe? Why did this expedition haunt the colonel so? More important, did it offer any clues into Laura's death?

Ursula put the letter back down carefully on the desk. She then got up and went to the bookshelf, scanning for her father's copy of Kelly's *Handbook to the Titled, Landed and Official Classes.* It was on the bottom shelf, next to the latest editions of Burke's *Peerage* and *Landed Gentry.* Robert Marlow wanted to ensure he always knew whom he was dealing with — socially as well as in business. Ursula pulled out the *Handbook* and flicked through the pages. There was a brief summary under "Radcliffe, William (Col.) VC, DSO": *Distinguished battlefield commander in the Transvaal and Sudan. Founding member of the Explorer's Club. Amateur anthropologist. Leader of three expeditions to South America.*

It was the last line of the summary that caught her eye.

Sole survivor of the massacre that occurred on April 11, 1888.

Ursula closed the book and sat down heavily in her father's leather armchair. So much seemed to center on this expedition, and yet she couldn't understand how her father was involved. Ursula had never even heard her father speak of Colonel Radcliffe or his family. He never intimated that he had any interest in South America. Indeed, she had no cause to suspect that her father had *any* other interests beside his business endeavors. Something tickled at the back of her mind, though . . . something from her childhood. She couldn't quite remember, but there was something, nothing more than a feeling, that convinced her that the expedition was the key. Ursula hugged her knees. Her head was starting to ache. Could it be that Colonel Radcliffe's fears were for his daughter? If so, was Laura's death somehow related to the events on the expedition nearly twenty years ago? Her mind began to drift.

She yawned, fighting back sleep. She heard the clock strike one and closed her eyes, trying to clear her mind. Sleep overcame her.

Ursula's dreams were filled with misshapen shadows, wraiths and shades from some surreal underworld that seemed to be waiting for her just on the periphery of sight. She stood alone in a hallway lined with black wooden doors. Each doorway she stepped though held worse horrors than the one before. Huge sightless eyes, gouged and red, peering out from a woman with grossly distorted lips. A naked man covered in blood. A room full of children, gray with death, piled high one upon the other. She closed each door and ran down the hallway, but she could not escape. Behind her was the *pad, pad, pad* of a dark cat of some kind. Following her. The hallway became a jungle. She was trying to fight her way though twisted vines. The flash of a knife. The scream of a monkey. She clutched her side, sobbing.

She was sure she must be awake, for the bedroom seemed so comfortingly familiar. She could see the pale moonlight filtering through the crack in the curtains. The light cast a shimmer on the mirror above the washstand. The green ceramic jug and basin were just discernible in the reflection. She heard a creak on the floorboard outside the door. The doorknob turned slowly, and she held her breath. Her mind felt cloudy and confused, for it seemed as if a shadow entered the room. She closed and opened her eyes again slowly. He was sitting there on the bed gazing down at her. Long fingers stroked her hair. She turned toward him as he lay down beside her. He was fully dressed, and as she nestled her head against him, she felt the fine wool of his dark gray frock coat against her cheek. She was so cold in her white cotton nightdress. She slid her body in close to his, burying herself in his warmth. She felt the smooth silk of his waistcoat against her palms. She stroked it gently, as she would a cat. The dark panther in her mind was pacing. Her eyes closed, and she was lulled back to sleep by the slow, measured sound of his breath.

The darkness beckoned.

Ursula could not resist his kiss. It tasted of burgundy wine, of hazelnuts and dark bitter chocolate.

She woke up.

There was a soft *tap-tap* on the study door. Ursula blinked, realizing she had actually fallen asleep in her father's armchair. She had only dreamed she was still in her bed. While her dreams dimmed, the memories of Lord Wrotham's image remained. The taste of him lingered. Although all reason dictated that what had occurred was not real, her senses refused to give him up. Ursula scrubbed her eyes with the back of her hand. She had to pull herself together.

"Miss . . . miss, it's me. . . ." came Julia's hushed voice from behind the door.

Ursula crossed the room quickly and opened the door.

Julia was in her nightdress and tartan dressing gown, carrying a white envelope on a silver tray.

"I couldn't sleep, so I came down to find something to read," Ursula blurted out, feeling that somehow she had to explain herself. Then she frowned. "Julia, what are you doing here?" she demanded.

"I was up getting myself a glass of water when we — I mean, Mr. Biggs and me — heard someone knocking on the back door. Well, there was this messenger boy standing there. Said it was real urgent, so I've brought you his message, and . . . well, miss, here it is." Julia handed her the tray.

Ursula took the envelope and opened it, making sure Julia wasn't looking over her shoulder. The message was scrawled in Winifred's hand:

Sully, I'm waiting out the back. We have to talk. Freddie.

"Julia," Ursula said quietly, "you may go back to bed."

"Are you sure, miss?"

"Perfectly. I will deal with this myself," Ursula replied, crumpling the note in her hands.

Julia's eyes widened. "Ooh! Is it a message from Tom?"

Ursula suppressed a shudder and shook her head. Julia's romantic notions were getting frightfully tiresome.

Julia said nothing more but left the room

and hastened back up the servants' stairs to her own bedroom.

"She'll have me eloping to Gretna Green next," Ursula muttered as she left the study, crossed the hallway, and hurried downstairs to the kitchen.

Biggs was sitting next to the fire, polishing his shoes. He shot Ursula a disapproving glare but said nothing.

Ursula passed through the kitchen and scullery and opened the back door. Winifred was standing there, bundled up in a large brown overcoat and stamping her feet to ward off the cold. She had a thick woolen scarf wrapped around her head, partially obscuring her face.

"Freddie!" Ursula exclaimed. "What on earth are you doing coming here?!" She ushered Winifred inside and shut the door behind her.

"I managed to sneak out the back of my place so the coppers didn't see me."

"You took a great risk —" Ursula began, but Winifred silenced her with a wave of her hand.

"I simply had to come. I couldn't stand not being able to see or talk to you! After all I put you through the other night . . ."

Biggs gave a polite cough and Ursula whirled around. He looked pointedly at the clock and Ursula grimaced. Her father was likely to be home any minute.

"Damn and blast! My father will have a fit if he finds you here. You'd better get going."

"But I'm not sure when I may be able to see you again. They're watching me all day and night, Sully." Winifred's voice caught in her throat. "I think they are going to have me arrested!"

Ursula clasped her friends arm. "Don't worry, Freddie! We're going to work this one out together. We can't stay here, though." Ursula thought for a moment. "Why don't we nip into the gardens — you can tell me everything there. Biggs won't give the game away." Ursula raised her voice. "Will you, Biggs?"

Biggs was sitting by the fire studiously reading the newspaper. He turned the page loudly.

"I think that's a no," Ursula whispered, and she reached out to take the garden gate key that hung on a hook by the scullery door. She and Winifred then walked out the back door and up the stairs that led to the street.

"Cripes, it's cold!" Ursula cried. She felt a tug on her sleeve, and Biggs silently handed her his heavy tweed overcoat and scarf.

"Just you take care," he said in low tones.

"Thanks, Biggs, you're a brick!" Ursula whispered in reply.

She led Winifred across Chester Square and into the enclosed garden. There were few signs of life except for the sound of an occasional carriage or delivery van in the distance. The wind picked up the pages of yesterday's *Evening Standard* and sent them spinning into the air. Ursula watched, fascinated, as the pages danced and twirled in and out of the lamplight, a whirligig of shadows, black text, white paper, corners flapping. She then shivered and pulled Biggs's coat closer.

She led Winifred to one of the park benches and sat down.

"So tell me, can you recall anything further about that night?" Ursula asked.

"God, Sully, I've told Lord Wrotham and Inspector Harrison everything I can remember. Laura and I were at a party — nothing remarkable about that. We left in a taxicab around one in the morning. Got home and then . . . then nothing. I remember going upstairs to bed and then nothing . . . nothing at all. It sounds unbelievable, I realize, but . . . all I know is that I could never have hurt her. Not Laura. She was . . . she was —"

"I know, Freddie. You don't have to tell me," Ursula interrupted. "Do you think you could have been drugged?"

Winifred gave a hollow laugh. "Oh, Sully, what do *you* know about drugs?"

"Nothing," Ursula replied candidly. "But it's a possibility, isn't it?"

Winifred was suddenly sober. "But who would do such a thing?"

"Someone who wanted Laura dead and wanted others to think you're the one who killed her. Freddie, before we go any further, there's something I must know: Is there any motive that the police might think you could possibly have?"

Winifred scratched her chin, and Ursula suddenly felt uncomfortable. Did she really want to know the sordid details of that night? So much had always been politely left unspoken in their relationship. All she knew was that, beyond their common intellectual pursuits and political interests, Freddie had a life that did not include Ursula. To Freddie it was as if Ursula were a beloved and spirited sister, protected from the dark longings that colored her other relationships. Ursula had always relied on her own imaginings when it came to the hidden desires that plagued Winifred — until now.

Ursula remembered the peculiar, fearful look that had come over Winifred's face when she found Ursula in the kitchen the night Laura died. There had always been a darkness, alluring and volatile, about the world Winifred inhabited. Ursula tried to shake off her fears. Winifred was, after all, her friend. She had taught her a great deal about the world and how to live in it. Even saved her from an angry mob of men who'd attacked them during a WSPU rally. Ursula could not doubt her now.

Winifred stared at her squarely before saying, with forced calmness, "The police found out that Laura and I quarreled that night, and witnesses at Madame Launois's confirmed it. The argument was about Laura seeing other people. She subscribed, you know, to a notion of 'free love,' and I . . . well, I was —"

"Unhappy about that?" Ursula asked quietly.

"Yes," Freddie responded after a momentary hesitation. "Actually more than unhappy. It's not hard to explain to you, because I'm sure you felt the same about Alexei." Ursula flushed slightly, but Winifred merely went on. "I simply didn't want to share Laura with anyone else."

"And so the police believe that you murdered Laura in a fit of jealousy?" Ursula asked, experiencing a strange sensation of both distaste and sympathy.

"Yes," Winifred replied, "and they also found out about my past experiences with various substances." Ursula frowned, not comprehending, but Winifred continued to speak. "Opium. Morphine. That kind of thing. So, you see, they do believe that drugs were involved — only that it was *I* who administered them!"

"What does Lord Wrotham think?"

"Despite some doubts, he is convinced I'll be arrested and, in all likelihood, will face trial for Laura's murder. He thinks that, given the evidence they're likely to produce about my 'degenerate lifestyle,' a jury could easily convict me. Wrotham has managed to keep it out of the papers. But there are rumors among the neighbors, of course. As soon as they make an arrest, I expect we will see it all splashed about on the front page of the *Daily Mirror*."

"Going back to that night — at Madame Launois's — was there anyone else there that . . ."

"Shh!" Winifred interrupted her. "I think someone else is *here*," she whispered hoarsely.

Ursula felt the hairs on the back of her neck prickle. The wind had died down, and the infamous London fog was starting to rise thick and dense around her. Its acrid yellow form gave the oak trees sinister proportions in the moonlight.

There was a strange, foreign scent of pungent tobacco and spice in the air. Winifred placed a warning hand on Ursula's shoulders. Ursula froze. There was no sound of movement. Everything was held in abeyance, like an animal waiting for the kill. Only the animal seemed to be the very air itself. The darkness itself. The fog and mist. Surrounding them.

Ursula felt something brush against her skirt. She opened her mouth to scream, and then everything went black.

FOUR

"Are you completely mad?! What possessed you to go with her there? You could have been killed!"

The police inspector coughed politely, and Lord Wrotham was silenced midstream. Ursula fought back the tears, threatened by Lord Wrotham's rebuke, unwilling to reveal her humiliation. The last thing she wanted was a display of "feminine frailty" at a time like this.

Ursula was sitting at home in the front parlor, a bandage around her head and a woolen blanket tucked across her shoulders. She was inhaling the vapors from the steaming cup of Earl Grey tea in her hands.

Lord Wrotham was pacing in front of the fireplace, tugging and straightening his jacket sleeve in an apparent attempt to regain his composure. The police inspector, whom Ursula now knew to be Harrison, stood in the middle of the room, appraising her with a gaze that suggested both skepticism and disquiet. He was younger than Ursula expected, with keen dark eyes and a neatly trimmed mustache. Her father sat white-faced in the satinwood armchair, staring at her incredulously. Ursula had fully expected her father's anger, but his continued silence was far worse. From where she was seated on the sofa, she could see the rain lashing down against the glass panes of the front bay windows, obscuring the view of Chester Square with a heavy mist. The sound of the rain was deafening compared to the apprehensive silence that had fallen in the room.

Harrison reached into the pocket of his navy blue coat and pulled out his pocketwatch.

"It's nearly midday," he remarked, his East End accent barely discernible. "Just a few more questions for Miss Marlow, and then, with your permission, I'd like to call in some of my boys to watch the place — just till we know what we're dealing with."

"Is that absolutely necessary?" Lord Wrotham asked, exchanging looks with Ursula's father.

"Surely concern over the young lady's safety outweighs such sensibilities," Harrison replied coolly.

Her father leaned forward in the chair, placing his head in his hands. Again Ursula was expecting to hear a reproach, but when none came, she found herself shivering despite the thick blanket wrapped around her. Lord Wrotham shifted his stance uncomfortably and turned to face the fire that was smoldering in the grate.

Harrison coughed again. "Agreed, then. . . . Now, Miss Marlow, I need to ask you a few more questions."

Ursula looked up as he opened his notebook and hunted in his pockets for a pencil. She still felt woozy and confused.

"Where is she? Freddie, I mean?" she asked

"Down at the Cannon Row police station," Harrison replied, flipping to a particular page in his notebook.

"You haven't arrested her, have you?" Ursula asked, dismayed.

"Not yet," Harrison answered curtly. "Miss Stanford-Jones arrived about half past one this morning, is that correct?"

Ursula took a deep breath, firmly trying to summon up the resolve to appear both poised and confident. "Yes, that's right."

"And you accompanied her into the gardens?"

"Yes, yes . . . she wanted to talk to me."

"About Miss Radcliffe?"

Ursula nodded reluctantly.

"You didn't think it a little odd that she should arrive at that time in the morning?"

Ursula shrugged.

"Why didn't you let her come inside?"

"Because I knew that my father would be upset. He doesn't like Freddie."

"Indeed," Harrison responded.

Ursula stared at Harrison blankly, but instead of replying, she surprised him by asking, "Why did you never interview me after Laura's death?"

Harrison gave an involuntary start and glanced uneasily at Lord Wrotham. "We felt . . . at the time . . . er . . . that there was no need to involve you unnecessarily in our inquiries." He then threw Lord Wrotham a pointed look. "We also had strong assurances that you had no relevant information at the time."

"I would have thought you'd want to verify that," Ursula replied dryly. Her father didn't seem to hear any of this exchange and remained silent, still sitting with his head in his hands.

After an awkward pause, Harrison returned to his questioning, "So how long have you known Miss Stanford-Jones?"

"About two years. She's a journalist, and

we met at a WSPU meeting at the Queen's Hall. I s'pose I really know her through that. Oh, and Oxford of course. We see each other now at rallies and meetings, that sort of thing."

Ursula saw Harrison grimace, so she continued, determined to make it clear where both her politics and her sympathies lay. "Winifred is very active in our cause and extremely highly regarded, y'know. Why, I was introduced to her by Mrs. Pankhurst herself —"

"The police are well acquainted with Mrs. Pankhurst and her kind," Harrison interjected. His pursed lips suggested that the Downing Street riots were still fresh in his mind.

"I believe that many of my colleagues are still feeling the ill effects of making that acquaintance," Ursula responded icily.

Harrison seemed momentarily startled into silence. "Did you see Miss Stanford-Jones socially — other than through your . . . er . . . suffragette activities?" he finally asked.

"No, not really. I don't think . . ." Ursula's voice trailed off, and Harrison looked at her curiously. Silently she cursed herself. For Freddie's sake she really must be careful what she said.

"Don't think what?" he prompted.

"Well, I don't think I'm really the type of girl —"

"I should think not," Lord Wrotham interrupted. "Why don't you keep to the relevant facts here, Harrison? This is not a question of Miss Marlow's relationship with Miss Stanford-Jones. Rather it's a question of the facts. We know that Miss Marlow is acquainted with Miss Stanford-Jones. We know she was called upon to assist her the night Laura Radcliffe died. Surely we should focus our attentions on what happened in the early hours of this morning."

Harrison flushed darkly. "M'lord," he replied stiffly.

"What I want to know," Ursula asked, her voice suddenly loud, "is why you aren't out there searching for the person who did this right now!"

Harrison snorted in exasperation. "Miss Marlow, the facts suggest that our chief suspect is Miss Stanford-Jones herself!"

"Harrison, you forget yourself." Lord Wrotham's warning was clear despite the evenness of his tone.

Ursula looked at them both mystified. "I don't understand," she said slowly. "What do you mean?"

Both men were silent.

"Inspector?" Ursula said quietly.

"The evidence, Miss Marlow," Harrison replied, his eyes watching her closely for any reaction, "implicates Miss Stanford-Jones in the Radcliffe murder as well as the attempt on your life."

Ursula felt as though a dull weight were suddenly placed on her chest, pressing down on her ribs so she could hardly breathe.

"The attempt on my life! But that wasn't Freddie — there was someone else there, in the gardens, I know there was! Wasn't Miss Stanford-Jones attacked as well?"

"When Biggs found you, Miss Stanford-Jones was also injured."

"See, I told you —" Ursula started to say.

"But I'm afraid we do not believe Miss Stanford-Jones's story. The way she tells it, someone knocked you unconscious and then attacked her. She argues that she managed to fend off whoever this was and that Biggs's arrival caused the perpetrator to run off. Biggs swears, however, that he saw no one. When he arrived, Miss Stanford-Jones was standing over you, and while yes, she had injuries consistent with having fended off some kind of attack, we believe that these were caused by your trying to defend yourself."

"But I have no . . . no recollection of that at all!"

Harrison ignored her protests. "You have suffered a nasty blow to the head, which no doubt prevents you from recalling precisely what occurred."

"But —" Ursula began, and was again interrupted. This time by Lord Wrotham.

"Ursula, please. Dr. Bentham has already examined you. It is his professional opinion that a concussion such as yours is bound to affect short-term memory."

"Dr. Bentham was here?" Ursula said in confusion, realizing that she had no recollection of anything before waking up on the sofa as her father looked down upon her.

"Coming back to the Laura Radcliffe case," Harrison said with a cough that indicated he had little time for these digressions. "We found a kitchen knife with Laura's blood on it and have identified Miss Stanford-Jones's fingerprints on that knife." He continued, "Lord Wrotham, however, is convinced that there is another explanation."

"Of course there is! I know Winifred is innocent!" Ursula exclaimed.

"I usually find," Harrison pressed on, ignoring her outburst, "that my first suspicions are correct. I've never been one to believe fanciful conspiracy theories." He gave Lord Wrotham a withering look, which seemed to have no noticeable impact. Ursula cast a glance across at her father in confusion. Nothing Harrison was saying made any sense.

"Given that there was no sign of a break-in or robbery," Harrison said, "our first thought was that Miss Stanford-Jones killed Miss Radcliffe and then called you in as a means of casting doubt over what had happened. What she didn't bargain on was that we would discover the syringe that was probably used to drug Miss Radcliffe or that we would uncover details about her past —"

"Harrison! You really do forget yourself!" Lord Wrotham exclaimed angrily. "Miss Stanford-Jones is my client. I insist you say nothing further to Miss Marlow. Do you want to scare her out of her wits, man?"

Robert Marlow looked up, startled by the outburst. Ursula inhaled sharply. A gust of wind rattled the windows, sending a cold draft of air across the room.

"Some information is surely necessary," Harrison said calmly. "For Miss Marlow's own protection, at least."

Lord Wrotham remained grim-faced but with a curt nod allowed Harrison to continue.

Ursula frowned and did not move from her seat. Her father excused himself, saying that the last thing he needed at this moment was further confirmation of how close his only daughter had been to the epitome of depravity and perversion.

Harrison cleared his throat. "We have information about Miss Stanford-Jones's past — and I caution you that this may come as a considerable shock — which indicates that this was not the first time she has displayed violent and perverse behavior. When she was sixteen, Miss Stanford-Jones was admitted to a private hospital. The diagnosis made by the alienist there was that she suffered from neurasthenia — an illness of the nerves. This ailment appeared to have been precipitated by a violent confrontation with her father, who, may I remind you, was a highly respected minister in the Methodist Church. She spent over a year in hospital receiving treatment, before returning to resume her education. At eighteen, however, she appeared to suffer a relapse and was admitted to the Wakefield Asylum. The concern at this time was even more serious than before. A neurophysical degeneration resulting in an aberration of sexual instinct. . . ."

Harrison, evidently discomfited by Ursula's candid gaze, let his voice trail off. This all sounded so surreal and strange that she could hardly believe what he was saying. She had always known that there were women who preferred the company of other women. At Mrs. Hopkins's School for Young Ladies in Skipton, many of her classmates had crushes on various members of the sixth form. When she first met Winifred, Ursula had chosen to think of Winifred's relationships in rather the same way.

How could she reconcile what Harrison had told her with the strong, confident Freddie she knew? It was because of Winifred's strength that their friendship had started in the first place. Ursula had been walking alongside Winifred at her first suffrage march when a man lunged at her from the mob screaming, *"Whore!"* There was the flash of a knife, and Ursula was pulled to the ground. The man managed to cut off some of Ursula's hair as a trophy for his lapel, but before he could proclaim any victory, Winifred set upon him, fists flying in the most unladylike fashion. The man retreated back, snarling and hurling abuses. Winifred had then coolly assisted Ursula to her feet, ignoring his shouts.

Lord Wrotham remained silent, staring

out the front windows with an impassive face.

Harrison ran his fingers through his hair. "It was at the Wakefield Asylum that she was first introduced to drugs such as sulphonal and valerinic acid — and we believe that a drug very similar to these was involved in the death of Laura Radcliffe. So can you now understand, with a psychiatric history such as hers, why we are concerned for your well-being? She is a dangerous woman, and we cannot begin to predict her actions. Until we have resolved the case, please, remain where my men can protect you, and avoid all further contact with her."

"You truly believe that I may be at risk?" Ursula asked incredulously.

"I do," Harrison replied.

Ursula turned to Lord Wrotham. "And what do you say?" she asked him sharply. He did not respond at first but rather walked back to the fireplace and straightened his jacket.

"Well?" Ursula demanded.

"Well indeed," Lord Wrotham replied coldly. "What can I, in the predicament I find myself, possibly say? It is you who charged me with the responsibility for this case. It was you who foisted this upon me. So what say I? Nothing. I can say nothing.

Advise nothing. It's a damnable position you have placed me in, Ursula."

Ursula was silent.

Robert Marlow returned, looking tired and worn. Surveying the room, he sighed before speaking. "Inspector Harrison — would you please leave us for a moment?"

Harrison's dark eyes narrowed, but he nodded his head.

"You are welcome to use the telephone to call Scotland Yard," Marlow continued. "Maybe you could make the necessary arrangements for a couple of officers to be posted . . ."

"Of course," Harrison replied before walking out of the room, straightening his jacket as he passed.

"I really must talk to Harrison about his tailor," Lord Wrotham said offhandedly as the door closed. He lit a cigarette, and though his outward composure had certainly returned, Ursula thought she detected a slight shake in his hands and suspected that his anger had not entirely faded.

Convinced that if she stood up, her knees would give way, Ursula remained seated. She placed the empty teacup carefully down on the side table and drew the blanket in tightly around her shoulders. The dull weight on her chest was of little comfort.

The rain outside continued to beat against the windows.

Robert Marlow paced in front of the fireplace, concern still deeply etched on his face.

"Do you really think a police guard outside will be of any help?" he asked Lord Wrotham. It was as if he had forgotten Ursula was there.

Lord Wrotham shrugged. "We can only hope. It gives us some time at least to . . ." He left the sentence unfinished.

She could have screamed. Damn it all, what was happening here?!

"I'm nearly killed, and now everyone is behaving as though I'm invisible," she muttered. As there was no reply, she continued, out loud this time, exclaiming, "You can't really believe that Freddie is some kind of a crazed murderer!"

"What about Pemberton?" Marlow asked, still seemingly oblivious to Ursula's presence.

"He has agreed to take the case. As you know, I'm not an expert in criminal matters, but Fenway speaks highly of him."

Fenway, Ursula knew, was her father's solicitor.

"We can't allow them to arrest her! She didn't do it!" Ursula said. Her father seemed startled by her voice.

"Quite frankly, I'm not sure we can stop them," Lord Wrotham replied, still standing by the fireplace. For a moment Ursula thought she saw a quiver of emotion in his normally cool blue-gray eyes. Was it sympathy? Concern? Pity, even? The moment soon passed, though, and Lord Wrotham's gaze became impenetrable once more.

"But you can't really think —" Ursula started to insist again.

"I don't know," Lord Wrotham replied tersely. "But it seems we must wait, whatever the outcome. Miss Stanford-Jones may have to go to trial. However, if there is someone else involved we have little choice except to wait for the murderer to reveal himself."

"Himself?"

Robert Marlow silenced her gently. "You must trust us," was all he said.

There was a knock on the door, and Biggs entered, unruffled as always. "Inspector Harrison wishes to know if he may return now."

Robert Marlow nodded. "Yes, yes . . ."

Harrison walked back into the room.

"There will be two of our best men posted outside," he announced. "One in the front. One out back. I'm sure that will suffice until we have made an arrest."

He sounded confident that this was close, Ursula thought.

"Miss Marlow." Harrison addressed her directly. "I must ask that you have no further contact with Miss Stanford-Jones. My lord" — he turned back to Lord Wrotham — "I expect you wish to be present when we resume our questioning. We have made arrangements to interview Miss Stanford-Jones later this afternoon."

Lord Wrotham extinguished his cigarette. "I will let David Pemberton know. He will be taking on the case —"

"Pemberton?" Harrison seemed impressed despite himself, and perhaps even a little unnerved by the prospect that one of the country's top criminal barristers was now involved in his case.

"Yes. Fenway has already sent over the brief, and I believe that Pemberton has already interviewed Miss Stanford-Jones."

"It's not every day that the likes of you or Pemberton gets involved in a case like this," Harrison said.

Lord Wrotham's eyes narrowed. "I am always willing to be of assistance where matters of family honor are at stake. You of all people should remember that."

Harrison flinched and, after a moment's

hesitation, turned to face Ursula.

"Miss Marlow, I think I've imposed on you enough for one day. Please be assured that my men will protect you. There is truly no need to worry. Regrettably, I will have to ask you some further questions. Perhaps it would be convenient for me to return tomorrow morning?"

Ursula sensed that a shift in power had somehow occurred. That whatever complicity lay between her father and Lord Wrotham now embraced her.

"Unfortunately, I will be in the East End all day. The vicar's wife and I volunteer once a month at a home for working and homeless girls in Stepney," she replied, and out of the corner of her eye she thought she saw Lord Wrotham smile. "Would Monday be convenient instead, Inspector Harrison?" she asked.

Harrison bowed his head. "Monday, then, Miss Marlow." He then took his leave.

Ursula watched the steam fog up the white-paned windows as she lay in the bath. She eased down, letting her head drift back to rest on the water, her knees raised slightly. Half submerged, she closed her eyes and felt a watery darkness descend. All her worries seemed to sink into that same darkness.

She wanted to hold them down, keep them immersed and distant. But it wasn't long before they pushed their way forward and the memories of the night Laura died came flooding back. Ursula sat up, shivering despite the heat of the bath, and held her knees in tight.

A kitchen knife and a syringe. Degeneration resulting in aberrant sexual instinct? Harrison's words were like fragments of shattered glass on a floor. Although she tried to pick them up carefully, tried to piece them together, nothing would fit. She knew deep inside that Winifred was no murderer. Somewhere out there was the real killer, and Ursula was determined to prove it.

FIVE

After an afternoon and evening of enforced bed rest, Ursula was finally allowed to leave the house and take a walk up to Green Park with one of Harrison's men in tow. Her father left early to visit his Lambeth dye factory. Mrs. Stewart and Julia had been pecking around her all morning like mother hens, driving Ursula to distraction. Finally she had declared that she "needed some air," grabbed her velveteen hat, her coat, and her scarf, and marched out the front door.

Chester Square was suffused with the pale light of a November sun. Ursula noticed that clouds were gathering over the rooftops and tugged her hat down low, concealing the bandage that covered the graze on the right side of her forehead. With long strides she crossed the square and was about to turn into Eccleston Street when a man called out to her from an Argyll taxicab that was parked on the sidewalk.

"Miss Marlow?"

Ursula ignored him and continued walking. Out of the corner of her eye, she saw Harrison's constable watching them closely.

"Anna asked me to come. Anna Proznitz."

Ursula stopped dead in her tracks and turned around. "Anna?" she said slowly.

The man got out of the cab, dropped a cigarette on the ground, and flattened it underfoot. He wore brown trousers, an unkempt necktie, and a flat cap.

"Which newspaper are you from?" Ursula asked shrewdly.

The man grinned. "You're a sharp one. Neville Hackett of the *Star*."

The *Star* was a radical newspaper run by an Irish Nationalist.

"Well, Mr. Hackett of the *Star,* what do you want with me?"

Ursula was on her guard. She hadn't spoken to Anna in over a year, and their last meeting had been acrimonious. Anna had never approved of her son's relationship with Ursula, and when Alexei decided to join Lenin in Paris in the winter of 1908, Anna held Ursula partially responsible.

"Just passing on a message," Hackett responded cheerfully. "Anna wants to know if you'll be at the meetin' today. She wants

103

to talk about Miss Stanford-Jones."

"And why would she want to do that?" Ursula asked.

The man grinned again. "Ain't you seen the newspapers yet?"

"No." Her father had taken the morning papers with him.

The man held up a copy of the *Daily Mail*. On the front page was a photograph of Winifred under the headline SUFFRAGETTE ARRESTED ON CHARGE OF MURDER.

Ursula closed her eyes. "Oh, God . . ." Her worst fears had been realized.

With trembling hands she took the newspaper from him and read.

Miss Winifred Stanford-Jones of Gower Street, Bloomsbury, was arrested last night in connection with the death of Miss Laura Radcliffe, daughter of the late Colonel William Radcliffe VC, DSO, of Radcliffe Hall, Surrey. Miss Radcliffe was found stabbed to death at Miss Stanford-Jones's house in the early hours of October 29. Miss Stanford-Jones, a well-known agitator in the "votes for women" campaign, has been imprisoned twice before for breaches of the peace. A representative of both the Women's Social and Political Union and the Women's Industrial Council, and a member of the Independent Labour Party, Miss Stanford-Jones is a frequent speaker on trade unionism and the role of women in socialism. Her arrest on charges of murder comes after a detailed investigation by the Metropolitan Police. Inspector Harrison of the Metropolitan Police declined to provide any further particulars of the case. Sources close to the Radcliffe family say that they are devastated by the sudden loss of both father and daughter.

See page 14 for Mrs. Humphrey Ward's editorial on women's suffrage: "A Dangerous Leap in the Dark."

"Arrested last night she was," the man continued. "Anyways, Anna wants to have a chat."

"Thank you. Tell her I'll meet her there."

He tipped his hat but lingered before getting into the motorcar. "Oy, how much do you know about this 'ere murder?"

"Not much," Ursula replied cagily.

"Just thought maybe you'd give me a bit of the inside scoop."

Ursula eyed him with distaste. Still, she thought, having someone from the press look into the possible link between Laura's death, Colonel Radcliffe, and the expedition could be helpful. Ursula rubbed her nose. Harrison's constable was still watching them closely.

"You ought to be looking at Colonel Radcliffe's death," she said as she started to walk away.

"Suicide, wasn't it? Death of a daughter hit him hard, that sort of thing?"

"I think there may be a bit more to it."

"*Do you,* now?"

"Yes," Ursula replied lightly, giving the police constable across the street a wave and a smile. "Maybe there's a link that the police haven't made."

"Right you are!" Mr. Hackett grinned. "Well, ta, luv. I'll look into it."

He got into the rear seat of the taxicab. Ursula straightened her coat and resumed walking. The cab drove off, and she hurried back home.

"Is everything all right, miss?" Bridget asked as Ursula burst into the house.

"Perfectly!" Ursula replied, grabbing her purse off the rosewood side table in the hallway. "Bridget, I'm going out for a couple of hours."

"Ooh, miss, wait up!" Bridget replied, dropping her dusting cloth in a fluster. "I'll 'ave to tell Mr. Biggs. Master said you're not to go traipsin' about on yer own —"

"Never you mind that!" Ursula replied firmly. "I won't be long." And with that she hurried out of the house and started walking briskly toward the Sloane Square Underground station.

Ursula exited the tube at South Kensington and boarded the double-decker motor bus for Albert Hall. Today's WSPU meeting was an important one. They were going to hear whether the prime minister, Mr. Asquith, would support passage of the Conciliation Bill, which would grant the vote to women householders, through the House of Commons.

Albert Hall was crowded with WSPU supporters. Ursula hunted around to see if Anna was anywhere close by. She soon spied her standing alone by one of the doors, her hands thrust deep in the pockets of her dark green jacket. Anna had a leather-bound notebook and a copy of *Woman Worker* wedged under her arm. A frequent contributor to the WSPU magazine *Votes for Women,* Anna had been one the first people to encourage Ursula to pursue a career in journalism (before she learned of her imprudent relationship with her son).

Ursula took a deep breath and then started

to nudge her way through the throng to greet her.

"Anna!" Ursula called out as she approached.

Anna looked up and caught her gaze with mournful brown eyes. Alexei's eyes.

"Last I heard, you were in Manchester working with the Women's Industrial Council. What brings you to London?" Ursula tried to sound nonchalant.

"Oh, this and that," Anna replied in her peculiar Russian-English accent, and shifted her gaze, obviously unwilling to say more.

"I got your message," Ursula said.

Anna nodded. There was an awkward pause.

"I hear you've been helping Freddie with this matter."

There was something in Anna's tone, an ill-concealed contempt, that irked Ursula.

"My father's paying for her defense, if that's what you mean," Ursula responded curtly to what hadn't been said.

"But you are, are you not, also trying to . . ." Anna searched for the appropriate word. "To . . . clear her . . . of these charges?"

"Yes. Yes, I am," Ursula replied simply.

"I wanted you to know that she still has many friends among us. If we can do anything, please let me know."

Ursula assumed that Anna was referring to the WSPU leadership when she said "us."

"Thank you," Ursula answered.

"No doubt the police are quick to pin it all on Fred."

"Yes, they certainly are."

"Typical! So what can we do?"

"Well . . ." Ursula paused for a moment before she continued. "It would be helpful to know who was at Madame Launois's that night. The police don't seem very interested, but I am. Perhaps another of Laura's lovers was there — who knows? I'd be glad for anything, really, that could provide a lead . . . something that could help clear up this wretched mess for poor old Freddie."

"I do know Laura by reputation. She had a number of lovers — and not just those of the female persuasion."

"I'm sorry?" Ursula stared at Anna blankly.

"She liked men too."

"Oh. Oh, I see." Ursula looked faintly embarrassed.

Anna laid a hand on her arm. "It's time we went in. How can I get in touch with you if I hear anything of interest?" Anna asked.

The crowd was moving quickly past them

now, so Ursula scurried to find one of her correspondence cards in her purse. "Here."

Anna looked at the Belgravia address with barely concealed distaste. "I'll let you know what I find out as soon as I can," she said.

"Thank you."

A lady passed them carrying a small purple banner emblazoned with the WSPU motto: DEEDS, NOT WORDS.

"Before you ask," Anna said, "I haven't heard from Alexei. As far as I know, he is still in Paris."

Ursula looked away.

"Good-bye, Ursula," Anna said, and Ursula thought (with some surprise) that she detected a note of sympathy. "I'll let you know if I find anything that may help Fred."

Ursula nodded. "Bye."

The atmosphere was tense and uncertain as Mrs. Emmeline Pankhurst rose to address the crowd. As soon as she read the prime minister's statement that the Conciliation Bill would not be heard until the next Parliament, there was a great outburst of indignation. Her daughter Christabel Pankhurst leaped to her feet and declared war against the government. Mrs. Pankhurst announced that she would lead a deputation to Downing Street, and the crowd rose to follow her. Ursula was swept up in the excitement. The crowd moved quickly, with Mrs. Pankhurst setting the pace. Banners were unfurled: FIGHT FOR THE VOTE! THE BILL MUST GO THROUGH!

Within a quarter of an hour, they reached Parliament Square and were joined by a crowd of WSPU supporters who had been waiting to march to the House of Commons. Ursula saw a police superintendent signal the formation of a human barricade across the entrance to Downing Street. Mrs. Pankhurst pushed steadily onward toward the line of men until suffragettes and police came face-to-face.

Ursula found herself in the midst of a surging crowd. She fought just to remain standing. A policeman grabbed her arm and she struggled in vain against him. He twisted her arm so hard she thought it might snap.

The crowd soon broke through this human barrier, and some women managed to make it up to the prime minister's house. Others struggled with the police. Ursula saw women violently pushed to the ground as the police endeavored to keep back the "masses." She saw a woman being carried away half conscious. Banners were torn to pieces, women struck down by blows. Everything was chaos.

Ursula saw Anna being dragged away by two policemen and bundled into the back of a police van.

Ursula's hair was down, and a mass of curls spilled over her face and eyes. Her dress was torn, and one of her sleeves had come loose at the seam. The policeman tried to grab her arm again and swore under his breath as she gave him a swift, sharp kick to the shin.

"Constable, I'll take it from here," a vaguely familiar voice called out.

Ursula stumbled to her knees as the police constable released her from his grasp. She looked up to see Inspector Harrison standing in front of her, arms crossed. His face looked pinched and grim. Ursula's gaze remained defiant as she picked herself up from the ground. By now the crowd was dispersing. A woman was lying near the pavement, her black coat spread over her. She was being tended to by a young man, who called out for assistance.

"This is an outrage!" he yelled to Harrison. "An absolute outrage! This poor woman must be well into her sixties."

Harrison ignored him and grasped Ursula by the arm.

"Are you arresting me?" she demanded.

Harrison's top lip curled. "I'm sure you'd

rather not embarrass your father any more than is necessary," he replied.

"I don't see how that is any business of yours." Ursula wrested her arm free. "I demand to be taken with the others!"

"Don't be so bloody ridiculous," Harrison scoffed. "No one's going to be arrested. You lot annoy me no end. Can't wait to be locked up. Can't wait to see the newspaper stories. That's what it's all about, isn't it? Not the vote, just to get your name in the papers. Disgusting, I call it. Like we don't 'ave enough to do around 'ere." Harrison's East End accent became more pronounced as he lost his composure.

Ursula's eyes narrowed, but before she could launch into a speech on the lofty principles of the WSPU, Harrison shoved her into the backseat of a motorcar.

"How dare you!" she spluttered as he closed the door behind her and got into the front passenger side.

"Go!" was all he said, and the unnamed driver sped off.

Ursula struggled to unlock the door, failed, and slumped resignedly against the back of the bench seat. How would it look to her fellow suffragettes, she wondered, to have been bundled off with a high-ranking member of the Metropolitan Police merely because of her father's influence? Angry tears pricked her eyes. Even at twenty-two, she was being treated like a recalcitrant child.

The motorcar pulled up at the Cannon Row police station adjacent to the red-and-white brick Gothic headquarters of the Metropolitan Police.

Ursula leaned forward. "I thought you weren't going to arrest me," she said.

Harrison got out of the car. "I'm not," he replied, "I just don't plan on going any more out of my way for the likes of you. . . . I'm sure you are aware, Miss Marlow, that I have a great deal of work to do. Until tomorrow."

Harrison slammed the door and instructed the driver to take the willful young suffragette home at once.

Six

Julia unfolded Ursula's pale yellow opera gown and laid it down carefully on the bed. Ursula was standing, looking out the bedroom window. The police outside the front door were still there and could hardly be considered discreet. Questions from neighbors and friends had prompted Robert Marlow to issue a brief statement describing the police presence as a "temporary but necessary" protection against threats made against him by "workers and hooligans." This sparked calls throughout the neighborhood for increased police protection, as everyone became convinced that socialists and anarchists lurked on every corner of Belgravia.

"Miss?" Julia prompted with a pointed look at the clock on the mantelpiece.

"Hmm? . . . Oh, cripes!" Ursula responded, realizing she hadn't finished unbuttoning her blouse.

"Here now, let me do that, miss," knowing that Ursula was notorious for popping buttons in her haste to get dressed and undressed.

Julia helped her step into the opera dress and then sat her down on the small silk-covered stool as she finished unpinning Ursula's hair. It felt good to have the weight lifted from the crown of her head. Ursula shook her head to loosen out the curls and was soon lost in her thoughts once more, oblivious to everything except the rhythmical brushing of her hair.

"I hear that the Abbotts have engaged a new lady's maid for Cecilia," Julia said as she started now to wind Ursula's hair up and around the padding that she used to create the upturned hairstyles that were currently so popular.

"Who told you that?" Ursula asked, called back to the present with a start. "John?"

Julia blushed slightly. Her burgeoning relationship with the Andersons' footman was the household's worst kept secret.

"He seems to know a great deal about everyone's affairs," Ursula began to say, but, seeing Julia's blush intensify, she decided not to continue.

Julia reached for the hairpins.

"So Lily has left the Abbotts," Ursula

mused. "I thought she was doing well there."

"Apparently," Julia said, two hairpins crammed in her mouth, "she *had* to leave, on account of her circumstances." She patted her abdomen meaningfully.

Ursula was silent, unsure of what to say. "What will happen to her now?" she asked quietly.

Julia clicked her tongue impatiently as she continued fixing her hair. "Don't you be wasting your pity on her, miss. Why, the tales that we heard after she'd gone. They say she isn't even sure who the father is!"

"But surely . . ." Ursula tried to restrain herself, although it was hard not to remember the dire stories she had read and heard. "Surely Lily needs our compassion, not our censure."

Julia looked at her mistress curiously. "What do they talk about at these meetings of yours?" she asked.

Ursula flushed.

Ever since she started accompanying Winifred to socialist party meetings, Ursula had become increasingly concerned about the plight of young, working-class women in London. Without education or access to appropriate medical care, they had no way of escaping the scandal of an unwanted preganancy. Although she vehemently opposed her father's views on eugenics, she agreed with him that some means of birth control was needed to liberate these poor women from the vicious cycle of childbirth and poverty. Julia, of course, had heard Ursula air her views on such matters, but for her own part she remained staunchly censorious over the sexual indiscretions of her peers.

"Anyway," Ursula changed the subject with a small cough. "You were saying that Cecilia has hired someone new. . . ."

Julia waved the brush in the air for dramatic effect. "A French maid — from Paris, no less."

"From Paris . . ." Ursula echoed, trying to hide the sudden envy she felt creeping into her voice. Julia's face fell, and Ursula hastily changed tack. "And to think Cecilia doesn't speak a word of French!"

Julia finished her mistress's hair, and Ursula reached over to apply almond oil to her hands and neck. She dabbed some perfume behind her ears and stood up.

"We must be sure to be up on all the latest fashions," Ursula said to Julia. "Can't have Cecilia's French lady's maid showing us up, now, can we?"

Julia's face brightened. "We cannot indeed. Have you seen the latest in the *Tatler*?

I have some ideas for hairstyles that will suit you perfectly."

Ursula couldn't help but smile.

That evening Ursula accompanied her father to the Royal Opera House. They arrived at Covent Garden just after seven. She loved to witness the spectacle of it all — sitting in a box and gazing across the circular vault with its magnificent chandelier, the luscious red and gold furnishings, and, best of all, watching society's elite mingle and chatter. It was hard to think of Julia's gossip and Lily's predicament and not feel the fragility of one's own circumstances. Even Winifred, despite her bohemian bravado, was now on the edge of what society was willing to accept. And she knew it. One more step and she could easily fall into that dark underworld that Ursula was dimly aware existed. It felt safe somehow, being here in her father's world.

Her father had purchased a box for the season, and tonight was Strauss's *Elektra*. Seated beside her father, Ursula trained her opera glasses across the domed theater. Familiar faces came in and out of focus as her gaze swept the room. Ursula scanned across to see who was seated in the other boxes, and her eyes soon alighted on Lord Wrotham at the other side of the hall. He was seated between two ladies, both of whom were unfamiliar to Ursula.

Cecilia Abbott came through the velvet curtains followed by her father and sat down on the chair next to Ursula. Daniel Abbott nodded briefly as he entered before tapping Ursula's father on the shoulder. Her father got up, and they both disappeared behind the curtain.

"Fa is such a beastly bore at the moment," Cecilia said crossly, watching them leave. "He knows how much I love going out, and he insists on arriving at the very last minute so I miss all the fun of seeing everyone arrive. And now he's toddled off to talk business. . . . Oh, and he forgot to leave me the glasses. What a beast he is!"

"Here." Ursula handed Cecilia her opera glasses. "Use mine."

Cecilia giggled. "I only want to check out the Andersons." Then, peering through the glasses, she laughed again. "I say, who's that old trout sitting next to Lord Wrotham? Ooh, do you think that's his mother? Fa said she may be in town."

Ursula shrugged. "I guess that's probably who it is, then," she said, trying to appear unconcerned. "Who's the other lady, d'you know?"

Cecilia gave a maddening smile, and

Ursula lifted her chin in the air and looked away with feigned indifference. Cecilia laughed, "It's no good pretending that you're not dying to know."

"Don't be ridiculous, Cissy," Ursula replied.

Cecilia edged closer to Ursula. "I have all the gossip — but if you don't want to know. . . . Ooh, is that Audrey Scott over there wearing last season's dress? Oh, Lord, don't tell me that's Sylvia! I wouldn't have recognized her — she looks positively ancient! But then I guess being jilted at twenty-one . . ."

"Cissy . . . ?" Ursula couldn't help herself. She had to know.

Cecilia laughed again and bent her head closer, conspiratorially. "That, my dear, is Lady Victoria Ashton, the extremely wealthy widow of the extremely wealthy Earl Ashton. I hear she's had some recent legal problems regarding his estate, and Lord Whatsit's been lending her a helping hand. Rumors are that's not all he's been doing. . . ."

Ursula tried to look nonchalant.

Cecilia grinned. "I shouldn't worry — she's almost twice your age. And I think if it's money he's after . . ."

"Really, Cissy!"

Cecilia snorted. "Stop dreaming, Sully —

you know the game. And from what I hear, Lord Wrotham could use a penny or two."

"Nonsense," Ursula replied with a frown.

"No, really." Cecilia's voice dropped to a whisper. "Apparently, when he inherited his brother's title after he died, he also inherited a heap of debt. Gambling, don't you know. I overheard Fa saying that Bromley Hall was nearly in ruins. The whole west wing's still closed to save on maintenance costs."

The orchestra began tuning up, and a few minutes later the house lights dimmed.

"Oh, I do wish Papa would hurry back," Ursula said. "He's going to miss the whole thing — it's only one act, you know."

Cecilia handed Ursula back her glasses. "Fa's been tetchy all day, so I wouldn't hold my breath. . . . Oh, hang on, here they are!"

Ursula's father and Daniel Abbott reappeared, looking somber.

Cecilia raised her eyebrows at Ursula and grimaced.

The vast hall grew dark; voices in the crowd subsided as the orchestra struck up. In minutes Ursula was transfixed by the music and the scene. A tragic story of all-consuming revenge, Elektra's tale stirred a deep visceral reaction within her. When Elektra was left, abandoned, to dig for the ax that had murdered Agamemnon, Ursula felt a stab of pain. As Orestes returned, she felt a momentary release, until the final scene robbed her of all breath as the frenetic dance ended and Elektra fell to the floor lifeless. Ursula stifled a quiet sob. The opera had taken her completely out of herself. Cecilia tried to muffle what sounded like a snort. As the lights came back up, Cecilia poked her in the ribs.

"Cissy, you really are a wretch," Ursula said.

"Well, stop being such a wet blanket. And do hurry up — Fa's booked the Cavendish for afters, and I'm starving!"

Ursula reluctantly got to her feet and followed Cecilia through the curtain and out into the crush of people trying to descend the stairs. Cecilia spotted a friend and attempted to reach her in the crowd. Ursula's father hung back, absorbed in conversation with Daniel Abbott. Ursula stepped aside, trying to overhear snatches of what was being said on the other side of the curtain.

"Are we sure it's him?" Abbott asked hoarsely.

"Who else could it be?"

"But what of this woman who was with Laura that night?"

"That sort of woman always is unhinged," Marlow replied, "but we cannot be sure of anything. There's the diary, for one thing."

"The threat made is real enough?"

"Aye, it's real enough." Her father sounded terse.

"Then we have no choice but to act," Abbott replied sharply.

Ursula heard movement suggesting they were about to leave. Quickly she turned to start down the stairs and was left to struggle against the crush of people as they descended into the lobby. She felt hot and constrained in her dress. The crowd was an ocean of faces and voices — surging and moving as if swept along by an unseen tide.

To Ursula's dismay her father had invited Mrs. Pomfrey-Smith and Tom Cumberland to join them all for supper at the Cavendish Hotel. Tom greeted her with a clammy handshake and a knowing smile. Her asking about Madame Launois seemed to have prompted an uneasy intimacy, and Ursula longed to disabuse him of any notion that she wanted or needed his further help.

As Ursula was being seated, Tom said in a low, conspiratorial voice, "Your father told me about that terrible incident the other night. I do hope you're all right."

"I'm fine, thank you," she said coolly, smoothing the linen napkin in her lap.

When she caught a glimpse of Lord Wrotham escorting his mother and Lady Ashton to a table across the room, this only intensified her annoyance. Her father was subdued and pensive, offering little in the way of conversation. This left Mrs. Pomfrey-Smith to entertain the table. Cecilia, with a mischievous glance at Ursula, seemed to relish the spectacle.

"Now, Cecilia here," Mrs. Pomfrey-Smith said with a flourish of her bejeweled hand, "has heeded my advice and has taken up golf — far more suitable for a young lady than certain other . . . pastimes." She gave Ursula a pointed look. "She will benefit greatly from the exercise, and it will provide an excellent opportunity to meet young men of the country."

Cecilia smothered a giggle with her napkin.

Tom leaned in closer to Ursula. "Don't worry," he whispered. "I think your work with those suffragette women is absolutely topping."

Ursula tried not to catch Cecilia's eye for fear she would laugh.

Mrs. Pomfrey-Smith turned to Robert Marlow. "Now, Bobbie, my dear, have you given any more thought to my little idea about a country house in Kent?"

Before Marlow could respond, she turned to Tom with a smile. "I thought it would be a charming addition to Mr. Marlow's interests. What could be finer than a country house for weekend shooting parties? It makes perfect business sense, don't you think, Tom? It provides an ideal opportunity to socialize and enjoy your colleagues' company away from the stresses of town."

"I already have Gray House — that's enough for me," Ursula's father replied gruffly.

Mrs. Pomfrey-Smith straightened one of the ostrich feathers in her hair. "Oh, Bobbie — that moldy old place. It's much too far north. . . . No, you need something closer, somewhere Ursula and you can go for weekends. Lancashire" — Mrs. Pomfrey-Smith barely suppressed a shudder — "is much too far. Can't think why you haven't got rid of the place by now —"

"It was Isabella's home," Robert Marlow interrupted her sharply. "I'm not selling it."

The mention of Ursula's mother silenced the table. Cecilia prodded the parfait de foie gras with her knife while Mrs. Pomfrey-Smith nervously fiddled with the black glass beading on her tulle evening dress.

It was Daniel Abbott who broke the silence by asking Mrs. Pomfrey-Smith if she thought Dr. Crippen might get a reprieve from the home secretary. Dr. Crippen had been found guilty of murdering his wife, Belle, only a few weeks earlier and was due to be executed. Mrs. Pomfrey-Smith seized the opportunity to air her views not just about the case but on the "utterly deplorable" state of England in general. Robert Marlow stirred himself and launched into a heated discussion with Tom and Daniel Abbott on the "degeneracy" permeating the English race.

Ursula knew better than to be drawn into such a debate. While she appreciated her father's concern over the deplorable health of working-class Englishmen, she could not countenance his views on selective breeding. To her this smacked of a dangerous, godlike arrogance — who, after all, had the right to make such a decision? Ursula closed her eyes briefly; the noise and chatter was starting to make her head ache. How she longed to be back home in Chester Square, where she could sit and think in peace and quiet. It was hard not to think of Winifred sitting in Holloway Prison awaiting her own trial and possible execution.

Ursula opened her eyes and caught sight of Lord Wrotham's reflection in the mirror on the wall. He was sitting between his mother and Lady Ashton (who were deep in conversation), a glass of whiskey in his hand. He rotated the glass, took a sip, and for the briefest of moments their eyes met.

Tom tapped Ursula's arm gently. She gave a start.

"Did you enjoy the chicken?"

His eyes flickered between the mirror and her face.

"Hmm?" Ursula replied. "Oh, yes."

"Because you haven't eaten any of it." Tom's hand remained on her arm.

"Excuse me for a moment," Robert Marlow announced as he got to his feet. "But I must have a quick word with Wrotham. The appeal in the Egyptian matter is being heard tomorrow, and Wrotham's clerk, Mr. Hargreaves, has chosen this most inopportune time to visit his mother in Bournemouth. . . . Ursula, I trust you can entertain our friends while I am gone."

Ursula flushed. She had clearly disappointed her father yet again by her behavior. Why could she not learn the art of small talk? She took a quick sip of champagne and smiled brightly. "Mrs. Pomfrey-Smith, have you seen the latest *La Mode*? I saw the most beautiful evening cape. . . ."

SEVEN

Winifred sat across from Ursula at the wooden table. Her dark green dress with white arrows marked her as a prisoner, while the circles under her eyes spoke of many sleepless nights in her small cell at Holloway Prison.

"How are you?" Ursula asked.

Winifred merely shrugged as reply.

"Are they treating you well?" Ursula knew she sounded foolish.

Winifred gave a wan smile. "Thanks for coming, Sully. I wasn't sure they were even going to allow me visitors. I had to wait four weeks last time, and they wouldn't even let me get any letters."

Winifred had been imprisoned twice for "breaches of the peace" related to her WSPU activities. The first time she had been arrested for trying to enter the House of Commons after a WSPU demonstration; the second arrest came after she took part in a march on Downing Street and was caught throwing stones through the window of the prime minister's house.

"I'm glad they allowed me to come," Ursula replied. "Not that my father knows I'm here. I came on the omnibus. But I wanted to let you know that I'm doing all I can to get you out of this mess."

"Has there been anything . . . ?" Winifred's voice trailed off.

Ursula shook her head sadly. "Nothing as yet. Inspector Harrison has ignored all my requests for information. Intolerable brute! I wish I knew what else to do. Everyone's treating me like an interfering schoolgirl. . . . I'm sorry, Winifred, I've been next to useless."

"Don't say that."

"Well, at least our sisters at the WSPU want to help. Believe it or not, I saw Anna just last week."

Winifred raised one eyebrow.

"Yes, it was strained," Ursula conceded. "But she wanted me to assure you that she would do all she could to help out. I asked her to ask around and see what anyone knew about Laura's other lovers."

Winifred's face clouded over, and Ursula immediately regretted her choice of words.

"Is there truly nothing more you can

remember?" Ursula asked.

Winifred shook her head. "I'm sorry."

"Was there anyone at Madame Launois's that night who could be involved?"

Again Winifred shook her head. "Laura was in a spiteful mood. She pointed out a number of people she claimed were ex-lovers, but Inspector Harrison said there was no one he suspected. Madame Launois's salons usually go all night. Most people probably didn't even leave there till five or six o'clock in the morning."

"Still, you never know what Anna may find out."

"Maybe." Winifred looked unconvinced, and Ursula reached out to clasp her friend's arm. A tap on the glass window by one of the prison guards forced her to pull away.

"Freddie, I need you to think hard. Did Laura ever talk about her father's travels? Did she ever mention the Radcliffe expedition?"

"The Radcliffe expedition? Never heard of it. Laura certainly never said anything to me about it, but then she rarely spoke of her father. According to her they weren't that close."

Ursula chewed her lip thoughtfully. "I don't know," she mused. "But something about Colonel Radcliffe's death doesn't make sense. Why did he kill himself? Did he feel guilty? Responsible for Laura's death somehow? There's something about him — and his relationship to my father. Yes, I know it's strange. I just have this feeling there's more to it all."

Winifred rubbed the back of her neck.

"Sorry, Freddie!" Ursula cried. "I've just been rambling on. Doesn't help you, now, does it? Anyway, looks like my time is up. I'd better get back home. I'll keep investigating, though. Keep your spirits up, old girl."

Winifred blinked back her tears. Ursula rose to her feet and was escorted out of the room.

"I have a one o'clock appointment with Lord Wrotham," Ursula said, stacking her gloves neatly on the desk before her.

The clerk pushed back his glasses and hastily scanned the appointment book in front of him. "I . . . I don't see anything here. Did you speak to Mr. Hargreaves? Are you sure you have an appointment?"

"Of course I'm sure," she replied, trying to appear nonchalant as she unpinned her hat. The clerk muttered under his breath, turning today's appointment page over and back again.

Ursula observed the clerk's confusion with

satisfaction. Less than an hour ago, she had overheard her father on the telephone (once again cursing Mr. Hargreaves's holiday in Bournemouth) demanding to know where Lord Wrotham could be found. Judging by the resultant confusion, Mr. Hargreaves's absence provided a perfect opportunity for Ursula to investigate Wrotham further. Her father had finally managed to arrange a luncheon meeting at Wrotham's club for half past twelve. Ursula furtively glanced at the clock mounted on the wall. It was now one o'clock. She wasn't sure how much time she had before Wrotham returned, but she was determined to seize the chance to look for any information that could assist Winifred. All she needed was to convince the clerk to let her wait in Wrotham's chambers — alone.

"Have you found it yet?" Ursula queried.

The clerk frowned. "I don't understand. . . . Lord Wrotham said nothing to me about any meeting. . . . I've been next door all morning attending to my usual duties, but I'm sure he would have left me a note if he knew. . . ." The clerk's voice kept drifting off as he hemmed and hawed. "Are you a client?" he asked, failing to keep the incredulity of that notion from creeping into his voice. "Where is your solicitor?"

"Lord Wrotham is a close personal adviser to my family," Ursula replied brusquely. "And our appointment is a long-standing one. Look, I am not easily refused — so why don't you just let me wait for Lord Wrotham in his chambers? No doubt he has merely been detained briefly and will be here for our appointment as planned."

The clerk stared at Ursula blankly.

"Well?" she prompted him.

A knock at the door brought an exasperated sigh from the clerk. He motioned Ursula to wait as he walked out from behind Mr. Hargreaves's desk. The door swung open to reveal a short, rotund man in a pinstriped frock coat.

"Where the blazes is Hargreaves?!" the man demanded. "I've got three briefs here for Wrotham, Masters, and Barnes, and nobody around here seems to know a dickey bird about 'em!"

Ursula coughed politely. The man glared at her from the doorway. Ursula returned his stare with the haughty raise of an eyebrow.

The clerk readjusted his glasses for a second time. "Miss Marlow," he turned and said wearily, "why don't you wait for his lordship inside while I attend to this?"

Ursula could barely conceal a smile of

satisfaction as she swept her way into Lord Wrotham's chambers with a deliberate flourish of her fur-trimmed cloak.

She closed the door quickly and hastily scanned the room. The bookshelves were lined with law reports and leather-bound books, all neatly arranged. Even the morning's *Times* had been painstakingly refolded and placed next to a black umbrella on one of the lower shelves. But despite the regulation and order that Lord Wrotham obviously exerted, there was still an undeniable undercurrent of decadence that intrigued her.

Ursula quietly crossed the room, placed her hat and gloves down on one of the leather armchairs, and leaned over Lord Wrotham's desk. It had a tooled-leather writing surface, and apart from a wooden desk tray, inkwell, silver cigarette box, and ashtray, the desk was spotlessly clear. Only a dark green Faber-Castell pencil carelessly left in the center disturbed the symmetry and order of the desktop. There were no piles of paper or case notes lying upon the desk, no noticeable signs of Winifred's (or anyone else's) case files. Wrotham would hardly be that obvious, Ursula thought ruefully. He was nothing if not methodical. Still, she thought, it was worth taking a look.

Ursula knelt down behind the desk, inching Wrotham's tall, barrel-backed chair out of the way, and slowly slid open the top drawer. Inside, there was a box of monogrammed letter paper and envelopes, an ink blotter, a gold-plated Waterman fountain pen, and a half-filled bottle of black ink. The next drawer down contained a wooden box with a neatly assembled collection of shirt collars and studs. She caught the faint yet distinctive scent she always associated with Lord Wrotham — a heady mixture of bergamot and tobacco — and closed the drawer quickly. In the third drawer there was a brass magnifying glass in a velvet-lined case. Ursula sighed — Lord Wrotham's life seemed even more mundane than expected.

She examined the bottom the desk, running her hand along the smooth wood to feel for any recesses or compartments. Nothing. A quick inspection of the remaining desk drawers, however, revealed nothing more than additional stationery and a dusty barrister's wig still in its box. She crawled over to the other side, slid open the top right-hand drawer, and peered in. What she saw made her recoil sharply, and she had to stifle a cry as she banged her elbow on the desk chair. Why on earth would Lord

Wrotham have a gun in his office?

Ursula gingerly picked up the Webley revolver by its handle. It was so much heavier than she would have imagined. She quelled a momentary flutter of panic before placing the revolver carefully back into the drawer next to a box of cartridges. She rubbed her elbow before closing the drawer. Suddenly Lord Wrotham's life didn't seem quite so dull.

She glanced about the room. She didn't have time to dwell on the matter of the gun. She needed to refocus on the task at hand. Where would Wrotham have put Winifred's files? she wondered. Surely he must have some information that could be of use, though it was hardly something he would let Mr. Hargreaves file. No, whatever he had he would keep close to him. Ursula felt sure of this. It was just a question of where.

Pacing the room, she ran her fingers absently along the antique globe that stood on a pedestal near the door to Lord Wrotham's antechamber. A few more steps and she reached the edge of the bookshelves. She laid a tentative hand on the stuffed bird perched on an artificial wooden branch. The brass plaque beneath it read "*Ara ararauna* — Blue and Gold Macaw." Ursula glided her fingers along the feathery-soft chest and murmured quietly to herself before crossing to the display case in the corner. Though the corner was dark, Ursula could see that the glass cabinet was scrupulously clean. There was not a speck of dust or smudge of a fingerprint. Cautiously she bent over, trying to ensure she didn't touch the glass. Displayed inside was an old vellum book, open to reveal a page bearing a miniature illumination of the Annunciation. On the opposite page was a prayer in Gothic German script with a wide ivy-leaf border. Again Ursula was taken off guard. Like the tapestry behind Lord Wrotham's desk, the manuscript seemed incongruous. There was something about both of them that suggested an aesthetic sensibility that she did not expect of him.

Ursula pursed her lips — all this ruminating was wasting valuable time. She was here to help Winifred, not ponder Lord Wrotham's decorating tastes. She turned away, angry at herself for being distracted so easily. As she turned, her skirt brushed against the case, and she heard the distinctive clang of a metal key hitting glass. She looked down and saw a small key inside a keyhole on the strip of wood that framed the glass case. Attached to this key was a much larger one, dangling from a dark red ribbon. It was the larger key that she had brushed against.

"I wonder . . ." Ursula mused, her gaze falling once more on the tapestry that hung behind Lord Wrotham's desk. She untied the larger key from the ribbon and crossed the room.

She carefully pulled the tapestry back and peered behind it. At first she could see nothing but the wood paneling. She ran her hands along the smooth wood until her finger caught a groove; she could just make out the faint outline of a keyhole embedded in a knot in one of the panels. Ursula hitched up her skirt and perched on the edge of a shelf as she tried to maneuver the key into the lock. The key turned easily, and with one brief tug the panel slid open. Inside was a small recessed hole, just big enough to hold a tin box. Ursula pulled out the box and laid it on the desk.

Exhaling slowly, she opened the box. Inside was a suede-covered book and a small stack of papers tied together with a leather band. Ursula opened the book and discovered that it was a diary. The title page said *The Radcliffe Expedition — A Journey Down the Orinoco* (the latter part had been scratched out and replaced with the ominous words *A Descent into Hell*). Mindful of the time, Ursula thumbed through the diary quickly, trying to ascertain whether it was relevant to the inquiry into Laura's death.

What started out as an orderly description of an expedition, however, seemed to swiftly deteriorate into a mess of scrawls and grotesque caricatures. One page caught her eye, for the caricature was of a man whom there was no mistaking. It was her father, hideously contorted, dangling from a hangman's noose. Ursula stared at it in horror. On the following page was another drawing, this time of a group of men — distorted but nevertheless unmistakable. There was her father and some of his colleagues sitting behind a long table. They were dining on a gruesome assortment of butchered animals. Beneath them were scrawled the words *Radcliffe's puppetmasters — may they dine in hell.* What, Ursula wondered, did her father have to do with a South American expedition? More puzzling was why Lord Wrotham was hiding this — was there a link between Laura Radcliffe's death and Colonel Radcliffe's involvement in this expedition? Ursula turned back to the front page. There was a name engraved there. *Ronald Henry Bates.* The name meant nothing to her. Her father had never mentioned such a man.

Ursula bit her lip and glanced at the clock — it was already half past one. Time was running out.

She put down the diary and untied the papers. The first of these were notes of the interview with Winifred, handwritten in Lord Wrotham's decisive script. Ursula tried to digest the information as quickly as possible. Nothing seemed remarkable except for his notations in the margin of the second page. Wrotham had written three questions:

What is she hiding?
Link with Bates?
How do we deal with Ursula?

Ursula tried to keep her self-control, but her anger was rising. However, there was no time, she told herself, to worry about that now. She needed to find out as much as she could as quickly as possible.

The second paper was a typed letter to Lord Wrotham from the permanent under-secretary of the Foreign Office, stating that inquiries were ongoing but as yet there was *No indication that the man you seek has entered Britain. Our agents have traced him to Venezuela, but no further information is available.* Ursula refolded this and turned to the next sheaf of paper, which seemed even more perplexing. There were four pages, and they appeared to be a list of her father's business interests. The most puzzling aspect was that the writing was Lord Wrotham's. Ursula scanned the list and could see nothing that appeared to relate to the case against Winifred. Lord Wrotham had circled some of the entries and scribbled comments next to others, but none of it made any sense to her. She was halfway down the list when a notation on the top of the page stopped her short. It was written in red ink and underlined: *How much is Marlow willing to pay?* Ursula was about to read the remaining papers when she heard voices outside.

She stifled an exclamation and hastily stuffed the papers and the diary back into the tin box. She shoved the box into the recess and pulled the tapestry into place. She was just replacing the key in the glass case when Lord Wrotham opened the door and strode inside.

"I was admiring your manuscript," Ursula said with a calmness that belied the thumping of her heart in her chest. She saw Wrotham glance at the desk, and the image of him holding the revolver suddenly came to mind. Perhaps the pencil had not been placed quite so carelessly, she thought.

"It's been in the family for generations," Wrotham replied evenly as he walked past and placed his hat down on the desk. Ursula was not deceived. She saw how he raised his hand to push back his hair and knew that for a moment at least he had been as unnerved as she.

"It's a Book of Hours dating back to 1475," Wrotham continued. "A gift from the Duke of Bavaria, or so I'm told."

"How very interesting," Ursula replied with icy politeness, her composure rapidly returning.

Wrotham took off his dark gray overcoat, opened the door to his antechamber, and hung it up on the coatrack just inside the doorway. As he returned and closed the door behind him, he drew out his pocket-watch and unlatched it from the fob chain. He then placed the watch in the top right-hand drawer, his eyes watching her closely. Ursula held a momentary breath. Lord Wrotham sat down behind his desk, reached for a cigarette from his silver cigarette box, and leaned back in his chair as he proceeded to light it.

"So, Miss Marlow," he began, "why are you here?" He gave her no time to respond before he continued. "I have no doubt that you knew I was meeting your father, so I'm left to wonder why you deceived poor old Chatterley out there that we had an appointment."

"Oh, I'm sure you know why I'm here," Ursula retorted smoothly, gathering up her hat and gloves from the armchair.

"I'm hardly likely to leave sensitive case files lying around in my office, now, am I?"

"Well, you have to give a girl full marks for trying," Ursula replied with a deadpan smile.

Lord Wrotham studied her face. "Satisfied, are we?" he asked.

"Not in the least! But in all seriousness, Lord Wrotham, I do apologize for my impromptu visit. When I last visited Miss Stanford-Jones, I noticed they had taken away all her books. I brought you my copy of *Women and Socialism* to give to her." Ursula fished the book out of her purse and handed it to him. "With Mr. Hargreaves away on holiday, I didn't feel comfortable leaving it with an unknown clerk."

"I see," Lord Wrotham replied, his eyes never leaving hers. "I will pass this on to Miss Stanford-Jones when I see her next."

"Thank you." She bowed her head as she pulled on her gloves one by one. "I really must be going."

"Of course," Lord Wrotham stood up and

walked over to the door. "Good day, Miss Marlow," he said in a voice laced with sarcasm. "I'm sure Miss Stanford-Jones will be touched by your concern for her."

Ursula edged past him, hurried down the stairs and out into the quadrangle, troubled by the fresh litany of unanswered questions her visit had raised.

EIGHT

"How the hell should I react, my girl, when I read such muck . . . such filth in the *Daily Mail?*"

Ursula was silent. Her father, enraged, was pounding his fist on the desk in frustration. He had summoned her to his office at Butler's Wharf, adjacent to the warehouses along Shad Thames, to berate her for talking to Mr. Hackett.

"I didn't tell him anything!" Ursula protested.

"But you did talk to him."

"Well, I can hardly deny it —"

"No, lassie, you damn well cannot. Harrison's man saw you. Damn it, Ursula, how could you be so foolish?!"

"What does the article say?" Ursula asked quietly.

Her father threw the newspaper across the desk. She picked it up carefully and started to read.

The article bore the banner THE CURSE OF THE RADCLIFFE EXPEDITION?

Two decades on, and the mystery surrounding the Radcliffe expedition continues to deepen, with the deaths of Laura and William Radcliffe last month. Colonel Radcliffe, who led the ill-fated expedition to Venezuela in 1888, was found on his Godalming estate with an apparently self-inflicted bullet wound to the head. His eldest daughter, Laura, was found only days earlier, the victim of a vicious knife attack. Although Miss Winifred Stanford-Jones, who stands trial for the murder of Laura Radcliffe, is a well-known violent proponent of the "vote for women" campaign, recent evidence has come to this paper's attention that suggests the Metropolitan Police may have been premature in dismissing accounts that Miss Radcliffe's death could be related to her father's expedition.

The Radcliffe expedition — which was funded by an endowment from some of the North's most successful businessmen; Mr. Robert Marlow, the prominent industrialist, provided the bulk of the finances to fund the expedition, along with his business associates Messrs Gerard Anderson (of Anderson & Stowe Ltd.) and Daniel Abbott (of Northern Railways fame) — ended in April 1888 with a brutal uprising by the native Indians that claimed the life of the botanist Ronald Henry Bates.

Ursula looked up and was about to protest further but was merely instructed to "read on."

She did as her father ordered, and it was then she fully realized why her father was so angry.

While the stated purpose of the expedition was to supply the British Natural History Museum with specimens for its tropical fauna and flora collections, one cannot help but speculate, with such wealthy and influential business concerns involved, if there wasn't a more lucrative objective in mind. The mystery surrounding the fate of the Radcliffe expedition deepens when one considers the lengths to which these businessmen continue to protect the expedition's secret. If the expedition has no bearing on the death of Laura Radcliffe, then why is Mr. Robert Marlow funding the defense of Miss Stanford-Jones?

Ursula finished reading and replaced the newspaper on her father's desk.

"He said he worked for the *Star*," she said quietly.

Her father sat down heavily in his chair, and Ursula felt a pang of regret. She certainly never intended that her comment to Mr. Hackett would lead to such speculation.

"I want you to promise me," Robert Marlow began, "that you will stop your interferin' right now!"

"But, Papa, I just want to help Freddie."

"Freddie be damned! I forbid you to look into this anymore! Do you hear me? No puttin' your nose in where it's not needed. You need to be thinkin' of your future. Can't have you playing detective when you should be finding yourself a husband!"

Ursula flushed, trying to restrain her anger and humiliation at being spoken to like this. She had never seen her father in such a state. Their relationship had always been so close. Hot tears started streaming down her face.

Her father reached out and then checked himself.

"Nay, lass," he said. "I mean it. Tears

won't help. You've got to promise me you'll leave well enough alone. Miss Stanford-Jones has the best lawyers. I should know — I'm payin' for them, for Christ's sake. That's got to be enough for you."

Ursula nodded, though in her heart she refused to give up.

"Well now, that's that." Her father was calming down. "Tom'll drive you home, and mind you don't linger. I need him back to help finalize the terms of the McClintock deal."

"Right," Ursula answered stiffly.

There was a knock, and Tom poked his head around the door as it opened. "You wanted me, sir? Sorry, it took me a while — I was just checking the load that came in from Cairo."

"Drive Ursula home, would you? And mind you be back before four. We still have a few more hours to put in before we get the McClintock deal finalized."

"Right ho!" Tom replied jovially.

Ursula winced. She had little doubt that Tom knew what her father had been saying to her all along.

Tom opened the door and led her out into the dim corridor that connected the office with the warehouse. There was a faint smell of spice in the air even though her father's warehouse held only bolts of cloth and linens. Her father had recently established a new venture to supply haberdashery to Mc-Clintock's department stores and had appointed Tom to oversee the deal.

Tom led Ursula into Copper Row, past two men unloading crates from the back of a horse-drawn delivery van.

"Like my new motorcar?" Tom asked, pointing out a compact two-seater motorcar that was parked behind the van. "It's a Humber. I bought it just last week."

"Very nice," Ursula answered coolly.

He helped her climb up onto the red leather bench seat. The car was open to the elements, so Ursula wrapped her scarf around her head before replacing her hat. Tom dug out a pair of driving goggles from beneath the driver's seat and pulled them on.

"You look ridiculous in those," Ursula commented as she jerked her gloves out of her coat pocket and tugged them on one at a time.

Tom made no comment. He merely started the car engine, grinned, and gave her the thumbs-up signal as he maneuvered the motorcar past the delivery van and out onto Tooley Street.

Once through Lambeth and over the New

Vauxhall Bridge, Tom started to talk. Ursula kept her eyes firmly on the road. She was in no mood to listen to his chatter.

"The McClintock deal is an important one, you know," he called out over the engine noise as they turned into Buckingham Palace Road, past Victoria Station and the Grosvenor Hotel. The traffic stopped to let a double-decker bus pull out from the pavement. "It's a great honor to be given such responsibility. I think it shows how well your father and I work together," Tom continued. "The new position also provides me with much greater opportunity for advancement, and, as I've told your father, I've now saved plenty of money to ensure you will be well provided for."

"Hmmm?" Ursula blinked. She hadn't been listening closely.

Tom turned the motorcar into Eccleston Street and pulled into Chester Square.

"What do you mean 'provided for'?" Ursula asked as Tom took off his driving goggles.

"I mean for a marriage settlement." Tom shook his head and ruffled his hair with his fingers.

"What? Me? Marry you?!" Ursula was incredulous.

"It's what your father wants."

"Oh, I think not!" she exclaimed.

"He told me just this morning how anxious he was to have you settled," Tom continued, smoothing his hair back in place. "He hinted that an offer from me would be well received."

"Did he, now?" Ursula responded coldly.

"Yes." Tom reached over and grabbed her hand. "Oh, Ursula, think of it. I've got the money and the opportunity to help your father run his company. Think what a relief it would be to him. To know that his right-hand man will also be his son-in-law. That your inheritance is safe and secure with me. You need never worry about anything. Oh, Ursula, we'd be perfect for each other!"

"I doubt that very much," Ursula replied, pulling her hand away. She started to climb down out of the car. Tom leaped out to assist, catching her around the waist as she lost her footing on the step.

She pushed him away angrily. "Really, Tom!" she admonished.

Tom's eyes flickered for a moment before he smiled once more. "Come on, old thing!" he said. "You know it's for the best. Dash it all, I'll even let you continue your 'vote for women' lark. There're not many husbands who would do that."

Ursula tried to quell her anger. "Tom,"

she said firmly, looking him dead in the eye, "I don't love you."

Tom brushed his sandy mustache with his thumb. She could see the boyish charm in his eyes fade, and his gaze grew cold and resolute. "That will change."

There seemed to be tension about him now. As if something tightly wound within him threatened to snap and break. Sensing his hostility, she took a step back.

"Promise me you'll think about it," he said with a fixed smile.

"I shall not promise you anything, Tom," Ursula replied, and turned away. She ran up the stairs, opened the front door, and closed it quickly behind her. Once inside, Ursula took off her scarf and leaned against the door. She closed her eyes for a moment, trying to calm herself. Really, she thought, I don't know whether to laugh or scream. Catching sight of Mrs. Stewart making her way down the stairs, she decided it was best to do neither and retreated into the front parlor to think in peace.

Ursula was curled up on the wing-backed sofa, notebook and pencil in hand. Despite her father's protestations, she wasn't about to give up her investigations. She tried to write down some notes, but nothing seemed to make any sense. She was thinking about the night Laura died and trying to decipher the limited information she had. If Laura had died sometime between one and four in the morning, then whatever drug was used must have been extremely powerful. It had left Winifred unconscious for at least three hours. And what of the open window? Surely that was the means of entry, but it would have taken considerable skill to scale the wall and get in through the window. Ursula had once arrived through the rear entrance to the house for a clandestine WSPU meeting and noticed that the white-painted brick wall at the rear of Winifred's house had nothing but a black downspout from the roof to the ground. There was also a small garden enclosure and an alley running along the back that the delivery vans and carts used. In the early morning, the alley would have been deserted.

Ursula chewed the end of the pencil lead thoughtfully. Try as she might, though, she couldn't concentrate on the matter at hand. She kept hearing her father's furious insistence that she cease her investigation into Laura's death. She couldn't in all conscience let the matter rest — she couldn't stand by and do nothing while her friend was tried for a murder she didn't commit. Ursula was unsettled by her father's anger and saddened that she had disappointed him once again. She was further unnerved by Tom's ridiculous proposal. She put down her notebook with a sigh. She was far too distracted to concentrate.

The telephone rang in the hall, and Ursula heard Biggs answer it with his usual solemnity (Biggs handled the telephone as if it were a precious piece of porcelain that could shatter and break if not treated with all due respect). Her ears pricked up when she heard him put down the receiver and walk up the hallway to the door of the front parlor.

Biggs knocked and opened the door. "A Mr. Neville Hackett on the telephone for you, miss," he said.

Ursula leaped up and hurried to the telephone that lay perched on the rosewood table at the base of the stairs. "Hello, Mr. Hackett?" she asked, leaning over the receiver.

"Ursula? Thought you might like to know I managed to get hold of a copy of the coroner's report. They couldn't identify the drug in Laura's body. The coroner classified it as a 'substance unknown.' "

"That could be very useful. Anything else?"

"Only a quick conversation with one of the constables on the case. I chatted him up over a pint or two at the Dog & Otter. Off the record, of course, but looks like what they found at Freddie's place was some morphine. Nothing else."

"So where did this 'unknown' substance come from?" Ursula asked.

"Exactly," was his reply.

NINE

"There," Julia said, pinning a large silver peacock brooch onto Ursula's bodice. "That finishes the outfit nicely."

"Oh, Julia," Ursula sighed. "I can't believe I have to go to this."

She still hadn't quite recovered from the impudence (and imprudence) of Tom's proposal that afternoon. She wanted neither to attend tonight's party nor to disappoint her father by refusing to go. This frustration was like a choker around her neck. Each moment she felt as if it were being tugged tighter and tighter, until there could be no escape.

"Now, miss," Julia replied with a mock reproving smile, "you know how much this means to your father. You owe it to him to accompany 'im — like a proper lady."

Ursula muttered under her breath but nevertheless was reconciled to facing the dinner party.

She had known her father's business associates and their families all her life. She had grown up with them, but still she felt somewhat removed and distant from their lives. After over a decade of working together, these men enjoyed a remarkable bond. From childhood, however, Ursula had always been aware that much of what defined this relationship went unsaid. She could never quite identify what it was; she knew only that there was a powerful bond, a solemn loyalty, that seemed to tie one man, one family, to another.

Sure to be there tonight was Daniel Abbott, Cecilia's father, who had already established a successful railway network in the Northwest when Ursula's father first met him in 1879, just before Marlow bought the Preston mills. With interests in America and Europe, the Abbotts now turned their attention to securing a lucrative marriage for their only daughter, Cecilia. Ursula loved how Cecilia flaunted her father's money and flouted his expectations.

"Will Cecilia be there tonight?" Ursula asked as she followed her father down the stairs. Julia was trailing two steps behind her with Ursula's violet evening jacket and gloves in her hands.

Marlow adjusted the lapels of his best

dress jacket as he descended, his coat and gloves neatly folded over his arm.

He did not bother to turn around to answer but merely said, "Seems that Cecilia has gotten involved with a Fabian — this one with even fewer prospects than the last. I expect Abbott's keeping a tight rein on her at the moment, so Cecilia's unlikely to attend."

Ursula's mood grew even more dreary at the prospect of an evening without anyone interesting to talk to. There would be no escaping the Andersons. The dinner was being held at their Kensington house after all. Gerard Anderson, a Scot, was as red-faced and stout as his wife, Elizabeth, was pasty and thin. Gerard looked less like an accountant and more like the local publican, but he was her father's financial adviser and, by his own account, a self-made millionaire (his investments in the Americas having proved extremely lucrative). The Andersons had four daughters. The eldest was Miranda, who was five years older than Ursula. She married a young artillery officer before she gained her majority but was widowed soon after when her husband fell in the Battle of Bakenlaagte in the Eastern Transvaal. Miranda's constant display of a martyr's superiority caused Ursula no end of aggravation. Next was Charlotte, only two years older than Ursula. Her decision to join the Sisters of St. Clare had been a cause of considerable mortification for the whole family. The two youngest Anderson daughters, Marianne and Emily, were not yet "out," and so their potential remained to be seen. But as Marianne was dimwitted and Emily was plain, Ursula wondered if money would be sufficient for them to forge any appropriate connection.

The sour-faced Obadiah Dobbs would also be at the dinner. The Dobbs family was the only one among Robert Marlow's business associates to have been blessed with a son. So far Christopher Dobbs showed the greatest promise for carrying on the family business. Obadiah, who went to sea when he was nine, had formed his own shipping line with capital provided by Daniel Abbott and Ursula's father, after the three met at a Mechanics Institute class in Liverpool in 1881. Although Christopher cut quite a dashing figure, Ursula found his obsession with ships a bore.

Ursula sighed as she and her father climbed into the backseat of Bertie. She wasn't sure which would be worse, putting up with the Anderson girls' banal chatter or Christopher's bravado.

She seemed engulfed in layers of patterned silk and velvet and was trying desperately to straighten both her skirt and jacket to make room for her father to sit down.

"I've invited Lord Wrotham as well," her father said, just as Ursula made herself as comfortable as she could in the narrow seat. She tugged on one of her pearl earrings with an agitated tremor.

"We may 'ave some business matters to attend to," her father continued as he eased into the seat and lapsed into the thick Lancashire accent he usually took pains to disguise. "Tha knows how it is. . . . So, lass, I may send you home early. There's nowt you'd be interested in anyway."

Her father could be so patronizing sometimes! But Ursula was inwardly relieved. This way she would have an excuse to leave early. Lord Wrotham's presence, however, only served to intensify her annoyance. Her father's dependency on him irritated her. She felt restless and cross.

Samuels parked the motorcar outside the Andersons' Kensington town house and then came around to assist Ursula and her father from the car. In his cap, greatcoat, and leather gloves, Samuels looked the quintessential chauffeur. Ursula couldn't resist a smile. She suspected that he was only too keen to leave them so he could pop down to the kitchen to share a cup of tea with the Andersons' new scullery maid, Mollie, who was (according to Julia) the "spitting image" of Lily Elsie, Samuels's favorite stage actress.

Ursula took her father's arm as they walked up to the black enamel front door with the large brass knocker. She looked up at the imposing four-story town house with its redbrick and tiled trim and wondered about the houses that had been demolished to make way for these "modern" mansions. Gerard Anderson had authorized demolition of a row of Georgian terrace houses in order to build this new development. Instead of being impressed by all the electricals and conveniences (why, the Andersons even had central heating!), Ursula felt saddened by the newness of the structure and found herself longing to know the history of the places that had come before, the families that had lived here, their love affairs and deaths. Her father gave her a poke to wake her from her thoughts and hurried her along inside as the door opened and they were welcomed in by John, the Andersons' footman.

He led them into the wood-paneled receiving room, where Elizabeth Anderson was waiting to greet them. She was standing between a deep-seated red damask sofa and the Tiffany standard lamp, rubbing the palms of her hands together. Usually Elizabeth took such pains with her appearance, but tonight there was a faint aura of unease about her. She looked uncomfortable in her dress, her hair had been too closely pinned, and the skin on her forehead was stretched taut.

"Mrs. Anderson," Ursula said with a smile and a perfunctory bow of her head.

"Miss Marlow!" Elizabeth exclaimed. "How beautiful you look this evening."

Ursula raised an eyebrow but did not comment. Elizabeth Anderson had never complimented her before on her appearance.

"Are Marianne and Emily not joining us this evening?" Ursula asked with feigned sweet temper. She had already noted that she seemed to be the only daughter present. On the far side of the room, Obadiah Dobbs stood with his back to her. Rigid and unyielding, his taut frame was silhouetted against the lamplight in the corner as he appeared to stare at the newly commissioned family portrait on the wall. Daniel Abbott was sitting in a high-backed chair, apparently absorbed in the whiskey and soda he held in his hands. He occasionally looked up and stared across at Dobbs, but all too soon his gaze returned once more to the drink in his hands. There was no sign of Gerard Anderson, but Ursula noticed how her father immediately left the room after no more than a cursory nod to Elizabeth. Ursula was uneasy; the atmosphere in the room was unlike that of any other dinner she had attended here.

"No," Elizabeth replied carefully, "they have gone abroad."

"Abroad?!" They might have gone to the moon, Ursula was that surprised. "But who is accompanying them? When did they leave? Where are they going? Papa never mentioned that you were planning a trip!"

Elizabeth looked unaccountably embarrassed. "Oh, it was quite a rushed enterprise. My sister and her husband were planning a trip to Constantinople, and the girls just simply fell in love with the idea. Miranda's going over there, too. Just think of it! They only left just yesterday, and the household has been in such a state."

"I can't believe that —" Ursula began, and then she noticed that Elizabeth would not meet her eye. "I'm surprised you agreed to hold this dinner at all," Ursula continued, watching Elizabeth closely. "You must be exhausted from all the arrangements!" Elizabeth went pink; Ursula suspected that she had replied inappropriately and said no more. How strange this was, that the Anderson girls should all be off on holiday so suddenly — with Christmas just weeks away, no less. Something was gravely amiss, Ursula thought.

It was then that the footman announced the arrival of Lord Oliver Wrotham.

To her surprise, Lord Wrotham did not come unaccompanied. He brought Lady Ashton with him, and as they entered the premises, Ursula felt a twinge of envy. She couldn't help but contrast Lord Wrotham's cool composure to Tom's florid eagerness. Lady Ashton also looked so sophisticated and composed in her tight blond curls — a marked contrast to Ursula's dark auburn hair and nervous energy.

Elizabeth led Lady Ashton across the room to introduce Ursula as Wrotham made his way to where Marlow and Gerard Anderson were drinking champagne.

"I have so longed to meet you. My Lord Wrotham has spoken of you often." Lady Ashton's voice warbled like a bird's as she spoke.

"Really? I find that most surprising,"

Ursula demurred.

Lady Ashton smiled, narrowed her pale blue-green eyes, and took in the room "Now, that's a particularly fine piece of Sèvres porcelain on display in the reproduction Sheraton cabinet. Don't you think?"

Ursula nodded and pretended to be looking at a portrait of Elizabeth by the Scottish painter Ranken while she tried to overhear Lord Wrotham and her father's conversation.

"We need to talk," Lord Wrotham said in a low tone.

Robert Marlow glanced around with apparent indifference. "Here?" he asked.

"No. But tonight."

"That urgent, eh?" Marlow's voice seemed strained. Ursula could tell that her father was only pretending to be unconcerned.

"Yes."

It seemed Ursula wasn't the only one interested in what they had to say. Dobbs, who was at the other side of the room, was eyeing her father and Lord Wrotham closely. He took a sip of whiskey as his eyes darted from Lord Wrotham's face to her father's.

Lady Ashton tapped Ursula lightly on the arm. "Tell me, my dear, are you interested in art?"

"Why, yes, yes I am," Ursula replied with

some surprise.

"Though I fancy your tastes are slightly different from Elizabeth Anderson's. What do you think about these avant-garde painters such as Picasso and Braque?"

"I think their work is very exciting." Ursula responded with genuine enthusiasm.

Lady Asthon smiled lazily. "*Bizarre cubiques,* is it not? You really must get to Paris sometime and see Montmartre. Such an inspiration," she drawled.

"Educating Miss Marlow on the value of modern art, Lady Ashton?"

Ursula jumped at the sound of his voice and Lady Ashton turned to Lord Wrotham with a flutter of her pale eyelashes. "Surely you don't disapprove? A girl with Miss Marlow's prospects should be encouraged to keep up with the very latest in art as well as fashion. Besides, I think Paris would suit her very well. . . ." Much to Ursula's horror, Lady Ashton gave her arm a playful poke.

"Of course . . ." Lord Wrotham demurred, giving Ursula a quick bow and offering her his greeting.

A gong sounded, signaling that dinner was served.

"Shall we?' Lord Wrotham asked, proffering his arm to Lady Ashton. His request prompted another flutter of eyelashes and a light trill of laughter. Both sent a shiver of irritation through Ursula that she found hard to hide. Her father held out his arm to escort her to the dining room. Dobbs excused himself briefly from the room to make a telephone call, while Daniel Abbott had to content himself with Elizabeth Anderson's company as they made their way to dinner.

Gerard Anderson always excelled when entertaining his business partners, and tonight was no exception. The first course was turtle soup, followed by turbot with lobster sauce. Then came the guinea fowls, a forequarter of lamb, and a roasted duck. Conversation over dinner focused on free trade and tariff reform, but Ursula was distracted. Seated opposite Lady Ashton she sensed throughout the meal that she was being critically appraised, like some prize pig at a fair.

Lady Ashton hardly spoke but seemed to be weighing something in her mind as she watched Ursula carefully. Ursula felt her gaze every time she placed her fork on the plate and with every sip of wine she took. It was only when her father started to engage Lady Ashton in conversation that Ursula felt her attention shift. Her father was on about one of his perennial topics, what he termed the "degeneration of England," when he asked Lady Ashton what her views were on the role of upper-class women in today's society. Ursula sighed; no doubt this line of questioning was designed to emphasize her father's displeasure at his own daughter's politics. Lady Ashton replied vaguely that she would have liked the opportunity to have a family, thereby contributing to the much-needed next generation. Ursula's father nodded vigorously, expressing his concern that while the birth rate among the educated and the wealthy continued to fall, the poor were overrun by poverty, disease, and squalor and they perpetuated this through an alarmingly high number of births.

"Havin' been brought up in the slums," Robert Marlow said with a wave of his knife, "I know what it's like to have nothing, tryin' to feed a family of eight on a mere miner's wage. Where I grew up children were taken by either disease or the workhouse. We cannot allow the national degradation to continue unchecked. Why once a criminal would have been merely hanged, now we provide him with soup kitchens and shelters. With attitudes like that we may as well all sleep out on benches in Green Park!"

Ursula sighed. She disagreed, but as they were in company she restrained herself from starting an argument. Besides, from the look on the faces of Anderson, Dobbs, and Abbott, her father's sentiments were more than shared. Lady Ashton, however, fell silent, her eyes once again moving to Ursula.

By the time the cheese soufflé was being served, Ursula began to sense an atmosphere of anticipation. Whatever it was, it remained unsaid and almost imperceptible, like a thin thread of cobweb hanging in the corner of a room.

After dessert Robert Marlow suggested that the ladies might like to retire for a bit while the gentlemen enjoyed port and cigars. Ursula stifled a groan — she always hated having to leave just when the discussion had any possibility of becoming interesting. Nevertheless, she quietly followed Elizabeth Anderson and Lady Victoria Ashton as they made their way out of the dining room and up the stairs in silence.

In the upstairs drawing room, each took a seat. Lady Ashton was the first to speak. "Tell me, Ursula, have you traveled much?"

Ursula was surprised by her abruptness.

Gone were the eyelash flutters and the smiles.

"No . . . hardly at all," Ursula replied slowly. "I've been to Scotland, of course, to visit my mother's family, but other than that I haven't. Why do you ask?"

"It is of no consequence," Lady Ashton replied quickly. Then, with a sly smile, she continued, "I hear that you have quite a wit — and a dangerous capacity for getting yourself into trouble."

"I'm sorry, Lady Ashton, I don't understand what you mean," Ursula replied, though she understood the woman's meaning perfectly. Winifred.

"I may be able to assist you and your father," Lady Ashton went on, unfazed.

"Assist?" Ursula echoed.

"Yes. I am in need of a companion — someone who can amuse me on my travels."

Ursula frowned. Surely all the complicity and silence was not about this? "I'm sorry, but I still fail to understand —"

Lady Ashton nodded and Elizabeth Anderson quietly left the room.

"Your father and Lord Wrotham believe that I may be able to help you at this difficult time. You must leave England, and I require a companion to accompany me abroad. How much simpler can this be?"

"But again you are mistaken," Ursula replied. "I have no desire to leave England. I'm sorry to say, but there really isn't anything that I need your assistance with."

Lady Ashton sighed and smiled. "Ursula, you will leave England. Your father will make sure of this. I'm just giving you an opportunity to see the world before your impending nuptials."

Ursula's stomach dropped. "There are no impending nuptials that I am aware of," she replied carefully.

Lady Ashton smiled again. "My dear," she replied, "everything has been arranged by your father. I would leave it in his hands if I were you."

Ursula's own hands gripped her skirt. "I don't know what you are talking about."

"Oh, really, aren't you over that Russian boy yet?! Your father has told me all about that ill-favored relationship. You need to accept the inevitable: Marriage to a man like Tom Cumberland would be the very best thing for a family such as yours."

Ursula's eyes narrowed. She heard the gentlemen's voices on the stairs. No sooner had they entered the drawing room to join the ladies than she rose to her feet and, with a defiant glare at Lady Ashton, pronounced that she was suddenly feeling "most unwell."

173

"Papa," Ursula instructed her father, "please take me home immediately."

"I don't think so, lass. You aren't going anywhere." Her father's reply was swift.

There was a shy knock on the open door, and a young maid entered, head bowed, carrying a tray of china cups and saucers and a large silver coffeepot. Nobody said a word until she had left.

"Papa, I insist." Ursula could barely contain her fury.

Her father ignored her. The others moved to take their seats. Lady Ashton busied herself straightening her brocade silk jacket. Humiliated and angry, Ursula was determined to thwart any plan that involved getting her wedded off to the insufferable Tom Cumberland.

She grabbed the side table, appearing to sway unsteadily.

"Papa . . . I . . ." she cried out softly, and with that she fainted to the floor, sending the china cups crashing.

Ursula opened her eyes to find herself in an unfamiliar bedroom. Lord Wrotham was bending over her, a curl of dark hair falling over his eyes as he loosened the buttons on the high collar of her blouse, and she could feel his breath, warm and steady against the nape of her neck.

"Neat trick," he commented, and Ursula couldn't repress a smile.

From the corner of her eye, she saw Elizabeth standing next to the bed wringing out a warm facecloth. She politely moved Lord Wrotham out of her way and placed the cloth on Ursula's forehead. As Lord Wrotham straightened up, Ursula noticed a hollowness around his eyes that belied his apparent lack of concern.

Just then her father hurried into the room.

"How is she?" he asked anxiously. Ursula felt a pang of guilt at deceiving him.

She tried to sit up slightly, saying, "I am feeling a little better, I think, Papa — please don't fret."

"Fret!" Her father exclaimed. "If you only knew what I feared!"

"Do not concern yourself, Robert." Lord Wrotham placed a reassuring hand on her father's arm. Ursula's eyes widened at Lord Wrotham's informality. "I assure you she is fine now," he continued. "I expect it was just the heat. The temperature in here is really quite infernal."

"Oh, dear," Elizabeth said. "Gerard will be angry. Can we . . . will Lady Ashton . . . ?"

"Nothing can be answered tonight," Robert Marlow replied, exasperated. "I must take Ursula home. Tell Gerard we will resume discussions tomorrow."

Ursula slowly tried to raise herself further. "And Lady Ashton?" Elizabeth asked.

"Leave her to me," was Lord Wrotham's harsh reply.

"Gerard is arranging for his footman and Samuels to carry you down to your car. Ah, here they are now."

As Ursula started to open her mouth to protest, she was lifted into the arms of the two young men and carried cautiously down the staircase, out of the house, and into the waiting car.

As they descended, she caught a glimpse of Lady Ashton following.

Robert Marlow and the others remained upstairs, deep in conversation. Ursula was deposited in the backseat of Bertie with a tartan rug placed over her knees to keep her warm.

"My dear." Lady Ashton's face appeared before her in the open window. "You needn't have resorted to such a spectacle."

"I don't know what you mean. . . ." Ursula replied tartly.

"Only that you should not have worried. About the nuptials, I mean." Lady Ashton smiled. "You are so very young and silly, m'dear, not to consent to my proposal. My offer would be the perfect opportunity for freedom before having to fulfill that particular obligation."

Ursula stared at her stonily. Voices could be heard coming closer.

"And to think," Lady Ashton concluded, "they were really concerned about your safety."

"Victoria?" Lord Wrotham asked, sounding very guarded.

"Just checking on the young'un," Lady Ashton replied breezily. "I think she's fine now."

The drive back home was tense and silent. Sitting beside her, her father seemed distant and preoccupied.

"Papa?" she prompted.

But her father just gazed out the car window, his face submerged in the dark shadows of London.

Ursula felt full of disappointment and fear. Her father lit a cigarette. She watched the blue wisps of smoke coil their way up and around his head, like a snake unfurling.

"I'm sorry," she finally said. "I just want everyone to leave us in peace."

"Peace would have been your acceptance of Lady Ashton's offer!" her father responded angrily.

Ursula choked back tears. "And what of Tom's offer?" she whispered.

Her father did not reply.

Would there be no respite, she wondered, from disappointing him? Perhaps in that, if in nothing else, she was constant. She could not be what he wanted her to be, but now she was certain of the pain this realization caused him. He was, after all, her father. Her heart longed at this moment to be true to his image of what she should be, to satisfy him in that regard at least. She felt adrift, longing for the comfort of his embrace, for the comfort of his approval.

"Papa, I want to know what everyone is so afraid of."

Her father looked dumbstruck.

"Why do you want me out of the country? Why have the Andersons sent their girls away? Does it have something to do with Laura's death?"

Her father's face, caught in the sudden glare of a streetlight, remained impassive.

"Oh, Papa, please tell me, I beg you! What really happened on the Radcliffe expedition? Why are you all so afraid?"

Her father did not answer.

The motorcar pulled up outside the house, and Samuels opened the curbside passenger door for Ursula before making his way around to the other side to assist her father.

"Never mind, Sam!" Robert Marlow snapped. "I've got it."

Samuels hurried back to Ursula. "Do you need me to help you inside, miss?" he asked kindly.

Ursula shook her head. "Run along, Sam, and tell Mrs. Stewart to put the kettle on if you would."

Samuels hurried down the stairs that led to the servants' entrance and went inside, leaving Ursula and her father alone.

She clambered out of the car awkwardly, the back of her silk court shoes catching on the slippery edge of the pavement. Straightening her skirt and pulling her coat closely around her shoulders, Ursula looked across the road, expecting to see the familiar face of Harrison's policeman standing opposite the house by the entrance to the Chester Square Gardens. The street, however, was empty and quiet. By then Biggs had opened the front door and let out a welcoming gleam of light that cheered her spirits.

Ursula walked tentatively up the steps, trying to avoid sliding on the ice that had already hardened on this cold November evening. At the top she waited for her father, framed against the light of the open doorway. She watched as he extinguished his cigarette underfoot before making his way up toward her, his greatcoat pulled in tight, collar lifted against the wind. Judging from her father's face, there seemed little chance for reconciliation between them tonight. Ursula sighed.

Suddenly the form of a man emerged from the shadows.

Her father turned quickly.

Ursula thought she saw the flash of metal as the stranger lifted something up and pointed it at her. The rest was a blur. Her father called out to her, but she seemed incapable of movement. Her father flung himself across her. Then there was a loud, resounding bang, and they both collapsed to the ground. Her father's weight was upon her.

"Papa . . ." She tried to speak, but she could hardly breathe.

Her father groaned as she tried to shift his weight. Ursula started to panic.

"Papa?" She managed to sit up. Her father's limbs felt heavy and dull as she struggled out from beneath him.

She looked down to see a dark stain spreading across her dress from where her father lay. There was blood on her hands, blood on her clothes, blood seeping out across the ice. She gathered him against her.

Her father looked up into her eyes and died in her arms.

TEN

Time had a peculiar resonance in London. Ursula could sense its passing as a rising swell beneath the earth. It uncovered the centuries before — as if an archaeological excavation were occurring before her eyes. She saw the hills of Roman Londinium rise up, felt the presence of a great sea of people coursing through the byways of a medieval town, like dark blood through the veins. She traveled with the ebb and flow of the Thames. She saw faces clouded in the mist, darkened images against a great fire. Smoke. Fog. Water. The elements of London past. She wondered now about her own past, of where she belonged and how she fit into the scheme of things. The shards of her world lay on the pavement before her. Her father was being taken away. A black hearse had arrived to take the body to the railway station. Men in dark coats moved around her. She was isolated in time. The tick of the clock meant nothing to her now. London moved to a separate time. Inside, she had stopped.

Ursula refused to receive any visitors. Their cards piled up on the table by the hat stand at the front door. The servants trod quietly, unobtrusively seeing to her needs, which were declining day by day. She shunned food. Drank only water. Lay in bed without bathing or dressing.

After nearly a week of this, she sensed that the household servants were determined to make a change. She felt it as surely as she felt London time echoing through the empty rooms. Mrs. Stewart became brisk and more demanding. She flung open curtains, cheerfully instructed her to get ready for the day. Ursula even started to obey. Mechanically and silently, she carried out the tasks of her existence. She dressed. She ate toast and marmalade. She drank tea. She allowed herself to be led downstairs.

Once the unpleasantness of a coronial inquiry had been completed, a funeral date was finally scheduled, and her father's last wishes would be fulfilled; he would be buried alongside his wife in Lancashire.

Lord Wrotham was to accompany Ursula on the train ride up to the Marlows' house in Whalley, the aptly named Gray House, for the funeral. Up till now Ursula had refused to see Lord Wrotham. Every day he called and left his card, and every day she instructed Julia to present her apologies. By the time she was due to leave for the funeral, though, she had lost the will to refuse him. When Lord Wrotham arrived at the appointed hour, he was clad in full mourning attire: jet-black three-button frock coat, stiff white shirt, slate gray waistcoat, and gray cravat held in place by a pin of white gold and onyx. As always he was the epitome of London present. Only Ursula noticed the tiny shaving cut on his jawline, just below his right ear.

She sat on the parlor sofa swathed in her black crepe dress, feeling weary.

"You should get some sleep," she said listlessly as Lord Wrotham made his way toward her. He knelt down and took her hand, first in one, then in both of his own.

No formalities. No paying of respects. He merely stared at her as she sat there, his eyes telling her what words could not. Ursula blinked back her tears.

"My lord," a voice from the doorway said, "I have placed Miss Marlow's trunk in the motorcar. We are ready to leave whenever you are."

"Thank you, James," Lord Wrotham replied, getting to his feet.

Lord Wrotham's chauffeur was driving them to Euston Station, where they were to catch the morning train to Manchester. Everyone except Julia had already been sent on ahead to open up the Gray House to prepare for the reception that would follow the funeral. As lady's maid, Julia had the privilege of accompanying Ursula and Lord Wrotham on the journey up north.

Ursula had rarely been back to her childhood home, her father keeping it only to have somewhere to stay when visiting his local mills and factories. Usually Miss Norris, Ursula's old nanny, would make any necessary arrangements for his stay. She lived alone in the back cottage and kept one bedroom and the drawing room aired and ready for whenever Ursula's father visited. Ursula could only imagine what manner of changes Mrs. Stewart and Biggs had now wrought. She had left all of the arrangements for the reception to them, giving them only two instructions. First, provision should be made for the workers likely to attend the funeral — brown ale and sandwiches, perhaps in the Co-operative Society Hall. Second, she wanted a formal reception to be held in the front drawing room of

Gray House, just as it had been for her mother.

"Ursula, we really should be going." Lord Wrotham's low voice brought her back from her thoughts. She nodded quickly, straightened out her skirt, adjusted her hat and veil, and got to her feet. On the small table beside her, she left unopened the note that had just arrived in the morning post from Winifred.

Julia was waiting by the front door in her woolen coat and knitted cap. She was white-faced and teary, but Ursula hadn't the strength to rally her spirits. As they got into the motorcar, Ursula thought she heard Lord Wrotham speak to Julia in low tones and was grateful for his compassion.

Euston Station, with its imposing Doric arch and great hall, was a cold and daunting place. The sound of whistles and steam engines put her nerves on edge, and already she felt dirty from the gritty coal dust that seemed to permeate the place. Ursula watched as her father's coffin was raised and placed in one of the rear carriages of the train. Lord Wrotham reached out quickly to steady her when he thought she might sway.

On the train ride, Julia sat opposite Ursula and Lord Wrotham in the first-class railway compartment that had been reserved for them, her hands tightly clasped in her lap. As the train pulled out of the station, Julia could not restrain her tears but managed to give Lord Wrotham a grateful, if awestruck, smile when he produced a crisp linen handkerchief from his coat pocket and handed it to her.

Ursula was thankful for his presence, but at the same time she found the closeness of it hard to bear. The way the edge of his coat touched her dress, the subtle smell of tobacco and bergamot about him — they served to remind her of her father. There were moments when it took all her will-power not to curl up beside him and bury her face in the soft folds of his coat, the way she did with her father when she was a child, tired from a long trip home.

For most of the journey, Ursula sat staring out the window, feeling as though her heart had turned to stone. She closed her eyes and leaned her forehead against the windowpane. She was so desperately tired. Tired of the endless questioning she had endured from Harrison. Tired of the pain she felt deep inside, cold and hollow with sadness and regret. The noise of the engine and the movement of the train as it lurched and sped its way across the countryside provided a strange source of comfort.

Samuels picked them up at Manchester's London Road Station and drove them to Whalley. Ursula took little notice of the journey but found that once she saw the old stone house her father had bought for her mother, she was suddenly awash in emotions. Anger, guilt, hopelessness, and grief flowed through her unchecked. She shrugged off all offers of assistance, insisting that she could take care of herself, as she stumbled up the stairs. She heard Lord Wrotham tell Samuels to drive him to the Shepherd's Inn, where he was staying. Ursula left strict instructions with Biggs that until the hearse arrived tomorrow, she wanted to be left alone, upstairs, in the pale green bedroom where she had spent so many happy years as a child.

By ten o'clock the next day all preparations were complete. The glass hearse with its black plumed horses stood outside, the pallbearers in their top hats and black gloves standing behind, ready to bear the coffin once they reached the church. Ursula had pulled the black lace veil down over her face and walked stiffly along the passageway to the front door. The servants lined up before her to pay their respects. Mrs. Stewart dabbed her eyes with a handkerchief, while

Julia wept openly. Bridget and Moira stood silently, heads bent, and as Ursula passed, she saw the rosary beads clutched between their fingers. They were like mirror images of each other, both crossing themselves when the coffin went by. Biggs stood by the front door, rigid and tall. His face was impassive, jaw set, hair smoothed back, eyes to the front. Ursula paused for a moment by his side, her lips quivering slightly as if she wanted to speak but couldn't. Only then did his eyes betray him, a mere flicker of anguish, but it was enough. Ursula gripped his arm with fierce resolution.

Again she seemed about to speak, but the words could not come. Lord Wrotham quietly walked up beside her.

"It's time," he said. "We must go."

Ursula watched the familiar landscape pass while they rode to the church as a stranger would view an alien wilderness. As they made their way over Closebrow, a bitter wind rattled the carriages. The horses threw back their dark heads and whinnied. Ursula could feel the icy drafts of air as her fingers clutched the side of the cold leather seat. She gazed out over the stone fences and leafless hedgerows and out across the bleak, rocky ground. The sky was grizzled and pale. The procession slowly made its way down past Lee Lane and onto Harwood Road. Just after they passed Norden Bridge, Ursula saw people lined along the streets. Families stopped on street corners, solemn young boys took off their caps, and as they swung into Blackburn Road, Ursula noticed a column of men with black armbands, their unfamiliar faces reddened and pinched in the cold. The Daisy Hill, Britannia, and Rishton mills were silent. The whistle from the Norden Fireclay Works shrieked once and stopped. The shops along the High Street remained closed. All she could hear was the pealing of the bells of the Church of St. Peter and St. Paul.

Once inside the church, Ursula recognized many of the faces, some hazily recalled from childhood, others sharp and painfully recent. George Barden from the Oldham mill was standing in the back corner, the only familiar face among a sea of unknown men in work clothes standing in the rear of the church. There were Gerard Anderson, Daniel Abbott, and Obadiah Dobbs standing in the middle pew alongside their wives. None of her generation were present, Cecilia Abbott having left for Ireland a week ago, while Marianne and Emily Anderson remained in Greece. Christopher Dobbs was rumored to be aboard his father's steam-

190

ship *Excelsior* en route to India.

As Ursula and Lord Wrotham followed the pallbearers with the coffin down the aisle, she also noticed some local dignitaries including David Shackleton, the local MP, and the mayor of Blackburn standing in one of the rows. Out of the corner of her eye, she saw Tom, standing respectfully at the end of the third row, his face partially hidden by the shadows.

Ursula took her place in the front pew just as the organ ceased playing and the Reverend Charles Harpur came forward to start the service. Seen from beneath her veil, everything was dim and dark within the church, the burning candles providing little light on this late-November morning.

Ursula felt cold and dead inside. The reverend's words meant nothing. The readings meant nothing. It was all she could do to rise to sing the final hymn, "Jerusalem," which had always been her father's favorite. As she looked around, the realization that she was now without any living family became even more profound. Her mother's family was conspicuous by its absence, so she had neither grandmother nor aunt there to console her. Her father had been the last remaining member of his family, so there was no one for her to turn to except Lord

Wrotham, who stood by her side.

After the service Ursula felt lost in the stream of black clothes and pale faces. Voices were heard, speaking of regret and of loss, but she could no longer listen. As the funeral party made its way up to the cemetery, her mind wanted to be quiet and alone — empty of thoughts, empty of memories. She wanted so much to be alone, to find a dark place to sit solitary and silent. Yet as the day progressed from the cemetery to the reception, once she had scattered the rose petals on her father's grave, after the tea and finger sandwiches had been consumed, she realized she already felt empty — that dark place had found itself inside her. As she crossed the threshold into the place where she had grown up, she found herself pacing down dim passages, lost among the doors and empty rooms. Neither the bustling company of Mrs. Stewart nor the warmth of an open fire could move her from that dark inner place. She drifted up the stairs late into the night, leaving Lord Wrotham slumped in an armchair in the drawing room, a glass of whiskey by his side. Julia helped her out of her clothes and into her nightdress and brought her a glass of warm milk, even though she knew she'd find it cold and untouched on Ursula's bedside table in the morning. All the lights were extinguished upstairs, leaving her to lie in the blackness of a moonless night, her body ice cold beneath the sheets, her eyes open but unseeing.

Downstairs, as the grandfather clock chimed midnight, Biggs sat at the large kitchen table, his head buried in his hands.

There was a place in her mind that Ursula liked to call home. It was a place where her mother was still alive, smiling as she sat by the fire. Her father would walk in, umbrella in hand, and Ursula would rush, a child, into his arms. This place existed only in her dreams, those dreams that came just before morning, while sleep was deep and sweet. Perhaps it was the warmth of her body beneath the bedclothes that made her imagine she was safe and home. She felt protected and secure as she lay there, pillows and blankets surrounding her. She tried to forget about the events of the previous weeks, tried to erase the fears that threatened to overwhelm her.

Ursula realized, however, as she woke fully, that she was not home. That she never could be home. This morning would be the final confirmation of that fact, as Fenway, her father's solicitor, was coming up from

London to read the will. It was at Lord Wrotham's suggestion that this should occur as soon as possible and should not wait for Ursula's return to London. Lord Wrotham also suggested that she should break up the return journey to stay at his estate in Northamptonshire. Given that his mother had relocated back to the family estate, there would be no impropriety in such a visit. His urging came after Mrs. Stewart and Julia had already expressed grave concerns over Ursula's health and, by the time Mrs. Norris and Biggs had concurred on the benefits of the good country air, Ursula had no strength left to refuse any of them.

Alistair Fenway arrived at Gray House at eleven o'clock and soon took his place in the front drawing room. Lord Wrotham sat beside him on a wooden chair Biggs had managed to procure, while Ursula sat alone wearing a black bombazine skirt and blouse on the large blue sofa under the bay window. A fire roared furiously in the cast-iron fireplace, and she felt cramped and hot in the stuffy room. Gerard Anderson arrived soon after Fenway. As her father's financial adviser, he had been requested to attend the reading of the will, but it was Ursula, of course, whom Fenway addressed as he opened the thick sheaf of parchment paper and read out the will's contents. The magnitude of her father's estate stunned Ursula. She had never really bothered to consider it in these terms before. To think that she was to receive a lump sum of £20,000 immediately was staggering. To realize that she stood to inherit an even vaster sum, most of which was held in trust for her, was an even greater shock. Fenway left, however, the worst shock of all until the very end. In his restrained, soft voice, he asked Ursula if she fully understood the terms of the will thus far. Ursula mutely nodded, and Fenway continued.

"Of course, my dear, the rationale for your father's trust is one of asset protection. He was mindful of your age and predicament — that is, your being unmarried at this time. Of course you will come into the trust at an appropriate time. Your father specified after marriage or upon reaching age thirty. At that time you will have full access to all available funds."

"Age thirty?" Ursula asked, puzzled.

"It is quite usual," Fenway replied crisply, "for a woman to come into her trust money at this age, there being obvious concerns about her ability to manage money until such time as she is mature enough to handle the responsibility."

"I see," Ursula responded with pursed lips.

"Of course, up until this time your father has appointed a trustee who is charged with the management of all trust assets and who will, of course, ensure that every provision is made for your needs."

"A trustee," Ursula repeated blankly.

"Yes. Did you not wonder why I asked Lord Wrotham here? Surely you must have realized. Your father appointed him to be your trustee."

The next morning Ursula visited one of the rows of terrace houses that her father had built for his mill workers in Rishton. She had heard of three families whose children were desperately ill with pneumonia and insisted that Dr. Guilfoyle, the local physician, accompany her. Ursula took along baskets of Hovis bread, meat-and-potato pies, and some of Cook's homemade scones and plum jam, which she left at the door (Dr. Guilfoyle refused to let her enter any of the houses for fear she might contract the disease). Samuels waited in Bertie at the end of Spring Street while Ursula walked up and down speaking with the locals as Dr. Guilfoyle finished his house calls.

It was midday, dinnertime for most of the workers, and a steady stream of them — men with their flat caps and neckties and women with their faces wrapped in woolen shawls — passed on their way home. The sound of their clogs echoed up and down the cobbled street. Few of the men acknowledged Ursula or gave more than a cursory tip of a cap, but she was used to their reticence; she had grown up with it, after all. She was approached by a group of young women — weavers, most likely — who asked her whether the mills would close on account of her father's death. Ursula reassured them that nothing would change, but she realized, as she spoke, the futility of her words. What say had she in her father's business? She would have no control over whether his mills would be kept running or whether his factories would continue to produce cottons and cloth. She had no idea what the future held, and she felt a rising frustration. Here there were children running around barefoot without any food in their bellies, and despite her inheritance she felt powerless to help them.

Dr. Guilfoyle came out from the last house, a "two-up, two-down" built of local stone. He waited until they were back in the motorcar before responding to Ursula's queries.

"Poor babby," he said quietly, taking off his wire-rimmed glasses and rubbing his eyes. "He's right poorly. But with them jammed in like sardines, it's no wonder. . . . Nay, nay, miss, dry up those tears. There's nowt you can do about it." His words only made Ursula feel even more helpless.

Samuels dropped Dr. Guilfoyle back at his surgery on Clifton Street before driving Ursula back to Whalley. She wrapped a tartan blanket around her knees and stared out as the terraced houses and chimney pots gave way to stone walls, farmhouses, and verdant fields.

As they turned into the driveway of Gray House, Ursula glanced at her gold pendant watch. It was just past one o'clock. Then she looked up and recognized the two motorcars parked in front of the house. There was Gerard Anderson's yellow Wolseley tonneau and Obadiah Dobbs's black Renault. Propped up against the side of the house was Daniel Abbott's Flying Merkel motorcycle.

Before Samuels had even switched off the engine, Ursula opened the rear door of the car and hastened up the broad stone steps to the house.

"I see we have visitors," she commented to Biggs as he opened the door.

Biggs nodded. "Yes, miss."

"How long have they been here?"

"Oh, about an hour, I'd say."

Ursula took off her gloves. "Is Lord Wrotham with them?"

"Yes, they are all meeting in the drawing room. His lordship asked that they not be disturbed."

"Did he?"

Biggs helped Ursula out of her tweed coat and hat and took a respectful step backward as she marched down the hallway, a look of grim determination on her face. The entrance to the drawing room was closed, but Ursula could hear the sounds of raised voices through the thick oak door. As the she swung open the door she recognized the unmistakable, strident tone of Obadiah Dobbs.

"I tell you we need to put more money into the venture. We're too close to give it up now!"

"Give up what now?" Ursula asked as she surveyed the room.

The men fell silent. Abbott and Anderson were sitting at the round table beneath the window, and each of them stood up as

Ursula entered. On the table was a pile of papers, a stack of ledger books, and a ceramic ashtray full of cigarette butts. Obadiah Dobbs was standing in the corner of the room, beside her father's old kneehole desk. With a scowl, Dobbs straightened his jacket. His face appeared ruddy and worn. Abbott and Anderson exchanged glances and sat back down.

Lord Wrotham was standing behind the table with his arms crossed. "Ursula," he said coolly. "To what do we owe this pleasure?"

"My apologies for the intrusion, gentlemen," she replied, and closed the door behind her. Her frustration had made her bold. "But as you chose to meet in my house, with my trustee, I assume that your subject is something that concerned my father. If it concerned him . . . well, it concerns me now." Ursula walked over and took a seat next to the fireplace, crossing her ankles to hide the fact that her knees were shaking. She could hear her father's voice in her mind, admonishing her for being both presumptuous and appallingly ill-mannered. But if she did not assert herself now, her resolve would be crushed. She would be subjugated entirely to these men.

"It's none of your business, that's what it

is!" Dobbs exclaimed, but Anderson quickly hushed him.

"Ursula," Abbott said gently, "you really should leave such matters to your trustee. Lord Wrotham has your best interests at heart."

Ursula clasped her hands, pressing her palms together tightly. "I am not a child, and I think under the circumstances I deserve to know what is happening."

"Ursula, this is business. Something a woman such as you can have no interest in. Truly, my dear, you should leave us."

Ursula grew all the more irritated by Daniel Abbott's fatherly tone.

Her eyes narrowed. "So despite the fact that I have been to Oxford," she began, with barely concealed scorn, "because I am a woman, I must be too stupid or too inconsequential to understand such things. Is that what you are saying?"

"No . . . no, of course not. We —" Abbott began soothingly, but Obadiah Dobbs interrupted him with a huff.

"You have no business bargin' in here! I always warned your father, I told him educating you, indulging your every curiosity, was a mistake!" Obadiah Dobbs spit out his words with bitter venom. "Now look at you, no manners, no womanly charm —

201

nothin'. You'll turn into a right bitter old maid. You should be findin' a husband instead of worryin' about this lot!"

"Yes, well, I see *your* manners haven't improved," Ursula responded archly, and Dobbs flushed darkly.

"Ursula, we were just discussing a venture that your father had decided against pursuing," Lord Wrotham explained calmly. He lit himself a cigarette and tossed the match into the fireplace. "I was just informing Dobbs that I could provide no further funds from the trust."

"And what *was* this venture?" Ursula asked.

Lord Wrotham shrugged. "Merely the importation of goods from South America."

Ursula's eyes narrowed, and Anderson spoke up. "Obadiah here has some contacts in South America that are interested in a joint development project. New chemical processes, dyes, medicinal elixirs — that sort of thing. Not something your father wanted to go into and, as we were just saying, not something Daniel or I feel is worth further investment. So there you have it — all very mundane and uninteresting, I'm sure, to a young woman such as yourself."

Ursula remained skeptical. She suspected she was being told only part of the story, just enough to sate her curiosity. She decided it was time to take matters into her own hands.

"Gentlemen, I'd prefer to talk about what's really going on." She steadied her voice. "I know all about the diary and the threat that's been made against your children. I can only assume you all believe that Bates is still alive and is responsible for the murder of Laura Radcliffe and my father. Now, since the bullet was clearly meant for me, I think I have a right to know what my father was involved in. Since my friend is about to stand trial for a murder she didn't commit, I think I also owe it to her to find out why you have all chosen to remain silent."

"Ursula . . ." Lord Wrotham warned, but her expression seemed to silence him.

"What are you all hiding?" she demanded. "What really happened on the Radcliffe expedition?"

Nobody spoke. Anderson drummed his fingers on top of the table. Abbott slumped back in his chair. The cigarette in his hand dropped ash onto the carpet. Dobbs stared at his boots, stony-faced.

"It was your father who first told me the story," Lord Wrotham said calmly. "On our way back from New York aboard the *Lusita-*

nia in 1905. He told me of an expedition to Venezuela that ended in the tragic death of a young botanist named Ronald Henry Bates. Your father was concerned that he and his business associates might be held accountable for what happened."

"Why would they be held accountable?" Ursula asked as Lord Wrotham paused. "It was supposedly an uprising by the native Indians."

"Indeed," Lord Wrotham replied. "But there seems to have been more to it than that. The expedition was supposed to find and bring back a variety of specimens of plants and wildlife but Colonel Radcliffe came to suspect Bates of unscrupulous dealings. Black market trading, that sort of thing. The journey seemed to have taken its toll on both men. Bates grew increasingly unstable while Radcliffe became paranoid that Bates was going to steal all that they discovered on the expedition. When the natives attacked, Bates was severely wounded. Radcliffe, injured himself, escaped with one of the Indian guides. No one ever went back to rescue Bates.

"Radcliffe was a superstitious man. He always believed that Bates had survived. Then, soon after the massacre, Bates's own wife and two sons fell ill, and all three succumbed to yellow fever in Trinidad. This weighed heavily on Radcliffe's conscience. In his later years, Radcliffe was convinced that Bates had not died and feared that one day he would resurface and exact his revenge.

"When Bates's diary arrived, we were then certain that he was alive and that Radcliffe's worst nightmares had indeed come to pass."

Ursula looked skeptical. "It strikes me that to be provoked to murder he must feel betrayed by you all."

Dobbs shifted his feet and coughed.

Ursula turned back to Lord Wrotham. "Why would my father confide all this in you?"

Lord Wrotham walked over to the table and stubbed his cigarette out in the ashtray. "He wanted me to use my sources in the Foreign Office to find out whether Bates was alive."

"And?" Ursula demanded

"At the time my sources couldn't confirm or deny it. There were rumors, but nothing more. We had no real evidence that Bates had survived until the diary appeared."

"And who knows who sent that . . ." Abbott interjected.

"My Foreign Office contacts have located Bates in Venezuela. They have no record of him arriving in England, but no one knows for sure. I've asked for more information, but in the current climate I doubt they will be of any assistance. The German menace is ever on their minds. Maintaining the Triple Entente is a tricky business. I'm not certain how much more help they will give us."

"So we don't even know if Bates is in England?" Ursula asked quietly.

"No," Abbott answered.

"But surely the diary is enough to prove foul play — to absolve Freddie for the murder and to link Laura's death to my father's."

"Unfortunately, no," said Lord Wrotham. "Harrison is convinced that these two terrible instances are in no way related. I've made him aware of the journal, but since anyone could have sent it or fabricated it, and since Bates is legally dead and cannot be accused of the crime, Scotland Yard has decided to rule out this theory."

There was a soft knock at the door.

"Yes," Lord Wrotham called out, and Ursula flinched. She wasn't even mistress in her own home.

Biggs peered around the door. "My lord, you asked me to let you know . . ."

"Is it two o'clock already?" Lord Wrotham asked. Biggs merely nodded. "My apologies, gentlemen, but I have a telephone call I must make. In my absence a colleague of mine has had to take over part of my caseload."

Anderson and Abbott rose to their feet. "We'd better be off," Anderson said, and Ursula detected some relief in his tone. He picked up the ledger and gave Dobbs a pointed look. "I think this matter is closed."

Dobbs picked up the papers from the table and stuffed them under his arm, muttering something inaudible.

Ursula got up from her chair and absently tucked a strand of hair back behind her ear.

"We really had best be going," Daniel Abbott said, and placed a hand on her arm. "All I ask is that you trust us. We have told Inspector Harrison everything we know. If only you would accept Lady Ashton's offer . . . You really would be safer out of England."

Lord Wrotham led Anderson and Abbott from the room, and Ursula thought she heard him lower his voice and murmur, "You need not fear, I will keep her safe."

"So headstrong . . ." Abbott sighed and turned back to look at Ursula. "She's as bad as my dear Cissy."

Anderson clutched the ledger books to his chest. "I would have trusted your father with my life," he said to her from the doorway, and then seemed unable to continue. Ursula felt a lump form in her throat.

Lord Wrotham, Abbott, and Anderson were halfway down the corridor by the time Obadiah Dobbs shuffled out of the drawing room. He and Ursula met face-to-face in the doorway. Ursula held open the door for him politely. He scowled as he passed her.

"You'd do well to accept young Cumberland's proposal," he said sourly. "For I doubt you'll receive another."

It took all of Ursula's self-control not to slam the door in his face.

ELEVEN

"Mrs. Stewart, please make the necessary arrangements with Biggs to get the access ladder up into the attic."

It was two days after her father's funeral and Ursula was determined that her mother's effects, which had remained stored in the attic of Gray House since her death, would finally be sorted through. There was little time left, for Ursula was due to leave with Lord Wrotham the following day.

"Oh, Miss Ursula," Mrs. Stewart replied, "you won't be wanting to do that. Your father, God rest his soul, he didn't let no one go up there. Perhaps if Mr. Biggs made arrangements . . ."

"Mrs. Stewart, are you questioning my instructions?" Ursula asked imperiously, and instantly regretted her tone. Mrs. Stewart was like a mother to her; she had known her all her life, since before the move to London when Ursula was only twelve.

"Forgive me, Mrs. Stewart, I didn't mean to be short with you." Ursula looked anxiously at Mrs. Stewart and was rewarded for her apology by a motherly smile.

"Now then, no doubt you're feeling tired after the funeral. You look pale. Why don't I ask Cook to make one of her lemon curd tarts. You did so love those as a child. And I'll get you a nice cuppa tea."

Ursula smiled. Mrs. Stewart was a strong believer in food as a cure for most ailments. "After I go through the chests in the attic, that would be lovely."

Mrs. Stewart nodded reluctantly and walked back along the hallway to the rear stairs. Ursula's father *had* never allowed anyone up in the attic to go through her mother's possessions, but now it was time, she thought, that the past was brought to rest.

Ursula was left standing alone on the landing. Julia was busy organizing the linen closet, which meant Ursula had a moment at least to be alone in her childhood bedroom. She had noticed how since the funeral she was never left alone — there was always Mrs. Stewart bustling about or Julia running in to ask her questions. Only Biggs seemed to keep his distance. Secretly she wondered if he didn't blame her for her father's death. After all, she blamed herself.

The pale green bedroom was bathed in a soft morning halo of light. It looked rather like a Vermeer interior, a play of light and reflections. The slant of sunshine through the window made Ursula look hazy and incomplete in the mirror above her old white dressing table. She was like a luminous breath, insubstantial and faint, making its way into the room.

A polite cough from behind her caused Ursula to spin around. Biggs was standing in the doorway.

"I have instructed Samuels to pull out the access ladder to the attic. It shouldn't take long. If you would like me to assist you . . . ?" Biggs left the question hanging, and as Ursula made no response, he continued, by way of explanation. "I was responsible for storage of your mother's effects. I have an inventory which I can use if there is something in particular . . . ?" Again the question was left open.

Ursula shook her head. "I shall see to this alone if you won't mind, Biggs. But thank you anyway, Biggs . . . for everything."

Biggs inclined his head stiffly, but his eyes looked troubled nevertheless.

Within the hour Ursula had put on one of Julia's aprons and climbed up the narrow ladder into the attic. She found herself crouching beneath the low ceiling staring at a pile of trunks and boxes that had lain there since her mother's death and remained untouched since. Everything was covered in a thick layer of dust, even the attic window, which as a result allowed only a feeble half-light to penetrate the shadows.

Ursula opened the largest trunk first. It still bore her mother's initials: IMM. Isabella Meara MacGregor. Her mother's maiden name. Ursula could hardly remember her mother — she was a faded photograph on the bedroom dresser, an image captured in her father's mind and passed on to her through stories and recollections. Ursula had few of her own memories to rely upon. Those that she had were misty and strange. Dark blue eyes gazing down upon her, a smile rising to a laugh, the smell of orange blossoms.

This first trunk contained only clothes — damask, silks, and linens — all hand-pressed and lovingly folded in tissue paper. Mrs. Stewart, undoubtedly. Biggs always said she was devoted to Ursula's mother. The next trunk was considerably smaller, bound with a brown leather strap and buckle. Inside, there were photographs, a bundle of letters tied with pink satin ribbon, and a series of books. Ursula opened with interest the leather wallet that contained the photographs. They seemed to comprise mainly portraits done of her mother's family in Scotland. Ursula recognized her grandmother, whom she had seen barely a handful of times since her mother's death, and her two aunts sitting beside her. It was a studio photograph, as were most of the other photographs in the wallet, all stilted and stiff, with high-collared men and primly dressed women. Only one of the photographs included her mother. She was kneeling in the front and couldn't have been much older than Ursula was now — which meant that this photograph must have been taken just before she met Ursula's father. Her mother's thick, dark curls were wound up and around the crown of her head, leaving ringlets cascading down her back and shoulders. She had on a white lace dress, white gloves, and black lace-up boots. Her eyes were candid and round, and in the hesitation of the moment her lips appeared partly open, as if on the verge a smile.

Ursula wasn't sure whether she should look at any of the letters — it seemed such an invasion of privacy that she hesitated to untie the ribbon that held the bundle together. But it was really too late for such sensibilities. She put the packet in the front apron pocket and walked over to the window. Stooping beneath the narrow angle of the roof, she rubbed the windowpane with a corner of her apron to remove the dust and allow more light. She then knelt down, careful not to get any splinters through her stockings from the rough-hewn floorboards beneath, and took the bundle from her pocket, untied it, and opened the first letter gingerly. It was dated March 1885.

My dearest Robert.
How I miss you when you are away. The house seems so very empty and cold without you here. When will your business in Liverpool be complete, do you think? I am trying very hard, but our neighbors seem wary of strangers, especially me, it seems. Could we not invite my sister Alice down for Easter? I would like so much to have company, especially if you must travel to Portsmouth next month. Young Mrs. Stewart, bless her, is taking care of the household beautifully, but I am feeling a little at a loss. Do not think that I complain, my love. I just want to make sure this house lives up to all your expectations. It is so large and the estate so new, perhaps you could

send word of your instructions?

The next in the pile was not her father's reply but rather another letter, this one dated a month later.

My dearest,
It seems ages since I heard from you, although I know how busy you must be with preparations for the expedition. I do hope your visit to Godalming and Colonel Radcliffe has proved a great success. Elizabeth Anderson came to visit yesterday. She is en route to Liverpool to join Gerard. She brought Charlotte with her, who is an absolutely adorable baby. Very saintly and quiet for such a young bairn. No doubt Fanny and Laura are growing up just as fast.

I am thinking of walking over to visit poor Mrs. Samuels tomorrow, as the rector's wife informs me that she is not much long for this world. Her son continues to cause mischief — why, Cook caught him just yesterday morning trying to steal one of her pies that was cooling on the window ledge. When we are finally blessed with a child, pray we will be spared such a demon! But I shall bother you no further with idle chatter.

I miss you and love you as dearly as ever. Let us hope that your business concludes successfully soon, for we all wish to see you home as quickly as can be.

Your loving wife, Isabella

Her father's reply to this was enclosed. His hand was rougher than her mother's, and the note was considerably shorter, indicative of her father's lack of comfort with writing letters of any kind.

Isabella, my love, you're an angel for tolerating my absence for so long. Look for my carriage on the evening of the sixth.

Your loving husband

Ursula flicked through the next few letters, which all seemed to concern similar absences from home.

There was something in the tone of all these letters that made Ursula frown. Perhaps it was that they revealed a wistful loneliness she had never attributed to her mother.

Ursula gently bundled all the letters and retied the ribbon that had held them together. It was then she noticed a small wooden box that lay at the very bottom of one of the trunks. Upon closer inspection she realized that it was a jewelry box, inlaid with an intricate rose pattern. She lifted the lid and picked up a delicate strand of pearls. It seemed puzzling that her mother's jewels had remained up here and not been placed in the safe or at the bank with her more valuable effects. There was a delicate rose gold knot pin, a blue enamel locket, a garnet necklace, and a small moonstone ring. Her mother must have had tiny hands just like Ursula, for when she placed the ring carefully on her middle finger, it fit perfectly. The final piece she found was a vermeil rose pendant. She fingered the pendant closely, but there was no sign of any opening.

Ursula picked up the enamel locket and pried it open instead. Inside, to her satisfaction, was a painted photograph of her father. He looked young and handsome in his somber gray suit and wing-collar shirt and striped tie. Ursula gazed at it, tears gathering in the corners of her eyes, and then placed it in her pocket. This she would have to keep close to her from now on.

She was about to return to the other trunks when she decided that she might as well take the whole jewelry box with her, and so she carefully placed it down next to the ladder before she set to opening the remaining trunks. The first trunk she pulled out had her father's name on the inside lid and was crammed with books. Ursula picked up a few of the volumes with interest. It puzzled her to think that her father would have left such books behind, given his keen interest in reading. One of the volumes was entitled *Natural Inheritance,* by Francis Galton, which Ursula briefly opened and then discarded. The next volume was a copy of Humboldt's *A Personal Narrative,* which sat side by side with Darwin's *Origin of Species.* There was also a glass case containing insect specimens of some kind, each mounted and labeled in her father's handwriting. Ursula placed the case and the books back in the trunk, having little time to contemplate these any further. It was her mother who consumed her thoughts.

The next trunk contained more clothes and also some photographs, wrapped in cloth. Ursula eagerly started to flick through these photographs, taking them once again to the light to see them in closer detail. There was a photograph of a group of people in front of a large marquee. She recognized Gerard Anderson standing next to his wife, Elizabeth, who had a baby in her arms. There was Daniel Abbott smiling as he sat on a wicker chair with his legs stretched out, next to an unknown man. Her father was standing to the left of the group, silhouetted in the sunlight while a stranger stood next to him, posing for the camera with a smile. The man had light-colored hair swept back from his forehead and was incredibly handsome, Ursula thought, despite the scar that traveled down his left cheek and his rugged and unwieldy beard. Something in his languid dark eyes struck Ursula as oddly familiar. She hesitated for a moment before turning the photograph over. There in her father's handwriting were the words *September 1887. Preparations under way. Bates, Anderson, and Abbott enjoying the sunshine.*

Ursula walked along the stone path and entered the cemetery gates. She was already growing tired, and since she had told no one at Gray House of her plans, she could only look forward to the prospect of a long walk back. Still, the fresh air revived her spirits a little, and being alone outside helped clear her mind. It was only a couple of days since the funeral, but it felt as if a lifetime had passed. Tomorrow she would depart for Lord Wrotham's estate, so this was the last chance she had to say a final good-bye to her father.

She kept her head bent, a woolen hat pulled down low against her ears, as she made her way along the path to her parents' grave. The wind had died down, and the oak tree that sheltered his tombstone now stood stock-still and silent, only the faint sound of winter birds on the moors interrupting her reverie.

Ursula wrapped her coat tight around her, for the air was cold and damp. She bent over to place a bunch of white lilies next to the wreath that lay on the fresh grave before her. The gray granite headstone glittered as the dying rays of sunlight caught its face. It was Aberdeen granite, just as her mother had wanted. Only now there were two names listed instead of one. The fact that the mason had already finished the engraving of the stone was testament to her father's status in the community. She ran a gloved hand over the letters in her father's name and felt an aching in her chest and in her throat.

"May you both rest in peace," Ursula whispered softly. She touched the headstone briefly with the palm of her hand as a last farewell and turned back to make her way past the lines of the dead to the cemetery gates.

TWELVE

Two days later Ursula stood on the grassy terrace of Lord Wrotham's estate, Bromley Hall, gazing out along the tree-lined avenue and the woodlands beyond. In the half-light of morning, the mist and fog barely risen, the grounds were scarcely visible. Dark oak and cypress rose up, wisps of clouds began to lift, and everything appeared immutable. The ancient language of the forest and valley spoke to her. She could stand here, she thought, spanning the centuries before and after, and nothing would ever change. The earth beneath her silk slippers was swollen and damp. She stood alone, oblivious to the cold, in only her silk nightdress and dressing gown.

Her thoughts were in turmoil. Numb from her experiences, Ursula had found it hard to sleep.

Winifred was in Holloway Prison facing trial in less than a month. Harrison seemed to think Robert Marlow's murderer was a disgruntled worker who had targeted him after being fired from one of the mills. Ursula couldn't convince him that there was any connection with Laura's death. The policeman who was supposed to be on guard that evening was subsequently suspended, his sharing a cup of tea with Bridget in the Marlows' basement kitchen having been regarded as an "error of judgment" on his part. At least his arrival on the scene soon after the shooting had, in Lord Wrotham's view, prevented any further shots being fired.

Lord Wrotham. Her trustee. This provided both a source of continued irritation as well as relief. Without anyone else to turn to, she found herself unnerved by the conflicting emotions he aroused. She despised the sense of dependency she now felt and was angered by the confusion his physical proximity seemed to create.

Bromley Hall had been the seat of the Wrotham family for over three hundred years. Originally a medieval manor house built around a courtyard, it reflected the additions and renovations carried out by successive generations. The most extensive of these occurred in 1570 with the addition of the east and west wings of the house in grand Renaissance style. Ursula first glimpsed the silver-gray limestone of the east wing, with its square chimneys, ornamental façade, and tall windows, as they drove along the curved avenue that led up to the hall. Nestled near Rockingham Forest, the entrance to the house bordered the original deer park established by the third Baron Wrotham to ensure a regular supply of venison for hunting. As the motorcar drew up at the gilded ironwork gate, Ursula could see deer grazing in the now-wild meadows.

Soon after she arrived at Bromley Hall, she discovered that relations between Lord Wrotham and his mother were so strained that the dowager Lady Adela Wrotham was more absent from their company than not. Ursula had been there nearly three days now and had seen the Dowager only once for dinner. She gained rare satisfaction out of observing Lord Wrotham's face as he suffered his mother's relentless complaints throughout the evening.

"It is so dreadfully, dreadfully dull here now," she had said with a sigh. "Why, when Fredrick took over the estate, he would have parties every weekend. Such manner of fun. You, on the contrary, have neglected me shockingly. Really, Oliver, you really are insufferable — to think that you'd deny your own mother!"

"I deny only what I must, Mother."

This was the first and only time Ursula had heard Lord Wrotham speak of his predicament, and from the look he shot her across the dining room table that night, it was clearly not a matter to be pursued. It was somewhat known that Fredrick, Wrotham's idle and free-spirited elder brother, had lavish tastes — tastes that he had apparently inherited from his mother, but tastes, nonetheless, that the estate could not sustain for long. That he had died in Naples of liver failure caused by "excessive living" was the source of ongoing discomfiture within the family.

"Here." Lord Wrotham's voice was low yet penetrating. It stirred Ursula from her reverie. She turned slightly as he placed a woolen shawl across her shoulders. "You'll catch your death out here," he said with a quiet firmness.

Ursula shrugged. She wasn't sure she cared too much about that anymore. In the past her father would have been the one to worry for her, always concerned that she could succumb to the consumption that had claimed her mother's life. How she remembered her father insisting that Mrs. Stewart bundle her up in a coat, muff, and velvet bonnet at the first hint of winter when she was a child.

"Trying to be my guardian, are we, now?" she asked lightly, aware suddenly of how exposed she must seem. "Isn't trustee enough?"

"I don't desire to be either," came the reply.

Lord Wrotham remained standing behind her, close enough for her to feel the warmth of his body through the soft folds of her shawl. He made no attempt to move closer to comfort her. She stood transfixed and cold, beyond his touch. The sun remained stubbornly behind the thick wall of clouds, a white glow barely visible in the winter sky.

"You really should come inside now." His voice was calm and clear, she thought. Like a stream running beneath her.

They stood in silence for some time. He seemed to be waiting for her to speak, but she had nothing to say. Ursula stared out across the broad steps that led down from the terrace. Statues, once resplendent, she was sure, stood hooded and wrapped against the winter air along the sides of the terrace. Remnants of one ancestor's failed attempt to transform a house into a Florentine palazzo.

"Most of this will have to go. Bromley Wood. The Eastern Meadow. I cannot sustain it all. When I succeeded my brother to the barony, I closed the entire west wing of the house. Most of the rooms remain in a state of disrepair. I hope that one day I will be able to restore each to its former glory. Even so, I have to face the fact that most of the gardens cannot be maintained. I hope to keep what I can, but gardens are, unfortunately, unproductive — and unproductive does not help me."

Ursula was surprised and endeared by his sudden candor. Bromley Hall had been surrounded at one time by formal gardens, a maze, and three ornamental lakes. The fifth Baron Wrotham had commissioned a copy of the Roman Temple of Vesta at Tivoli to be built around one of the great pools after he returned from his grand tour of the Continent. Ursula could still see the ruins of the temple from the terrace, partially visible between the oak trees.

She suddenly shivered, and this time Lord Wrotham moved in, wrapping the shawl tightly around her. Ursula felt a tremor of excitement as he drew near. She looked to him, and he stepped back quickly, as if he, too, had felt the attraction.

They stood there, gazing over the terrace

in silence. Time passed. The mist lay heavy and still, the sun barely discernible.

"Was it truly my father's wish that I marry Tom?" Ursula finally asked.

"He spoke of it, yes," Lord Wrotham answered.

"Tom asked me before, you know, and I refused, but now I . . . I . . . do not know whether —"

"You must trust your own feelings in this matter," Lord Wrotham interrupted her brusquely. "I cannot advise you."

Ursula flushed slightly at the rebuff. "Of course," she continued, "Tom is hardworking, ambitious, and not altogether unattractive. He built himself from nothing, and in this regard he is precisely the kind of man my father would consider suitable."

"Oh, yes, he is exactly the sort your father would find suitable," Lord Wrotham said dryly.

"You find fault with him?" Ursula asked in feigned surprise.

"I find no fault with him at all. You misunderstand me."

"Really? I thought your meaning was clear. Tom is not the sort you would consider a suitable match if you had a daughter."

"I am hardly the person to ask," Lord

Wrotham replied enigmatically. He shifted from one foot to the other. "All I mean to say is that you do not seem to be the kind of woman to accept a marriage based solely on your father's considerations. . . ." headded, his tone softening as if he guessed her thoughts.

"But if it was my father's dying wish . . ." she began to say, and stopped.

Ursula could not look Lord Wrotham in the eye. She knew it would be her undoing. Instead she stared at the wet grass around his feet, noticing how the slivers of morning light played across the droplets of dew. Inside, she felt despair mounting. If she did accept marriage to Tom Cumberland, a man she did not love would have control over her future and her fortunes. If she refused Tom's proposal, she would be acting against her father's last wishes. No matter her decision, she would not be free.

Ursula watched the wisps of her breath in the cold morning air. She heard the crunch of gravel and the sound of a door close. There were murmurs and voices, the sounds and movements of a household awakened and preparing itself for the day. Not wanting to make too much of a spectacle of herself, Ursula pulled the shawl in tight and straightened up.

"I think I had better go inside," she said. As she hurried indoors, she couldn't resist turning back just once, and, seeing the figure of Lord Wrotham steadily gazing back out across the gardens, she felt an inexplicable pang of loss.

THIRTEEN

That evening the Dowager Lady Wrotham decided to grace them with her presence at dinner once more. She arrived just as Ursula was closing the door to the private drawing room in which both she and Lord Wrotham had spent most evenings before adjourning for dinner in the adjacent dining room. Lord Wrotham was standing in front of the scagliola fireplace, holding a book in his hands. No sooner had Ursula paused at the threshold, opening her mouth to speak, than the Dowager came bustling in behind her in a haze of embroidered tulle.

"Do put that book down, Oliver. You know I cannot abide you reading before dinner. Miss Marlow, if you only knew how many silent evenings I have had to face sitting in this very room. I really must apologize — my son has little in the way of conversation. I am surprised you even bother to come down at all. It must be so dreadfully dull for you here." As always, the Dowager's words tumbled forth in a torrent.

"Mother," Lord Wrotham replied, inclining his head slightly in mock deference, "I was about to give this to Miss Marlow. It just arrived in my shipment from Hatchards." He handed Ursula the book, a copy of E. M. Forster's latest, *Howards End,* and murmured, "I hope you approve."

"What was that you said, Oliver?" the Dowager demanded. "You really must speak up!"

Ursula smiled slightly, but the day had left her too exhausted to have much patience for the Dowager and her petty trifles.

The Dowager was, however, determined to have her entertainment. Made restless by her sojourn in the country, she sat down and immediately started to question Ursula about her acquaintances in "London society."

Patting the seat next to her on the settee, she insisted that Ursula join her. Ursula obliged with a glance at Lord Wrotham, who now appeared absorbed in reading a copy of the *Spectator* as he stood in front of the fire. Ursula raised her eyebrows but was unable to comment before the Dowager launched into a stream of questions about the many friends she had in Belgravia. The

Dowager's lined face became animated, almost girlish, as she spoke.

"Why, you must surely know the Campbell-Grays! They live just across the square. Next to Lady Davenport, although she spends very little time in London anymore, so I'm not surprised you haven't been introduced. The weather plays havoc with her rheumatism, and I believe she now spends the season in Lytham St. Annes. But maybe you know —"

"Mother, please!" Lord Wrotham interrupted, tossing his magazine onto a side table. "Miss Marlow can scarcely wish to engage in such idle chatter."

The Dowager gave a disgruntled snort, prompting Ursula to say with uncharacteristic politeness, "Lady Wrotham, I'm afraid I must disappoint you. My acquaintances in what you call London society are only slight. My father was not a gentleman, you see —"

"Not a gentleman?!" The Dowager looked suitably shocked.

"No. The son of a coal miner, I'm afraid," Ursula couldn't help but reply.

"The son of a . . . ? Well I never!"

"And a man whose combined wealth probably exceeded that of Lord Northcliffe himself. I'd say that gives Miss Marlow here a perfect entrée into polite society, wouldn't you, Mother?" Wrotham chimed in.

Ayres, Wrotham's butler, opened the dining room doors and announced that dinner was served, cutting off any further comment.

Ursula sat opposite the Dowager beneath the cut-glass chandelier. Lord Wrotham took his position at the head of the long mahogany dining table and signaled Ayres that they were ready to be served. At one time this house had a full complement of staff, but these days Ayres had grown accustomed to doing a host of jobs that might have seemed inappropriate at any other table. It was with great ease that he now presented Lord Wrotham with a bottle of 1908 Lafite Rothschild and, once it was approved, proceeded to decant it into a crystal and silver decanter.

The Dowager gave a conspicuous sniff but said nothing as Ayres and a young maid whom Ursula had not seen before came in and placed the soup bowls down carefully on the silver chargers. Ayres then came around to each of them with a large silver soup tureen as the maid served them the lobster bisque.

There was silence as the soup was consumed. The Dowager gave Ursula a shrewd appraising look as Ayres and the maid returned to present the main course, roasted pheasant.

"The gal reminds me of someone," she said, and paused as if considering. "Yes. Who is it now . . . ? Of course!" she finished with a look of satisfaction. "She is the very image of Lizzie Wexcombe!"

Lord Wrotham looked as if his meal had turned to ashes in his mouth. Ursula glanced back and forth between mother and son, waiting for the inevitable outburst, but it never came.

"Lizzie was blonde," was all Lord Wrotham replied.

The Dowager sat back in her chair, placing her knife and fork down carefully on her plate. Ursula had already noticed the specially commissioned china that bore the family crest.

"Of course, but still she has a look of Lizzie, that's for sure. Maybe it's in the eyes, or perhaps the cut of her mouth. Poor, dear Lizzie . . ."

"Mother," Lord Wrotham said, and Ursula thought she detected a warning tone in his voice. Oblivious or not, the Dowager continued to chatter on. "Poor, poor Lizzie. I expect you know, Miss Marlow. So sad . . .

but still she would be such a headstrong gal!"

"What happened to her?" asked Ursula, feeling the full weight of the Dowager's stare upon her and not knowing what else to say. She remembered that Cecilia had intimated there was some tragedy in Lord Wrotham's past, but no one would ever tell her the details.

"But, my dear, I thought you would have known. Riding accident. Tragic. Absolutely tragic. And to think they had only just become betrothed."

A cold silence fell over the dinner table. Ursula wondered, though, if she didn't detect a glint of satisfaction in the Dowager's eyes as Lord Wrotham removed himself from the dining room before dessert arrived.

Thankfully, the Dowager decided to retire for the evening very soon after coffee was served in the drawing room. Ursula was only too pleased to be left alone, but when Lord Wrotham had not returned after some time, she decided to ring for Ayres to see if he could be of any assistance in locating him.

Ayres was the epitome of stiff propriety, responding with a cool, "I shall endeavor to find his lordship." A response which only indicated to Ursula that Ayres knew precisely where his lordship was.

"Actually, Ayres, I'd appreciate it if you could take me to him. To be honest, I'm sick to death of being cooped up in this drawing room."

Ayres seemed to be weighing his response to this before finally nodding and leading her out of the room and up the main staircase. Ursula followed him along the landing and through the long picture gallery that led to the west wing of the hall. She had never come to this part of the house; the west wing was, as far as she was aware, shut up entirely.

Ayres paused outside a heavy oak door. "I believe his lordship is inside. Would you care for me to announce you?"

"I should like to announce myself, if you don't mind," Ursula replied, with her most charming smile. "What is this room?" she asked as Ayres turned to leave.

"Why, miss, it was his lordship — I mean the sixth Baron Wrotham's library."

"Lord Wrotham's father, you mean."

"A great man, his father. Breaks my heart to see the library in its current state. I can tell it affects his lordship, too. Comes here often when the Dowager is visitin'." Ayres checked himself suddenly, and Ursula realized he thought he had given away too much.

"Thank you, Ayres," Ursula replied. "I think I understand."

Ayres bowed briefly before disappearing along the long gallery and down the central stairs.

Ursula knocked softly, then opened the door and entered.

Inside, Lord Wrotham rose to his feet from a deep leather armchair. He was in a peculiar state of dishevelment for him, with his evening jacket discarded and his tie undone. On the floor beside the chair was a glass and a half-empty decanter of red wine.

"I hope I am not intruding," Ursula said, mindful of her own embarrassment. The library was little more than a shell. Most of the furniture was covered in dust sheets, except for a large oak desk and the leather armchair. The bookshelves that rose to the ceiling were nearly bare, and yet on the floor there were books piled high. Ursula wasn't sure if they were being removed or in the process of being replaced.

"As you can see, I am alone," Lord Wrotham replied curtly.

A fire in the huge stone fireplace roared furiously.

Lord Wrotham refilled his glass and moved to stand by the fire. He seemed irritated by her intrusion. For a moment she wished she had not entered; however, something in the way he stared bleakly into the fire stirred her compassion. She had never seen him look so vulnerable. Instinctively, she walked over to be closer to him.

"Tell me about Lizzie," Ursula asked softly.

Lord Wrotham merely continued to stare at the fire.

"Your mother said —" she continued, but Lord Wrotham cut her off.

"My mother!" He nearly spit the words out. "My mother wants you to think that I suffer from the torment of some long-lost love!"

"And you don't?" Ursula asked quietly.

"No," he replied coldly.

Ursula was confused. What she saw in his eyes belied his words.

"Then why . . . ?" She let the question hang in the air.

Lord Wrotham prodded the fire with the iron poker impatiently. "My mother enjoys dragging up the past. I was nineteen. Lizzie was the sister of a good friend of mine at Cambridge. Only our families knew of the betrothal. A few months after we became engaged, Lizzie, headstrong as always, agreed to a wager — that she would beat her cousin in a race from here to Corby. Her horse failed to make it over a fence. She was left in a coma and subsequently died."

Ursula extended her hand to touch his arm, but Lord Wrotham pulled away sharply.

"I found out the truth soon after her death." His words were laced with bitterness. "She never loved me. She was used to spreading her favors among many. Oh, her family knew, all right. Only I was blind to it all. The youngest son, with no prospect of wealth or title — I was a fool not to have guessed."

Ursula found herself gazing into unfamiliar eyes, eyes that were fierce and watchful, reflecting a struggle to hold back emotions that threatened to flood over them both.

"You are too young to understand," he finally said, and his lips pursed in apparent disdain.

Ursula flushed. "You think I don't understand!" she cried. "After everything that has happened, you still have the temerity to insinuate that I don't understand loss? I who have lost everything!"

Ursula's eyes stung with tears. Lord

Wrotham was standing no more than two feet away, but the gulf between them had never seemed wider than at this moment.

"Now you have your title, my lord," she continued, her voice breaking as she tried to maintain self-control. "I'm sure there are many girls who would marry you for it. Maybe you will find yourself an American heiress or a gaiety girl? Or maybe a widow like Lady Ashton."

Lord Wrotham blinked. "Lady Ashton?"

"I'm not some helpless young creature in need of your protection!" Ursula exclaimed wildly.

Lord Wrotham arched one eyebrow. "I never said you were."

"And I certainly don't need to have marriage to Tom Cumberland thrust down my throat!"

Lord Wrotham stared at her for a moment. "You think I want you to marry Tom Cumberland?!"

Ursula could feel the ferocious heat of the fire through the folds of her dress. The atmosphere in the room prickled with anticipation. She felt a frisson of electricity surge between them. Then, like a flash of lightning, it was gone.

"I do not know what to think." She searched his face, but he was stern in his resolve. "I'm sorry for having intruded upon you. I really must be getting to bed. Good evening, Lord Wrotham."

"Good evening, Ursula."

Later that night she heard footsteps along the landing. They stopped just outside her door; she could see a shadow cast by the light of a lamp being carried. Ursula rose silently and picked up one of the pewter candlesticks from the table under the window. She drew it up above her shoulders and moved toward the doorway. She half expected some ghoul to fling open the door and gun her down just as her father had been. She waited, beside the door, her breath shallow and fast.

At length the shadow moved away from the door, and she heard footsteps retreating down the hallway. Uncertain, Ursula continued to hold the candlestick in one hand but slowly turned the handle of the door with the other and peered out into the hallway.

The narrow corridor was gray and gloomy, except for the dim glow of a light disappearing down the hall. She almost laughed with relief. Then there was a momentary flutter — what had Lord Wrotham been thinking as he paused outside her bedroom door? Ursula closed the door quietly. There was no fire to warm her, so she quickly got under the covers and pulled them around her. She lay still, trying to quiet her mind and let sleep return, but instead she found herself imagining over and over what might have happened if Lord Wrotham had opened the bedroom door.

FOURTEEN

After an unsettled night of obscure and tangled dreams, Ursula awoke with a dull headache. She rang for some hot water and fresh towels and then attended to trying to make herself look less wretched. She moved quickly, for the bedroom was chilly despite the new fire that had been lit that morning. She saw that the Dowager Wrotham's maid had washed, ironed, and laid out her dark indigo walking suit. Still in mourning, Ursula also wore a dark blue blouse and placed her mother's enamel locket, the one that contained her father's photograph, on a rose gold chain around her neck. After dressing she pulled on her sturdy brown walking boots and made her way downstairs.

The grandfather clock in the passage chimed nine o'clock. Ursula wasn't usually this late, and as the Dowager had taken to having all her meals in her room, Ursula found herself alone in the private dining room. She helped herself to some kippers and scrambled eggs from the breakfast warmer on the mahogany sideboard and poured herself a strong cup of tea from the silver pot, but she took barely two bites of food before pushing her plate away. She tried to clear her mind of thoughts, but she was overcome with memories of London. She saw her father's body lying beside her, his eyes glassy and cold. She heard Mrs. Stewart screaming, felt herself being torn away from her father's side. Ursula massaged her temples fiercely. She needed to be brave. She couldn't afford to be maudlin at a time like this.

Usually at this time of the morning, before the breakfast items had been removed, Lord Wrotham could be seen returning from his early walk, his two Scotch collies by his side. Gazing out the French doors that led from the picture gallery onto the terrace, Ursula could see no sign of him this morning.

It was then she noticed voices coming from beyond the anteroom that connected the picture gallery to Lord Wrotham's private study. Ursula quickly made her way down the passage, but as she came through the anteroom, before she could enter the study, she heard the distinctive voices of Inspector Harrison and Lord Wrotham.

Both their tone and their words made her stop in midstride and prick up her ears.

"What have you got for me?" Harrison asked.

"An offer of five thousand pounds."

"To buy his silence on the Radcliffe expedition?"

"Yes."

"An allegation of conspiracy to murder, even one over twenty years old, is not something easy to ignore."

"You heard the offer."

Ursula did not hear Harrison's reply. There was a pause before she heard Harrison again, this time in a voice loud and clear. "And the charges against Miss Stanford-Jones?"

"My only concern," Lord Wrotham responded, "is that the Marlow family's reputation is not sullied by any of this. Do what you will with Miss Stanford-Jones. She is Pemberton's concern now, not mine."

Harrison's familiarity of tone surprised Ursula. This was quite a different exchange from what had taken place in front of her that morning in the parlor at home in Chester Square.

She couldn't make out what was discussed next, until Harrison raised his voice and said, "Of course I understand. I have not forgotten my loyalty to you — how could I after all that you did for my family — but you must realize that in this matter my hands are tied. Bates is nowhere to be found. Sources say he could be halfway 'round the world by now."

"I know, and believe me, I appreciate all that you've done."

Appreciate all that you've done! Ursula thought angrily. When Harrison is happy to let Freddie hang for a crime she did not commit, when he is willing to let Bates go free and be bribed just to silence the investigation into the Radcliffe expedition!

Suddenly Ursula heard movement of chairs and footsteps — sounds indicating that Harrison was making ready to leave. Quickly she moved behind one of the marble pillars in the anteroom and kept out of sight.

Harrison and Lord Wrotham proceeded to the front door.

"I'll see you out myself. Thanks for coming all this way," Lord Wrotham said.

"If you hadn't removed yourself and Miss Marlow here, I would have visited you in town," Harrison replied sharply.

Lord Wrotham sighed and opened the door. "I'm glad Ursula's out of London. She can at least be spared the indignity of seeing her father's name vilified in the press."

"One last thing, m'lord," Harrison said as he walked through the doorway. "About Miss Marlow. Is she likely to be leaving the country soon? I don't wish to seem impertinent, but I had heard she may be accompanying Lady Ashton abroad — then I also heard that there was the possibility of an engagement to a man called Tom Cumberland . . . ?"

The question hung in the air.

Ursula could not see Wrotham's reaction. He did not reply at all.

Harrison coughed. "Of course, it's really none of my business . . . but I had to ask. Miss Marlow will have to be available to testify at Miss Stanford-Jones's trial next month. I trust you will ensure she does so."

"But of course."

Ursula waited until she heard the sound of Harrison's motorcar start and Wrotham close the front door and retreat back to his study before hurrying to make her way to her room, undetected. She snuck into the picture gallery, only to run straight into Ayres coming out of the doorway that led to the servants' stair.

"Miss Marlow," he said before she could

utter a word. "You have a visitor. Mr. Tom Cumberland is waiting for you in the drawing room."

"Oh." Ursula drew in a deep breath. Tom was the last person she wanted to see. After two unanswered letters from him, she had little doubt about the reason for his visit. "Just give me a moment, Ayres."

Ayres bowed his head and took a step backward. Ursula ran her fingers across the bridge of her nose and rubbed her eyes. She glimpsed a dim reflection of herself in the dark bronze urn that was perched on the side table beneath a portrait by Sir Joshua Reynolds. She looked disheveled and tired, her throat pale and white against the deep whorls of ornamentation.

The drawing room was aptly called the Green Room, for its walls were papered with pale green quatrefoil wallpaper and adorned with gilt-framed portraits. Two Louis XIV carved walnut armchairs and a green velvet parlor sofa stood in the center, framed by the tall windows that looked out over the front of the estate. A fire roared in the Carrara marble fireplace on the west wall.

Tom was standing with his back to the fire, hands clasped behind him, surveying the room.

"Ursula!" he exclaimed with a thin-lipped smile that never quite reached his eyes.

Ursula was all politeness. "Tom. It was good of you to come, but you really should have telephoned."

"I've been wanting to come for days but was called away on business. When you didn't answer my letters, I knew I couldn't wait another moment and had to come right away to see how you were holding up."

Ursula took a seat on the sofa, tucking in the skirt of her walking suit as she sat down. "Well, as you can see, I'm holding up as well as can be expected."

Tom remained standing. There was something in his stance, the way he was framed in the light from the tall windows, that tickled a memory in the back of her mind. Ursula dismissed it from her thoughts. She knew what she had to do.

"I'm sorry I haven't replied to your letters," she began awkwardly. "I'm sure you would like an answer. You deserve an answer."

"Well, of course, but I understand completely if you need more time . . . in the circumstances."

"No, no . . . it's fine. I don't need any more time." Ursula felt sick to the stomach, but she knew she had to continue. "It was my father's wish that I marry you . . . and I . . . I do want to abide by his wishes. . . ." She hesitated.

Tom was by her side in an instant. He clasped her hands in his. They felt clammy and hot. His thigh pressed against hers as he leaned over and kissed her fingers. "Oh, Ursula!"

Ursula tried to extricate her hands, but he merely bent over and kissed them again.

"We must marry as soon as we can!" he murmured into the folds of her skirt. "There can be no delay." As Tom raised his head, a stray curl of sandy blond hair fell onto his forehead. It was slick and sinuous, and Ursula could smell the sweet and sickly scent of macassar oil.

"Tom, please, can you not be content to wait? You have my answer, but the thought of marriage so soon after my father's death. . . . No . . . we must wait. Let this just be between us . . . for now. . . ." Ursula stammered.

"But I can't wait to show you off to the world," Tom said earnestly, trying to catch her eye. "We shall plan a grand tour, yes, that's what we shall do," he continued. "I want to take you away from all this — imagine, Paris, Rome, Constantinople . . . You can forget all about England. Forget all your troubles. Forget everything."

"But what of Winifred's trial? She needs me more than ever now. . . ."

"Miss Stanford-Jones . . ." Tom mused. "I had all but forgotten about her."

"Well I certainly haven't!" Ursula cried and pushed him away as he leaned in again toward her.

Tom straightened up. "Dash it all, Ursula, I'm just so excited! Can't think straight at all. You must do as you will. . . ."

"And besides," Ursula continued, "I may be going abroad as a companion to Lady Ashton after the trial."

Tom's eyes narrowed slightly but his demeanor didn't change. He still assumed an air of casual conviviality.

"But of course, you can start the wedding plans while I am gone . . ." she continued lamely.

"An excellent idea, my darling!" Tom exclaimed. "Some time with Lady Ashton will be good for you. Clear your head and all that — is it to be Europe then?"

"America, actually," Ursula replied. "I spoke to Lady Ashton yesterday and she has had to change her plans. An elderly aunt is dying and she wants us to visit her in Rhode Island."

He pulled out his pocketwatch. "Well, my

dear," he said lightly. "I really must be off. I need to be in London by tonight. McClintock wants to meet early tomorrow morning." He bent over Ursula and kissed her on the cheek. "Now I can reassure him that the Marlow empire is in good hands."

Ursula remained silent, determined to conceal her unhappiness.

Tom cupped her face in his hands and tried to kiss her once more. Ursula turned slightly so his lips brushed her cheek instead.

"I'll call on you in Chester Square. You are back next week, are you not?"

Without waiting for a response, Tom hastened across the room, pulled open the door, and bade her adieu. Ursula waited a few minutes before exiting the drawing room. She wiped her hands discreetly on her skirt. But they still felt damp and dirty.

A sudden draft of cold air caused her to spin around. Coming in from the garden, Lord Wrotham was holding open one of the French doors at the end of the picture gallery. His two dogs bounded in and shook their sable-and-white coats, sending a shower of water across the wooden floorboards. Lord Wrotham straightened up, unbuttoned his Norfolk jacket, and smoothed down his hair with the palm of his hand. He caught sight of Ursula and gave her a questioning frown. Their eyes met. Ursula steadied herself, assumed a look of calm indifference, and turned away.

That night after dinner, Ursula accompanied Lord Wrotham to the drawing room. It felt uncomfortable to be back in the room where she had received Tom's unwanted proposal, but Ursula pretended as though nothing had happened. Lord Wrotham walked over to the sideboard and poured two glasses of port. He offered one to Ursula before taking a seat in the walnut armchair opposite her, stretching out his legs to warm them by the fire.

"Ayres told me that Inspector Harrison was in this morning," ventured Ursula, taking a sip from her glass.

Wrotham nodded.

"Any news of Freddie's case? Have they managed to track down Bates?" Ursula tried to keep her tone light.

"No, I'm afraid not . . ." Wrotham feigned distraction as he picked up a book from the table beside his chair. "How is Mr. Cumberland these days?" he asked with apparent indifference.

Ursula smoothed down her skirt. "He's fine."

"So it was a pleasant visit?"

"I guess . . ." Ursula stared blankly at the fire. "I've agreed to marry him in the spring." She spoke matter-of-factly enough but a cold pit formed in her stomach. "Don't worry," she said with forced nonchalance. "I know what I'm getting myself into."

Lord Wrotham rose swiftly and walked over to the fireplace.

"Do you?" he asked with his back to her.

"I am well aware that in the past Tom frequented Madame Launois's establishment," she responded. "If that's what you mean."

Lord Wrotham continued to stand staring into the fire.

"And I know what vices are often indulged on the upper floors of her salon," Ursula continued with measured tones. "But attending such a place are hardly grounds to prevent a marriage."

Lord Wrotham spun around. His face was white.

"Don't look at me like that," Ursula retorted, feeling her anger starting to rise.

There was a sharp knock on the door, and Ayres entered the room carrying a silver tray with a blue envelope on it. Ursula took the opportunity to get up and move across the room. She looked to all appearances engrossed in the spines of some books on the bottom shelf of a tall bookcase.

"A telegram, my lord," Ayres announced.

Ursula felt all the heat drain from her face.

Lord Wrotham bade Ayres, "Leave it on the desk," before signaling him to go.

Ayres responded with a formal bow before retreating from the room. Lord Wrotham walked over to the desk and picked up the telegram.

Ursula's embarrassment fell away as she watched him read and then crumple the telegram in his fist.

"Who?" was all she asked.

Lord Wrotham hesitated before answering. "Cecilia Abbott."

Ursula clutched the side of the bookcase.

"Tell me," she asked softly.

"She left for Ireland last week. They found her body in a Dublin backstreet. She had been strangled."

Ursula crumpled forward, silent tears streaming down her face.

Lord Wrotham tossed the telegram into the fire.

"You must leave England immediately," he said.

"What would be the point?" Ursula yelled. "Cissy wasn't safe in Ireland. Do you think Marianne or Emily is safe in Greece? Do you think any of us are safe anywhere?"

Lord Wrotham bent his head, his face silhouetted against the flickering light of the fire. One of the logs in the hearth crashed forward, sending sparks flying across the floor. With a sob Ursula rushed from the room.

She insisted on leaving Bromley Hall the next morning. Her departure took Lord Wrotham by surprise, but he did not question her decision. He merely placed a call to ensure one of Harrison's men would be watching over her in London. Ayres made arrangements for Lord Wrotham's driver, James, to take her in his lordship's Daimler. It was time, Ursula told herself — time she found the courage to look after herself.

FIFTEEN

Ursula stood in the Grafton Gallery in front of a Gauguin picture entitled *L'esprit du Mal,* ostensibly viewing the latest London sensation, the exhibition of Manet and the Post-impressionists. She had come here to try and clear her mind, but the looming worry of Winifred's trial, due to start on January 3, was never far from her thoughts. Besides, it was nearly Christmas and the suggestion that she spend it with Gerald and Elizabeth Anderson was almost too depressing to bear. She found herself desperate for the kind of consolation that only came from immersing herself in art or literature.

Ursula remained in front of the picture, mesmerized by the scene. There was a girl standing in a pool of pink, holding a piece of cloth in front of her. Ursula wasn't entirely sure if it was a gesture of modesty or not. Behind her, a seated man stared out of the canvas. The title of the painting,

Words of the Devil, struck Ursula as ominous.

She forced herself to look away, and in doing so, caught sight of the plainclothes detective Harrison had assigned to follow her out of the corner of her eye. He was standing outside the gallery entrance, obviously bored witless, extinguishing a cigarette beneath his feet.

Ursula sighed and resumed her tour of the gallery. She let her eyes travel back to the rich hues of the canvases before her. On her right were the vivid colors and bold brush strokes of the unmistakable Van Gogh painting. Ursula leaned in to read the title, *Crows in the Wheatfield,* before taking two steps back so she could admire the painting more fully. It was then she caught sight of his tall, lean frame. He was standing before another of Gauguin's paintings — *L'esprit du morts veille.* Although she could see him only in profile, it was clear from the intensity of his gaze that he was oblivious to her presence. Ursula hestitated for a moment, unsure whether to approach or not. A man walking past muttered "Barbaric!" to his companion and Lord Wrotham's concentration was broken. He turned his head and saw her.

"I'm surprised to find you here," Ursula

commented as she drew nearer. "I would not have expected it."

Lord Wrotham raised one eyebrow. "Perhaps you don't know me as well as you think."

Ursula didn't reply — she wasn't sure whether he was being flippant or not.

"I often find myself here," Lord Wrotham continued, "when I need to think through a difficult problem. I find art helps distract the mind . . . allows a solution to reveal itself."

Ursula straightened the sleeve of her sage green jacket and pretended to study the Gauguin with a critical eye. She was surprised by his candor. She found his appreciation of modern art both surprising and endearing.

"Does being here mean you currently have a difficult problem?" she ventured.

"Perhaps."

"Is it something that concerns Freddie?" Ursula inquired anxiously.

He gestured to her to accompany him as he made his way toward the exit. "I was actually on my way to speak with you about this matter," he said in a low tone, hestitating by the door. "But this isn't something we want to discuss in public. Let me take you home. We can talk about the matter there."

He held the door open for her as they headed out onto Grafton Street. Ursula buttoned up her jacket against the chill December air. Her green and black striped skirt billowed out in a sudden gust of wind, and she hastened to hold onto it as her other hand grabbed her moiré silk hat to prevent it from blowing away.

"James is just over here," Lord Wrotham said as the Daimler pulled up to the pavement. He motioned to the plainclothes policeman. "I can take it from here."

"Right you are, milord," Harrison's man said with a tip of his cap. Ursula nodded politely, though being forced to rely on these men for "protection" grated on her nerves deep down.

Once they were settled in the backseat of the motorcar, Lord Wrotham signaled James and the engine revved as they set off toward Bond Street.

"So what is this all about?"

"I would rather wait till we get you home, but I see from your expression that won't suffice." Lord Wrotham drummed his fingertips on the leather seat beside him. "Pemberton and I have just met with Miss Stanford-Jones and she informed us that she plans to plead not guilty to the murder of Laura Radcliffe by reason of insanity."

Ursula stared at Lord Wrotham. "This means," he continued, ignoring her, "that she will be transferred to Broadmoor for evaluation."

"But —" Ursula started to say.

"Believe me," Lord Wrotham interrupted her sharply. "Pemberton and I are as astounded by her decision as you."

Ursula stared blankly out of the window as the motorcar passed Green Park and turned down Grosvenor Place.

"In many ways, though, it is the best decision as far as you are concerned. Have you no thought for the damage that would be done, indeed which has already been done, to your good name and reputation if you had taken the stand and testified on Miss Stanford-Jones's behalf?"

Ursula turned back to face him.

"I'm not sure I understand . . ." she said slowly.

"Think about it!" he responded. "How would you have handled being cross-examined about your relationship with Miss Stanford-Jones? Questioned about how you came to be called upon at five o'clock in the morning to assist her? How you regularly attend meetings of the Women's Social and Political Union, a group which actively promotes disorder and violence? Do you really think your reputation would survive that sort of interrogation?"

The Daimler pulled up outside the Marlow home in Chester Square. Ursula gripped the handle of the passenger door. She was too angry to speak.

"It may seem harsh," Lord Wrotham continued. "But at least Miss Stanford-Jones's decision grants us some more time to find out whether Bates is still alive and responsible for these tragic deaths."

Ursula held up her hand to silence him before she turned the handle and opened the car door. "Spare me the lecture! I do not believe you or Harrison really want to discover the truth." She almost choked on the words. "You dare talk to me about risks? What risks have either of you taken to find Bates?!"

Ursula got out of the car, shaking with fury. Lord Wrotham leaned across the backseat.

"Ursula, please. You have a wildness of spirit that I fear will be your undoing."

"And you really think you'll tame me?" Ursula said, exasperated. "Well, it's too late for that. You, Lord Wrotham, are nothing more than a brute and a bully!"

And with that Ursula slammed the car door.

Sixteen

*Atlantic Crossing Aboard the RMS Mauretania
January 1911*
Ursula stood aboard the deck of the RMS *Mauretania* leaning against the railing and gazing out over the open sea. After three days of bad weather, the ocean was finally calm beneath a clear, starlit sky. She tried not to think of England and the turmoil of the past few weeks, but remembrances came unbidden, like intruders in her mind. She saw that final glimpse of Winifred being escorted from court. How Winifred's eyes betrayed all that her letter would later explain.

I could not bear the thought of you on the witness stand, knowing the scandal it would bring. Now I must face the consequences alone. My bravest and truest of friends. You have all the courage you need to discover the truth. Go now and seek your answers.

It pained Ursula to think of Winifred incarcerated at Broadmoor for the next few months. Her fate was now in the hands of psychiatrists and doctors evaluating her state of mind and determining her fitness for trial. Ursula was not even allowed to visit her to offer comfort or support, but Winifred's letter provided the final seal on Ursula's plans. She was more determined than ever to travel to Venezuela to prove that Bates was alive. She could think of no other way to find out the truth — the truth that she hoped would reveal her father's true killer and acquit Winifred of Laura's death.

However, standing there, staring out across the black expanse of ocean, Ursula sensed all her hopes receding. The world had changed, the security of her youth was gone, and she felt as though she stood on the shore of a dark and unknown territory, afraid as she had never been before of what the future would hold.

At first Lady Ashton's arrangements for their journey to America provided a welcome diversion from her worries. Ursula seized the opportunity to finalize her plans. She arranged passage on the Atlantic and Caribbean Navigation Company's steamer-ship the *Zulia* for the ten-day journey from New York to Curaçao. There she would need to arrange passage to Ciudad Bolívar on the southern bank of the Orinoco. Aware of the improprieties — and infinite dangers — of a single woman's traveling to Venezuela, her only hope was to disguise her identity and attempt this portion of the journey dressed as a man.

Ursula had arrived at Miss Tennant's house in Chelsea full of trepidation. Winifred had spoken of this eccentric old woman who'd costumed her in men's clothing for years. Ursula walked along Cheyne Walk, through an iron gate and small garden, up to the white-painted door of a redbrick Victorian town house. She knocked twice with the black cast-iron door knocker. Miss Tennant turned out to be a wiry gray-haired lady in her early sixties wearing khaki bloomers, sturdy brown shoes, a high-throated white shirt, and a tartan wraparound shawl pinned at the shoulder with a silver brooch and a peacock feather. Ursula's gaping stare met a pair of intelligent brown eyes gazing at her quizzically from beneath a fringe of tight curls.

"Miss Marlow?" Miss Tennant demanded, looking Ursula up and down critically.

Ursula nodded.

"Guess you'd better come in, then."

Ursula soon found herself in a room filled with souvenirs of Miss Tennant's own travels. There was a stuffed tiger's head above the fireplace and an open crate filled with straw and African masks beneath the window. On the walls were prints and paintings depicting ruins and tombs across Egypt. Ursula felt particularly self-conscious standing in such a room all tightly corseted up in her narrow hobble skirt. Miss Tennant sat herself down on the red velvet divan and gave Ursula another appraising stare.

"You're in need of some men's clothing."

"Yes," Ursula answered. After a quick look around the room at all the exotic artifacts of travels abroad, Ursula decided to tell Miss Tennant the truth.

"Well then," the older woman said when Ursula was done, "we'd better get cracking. You'll need more than just a few pairs of trousers. Ever been to the tropics?" Ursula shook her head, and Miss Tennant sighed. "You'll need all the help I can give you, then. . . . Don't worry. I've decided that I like you. Yes. You don't seem like a ninny or a dimwit, so you may even survive the journey! Come with me, let's measure you up."

Miss Tennant walked past Ursula and into the adjoining hallway, calling out behind her (as Ursula struggled to keep up), "Ever tried dressing like a man before? . . . Thought not! How long have you got? . . . Three weeks! We'd better hurry. I've a tailor in the West End who is fast, but he's not cheap. Not that you look like money's a problem, but you'd better be prepared. Oh, and I'll need to see you again. If you're going to pull this one off you've got to walk, talk, and act like a man as well. No use just wearing the clothes!"

Miss Tennant stopped suddenly and turned around. She jabbed her finger in the air. "Just so you know, I haven't got the time for cowards. If you say you are going, then by Jove you'd better be prepared to go."

"I am."

"Then let's get started, shall we?"

Ursula had left Miss Tennant's nearly three hours later, armed with addresses of outfitters who would ensure she had all the equipment and medicines she needed to embark on her adventure. In less than a fortnight, she would return to pick up the three suits, five shirts, and various other accoutrements necessary for her disguise. Miss Tennant showed her how to bind her chest, how to swagger when she walked, even how to smoke a cigar. Ursula had bought herself collars and cuffs, men's cologne, and hair oil. She'd hidden everything in a separate trunk.

Now she touched her hair self-consciously. She tasted salt on her lips from the fine spray coming off the bow of the ocean liner as it cut its way though the dark, still sea. Her hair had been curled and rolled into the latest style, with coronets of braids at the back and Regency-like curls framing her face. She felt suddenly both foolish and naïve. What did she think she was doing? She would never be able to succeed with the charade. Did she really think herself capable of finding Bates? And even then, what was she to really say or do? The strength she had departing England seemed to be leaving her — to be replaced by self-doubt and fear. Ursula inhaled deeply and wound the wide silk scarf about her shoulders.

Deep in thought, she did not notice the tap on her shoulder until she heard a murmured "Miss . . ." from behind her. It was Violet, Lady Ashton's maid.

"Sorry, miss, But Lady Ashton's waiting in the lounge. She wondered if you were joining her for cocktails."

Ursula nodded. She knew better than to

keep Lady Ashton waiting. "Tell Lady Ashton I'll be there in just a moment."

Lady Ashton had arranged for Violet's cousin Ellen to act as Ursula's lady's maid. Ursula had been afraid that Julia would want to come along for the journey to New York and was relieved when she expressed her terror of the sea, enabling Ursula to make other arrangements. She didn't want Julia to be caught up in her plans to find Bates. Violet bobbed a curtsy and scuttled off the deck, her pallor still tinged green. Ellen was no doubt ensconced in Ursula's suite, neatly folding and putting away her freshly laundered clothes. Ellen seemed to revel in all the finery of the *Mauretania.* Ursula often caught her staring wide-eyed at its extravagances. "Ooh, miss!" she would say. "They have electric lifts . . . and did you see the grand staircase? And the ceiling in the dining saloon? Amazin' it is . . . they even have fresh flowers every day. . . ." Ursula had scarcely noticed her opulent surroundings, intent as she was on the journey that lay ahead.

Ursula walked back along the wooden deck, turning as she was about to enter the passageway for a final glimpse of the night sky. After three days of bad weather, the first-class passengers were starting to emerge. Many were now taking a hesitant promenade before dinner. Decked out in their evening finery, with the ship's lights in full glare, they looked like bejeweled insects, buzzing about an open flame.

Lord Wrotham strode in through the French doors after a long walk around the grounds of Bromley Hall.

"Mr. Anderson is waiting for you in the Green Room, m'lord," Ayres informed him.

Lord Wrotham stripped off his mackintosh and scarf and handed them to Ayres with a grunt. "How long has he been waiting?"

"Nearly an hour. I'm sorry, m'lord, but I had no idea you were planning such a long walk."

Lord Wrotham had been taking a good many long walks in recent weeks, though none of the household staff dared to comment. His mother the Dowager, however, needled him constantly. She warned him that he was in danger of becoming "a horrid bore, a recluse, and a thundering nuisance."

"Next you'll be turning up to the Derby ball in your Wellington boots," she told him severely, before she pleaded with him yet again to allow her to return to London.

"Nonsense, Mother," was Lord Wrotham's standard response. "You know as well as I that London society have all but disappeared to their country houses."

This inevitably prompted the suggestion of a shooting party, which only darkened Lord Wrotham's countenance even further.

Gerard Anderson was waiting in the green receiving room, sprawled on the green velvet sofa and reading the newspaper by the fire.

"Sorry about the wait," Lord Wrotham said brusquely as he walked in.

"My dear chap, no problem at all."

"What have you got for me?"

"News of Obadiah. Just as you thought — he's still angling for money to keep quiet. He knows we can't risk anything more being said in the press. Our business reputations are too important for that."

Lord Wrotham pulled out a cigarette case from his jacket pocket and offered one to Anderson, who shook his head.

"I think I may have a few words with Dobbs," Lord Wrotham replied, lighting his cigarette.

"Well, good luck finding him. Abbott and I haven't had sight nor sound of him since we received his demand."

"Don't worry," Lord Wrotham said grimly. "I'll find him."

"And what of Bates? Have your contacts

made the necessary arrangements?"

"Finally. There's great interest in Caracas in capturing him."

"Can your Foreign Office contacts help?"

"Don't worry. It's all in hand."

Anderson visibly relaxed. He pulled out a cigar from his coat pocket, and Lord Wrotham tossed him over a box of matches.

Anderson lit his cigar and savored its aroma. "Any news from Lady Ashton?" he prompted.

"Nothing since a wire telling me they were safely on board the *Mauretania*."

"Ursula will do well to be away from England for a spell. She's suffered enough, poor girl. First her mother, then Robert . . ." Anderson fell silent.

"I remember Robert telling me about Isabella," Lord Wrotham said suddenly, "about how his greatest fear had always been Bates." He was gazing back out the window, distracted by the memory of Robert Marlow that night on board the RMS *Lusitania* as they made their way across the Atlantic.

"He never knew for sure," Anderson said quietly. "But by the time the expedition left, I think he suspected."

"He said to me that night that his greatest fear was that he could lose her. He told me how Isabella came to him the day the expedition was due to leave Southampton and informed him she was with child. She was so excited I think it reassured him somehow. Reassured him that Bates meant nothing to her now. . . . I tried to ask more, but he broke down as he remembered Isabella lying in the sanatorium dying, and yet still all she wanted was him and Ursula by her side."

"You only have to look at Ursula," Anderson added soberly, "to know Isabella. She is the very image of her. I worried at first that Bob would never accept her because of it, but I think the more he saw Isabella in her, the more he had to have her close. Ursula was everything to him . . . and as Isabella's family refused to have anything to do with Marlow after her death, he was all Ursula had, too."

The past hung heavy around them. Anderson was just about to say something to try to break the silence when Ayres entered.

"M'lord, a telephone call for you, from London. A Mr. Biggs. Said he's received a telegram and must speak to you urgently."

Lord Wrotham threw the cigarette into the fireplace and hurried out of the room. Anderson fell back into his chair, dull dread in his eyes.

Lord Wrotham had left the door open, and

through the doorway Anderson could see him standing, telephone receiver in hand, in his study across the hall. Although his back was turned, there was no mistaking his stance. It was one of both surprise and anger. Anderson nervously drummed his fingers on the table beside his chair.

"Damnation!" Lord Wrotham swore, and slammed the receiver down. Even in his anxiety, Anderson had to suppress a smile, for he wasn't sure he'd ever heard Lord Wrotham swear before. Lord Wrotham walked back into the Green Room, trying to regain his composure. By the time he had returned and sat down, his face had become as implacable as stone. His eyes however, were hard as flint.

Anderson rubbed the tip of his nose and asked, "Ursula?"

"She's disappeared."

SEVENTEEN

A week later Ursula was standing in her cabin aboard the steamship *Almirante,* appraising herself in the mirror.

The *Almirante* was a small passenger steamer, considerably smaller than the *Zulia,* aboard which she had sailed to Curaçao, and of no importance at all when compared to the luxurious fineries of the RMS *Mauretania.* Nevertheless, it was aboard the *Almirante* that Ursula felt the most at home.

Tonight she would dine at the captain's table as they welcomed aboard the new passengers who had joined them in Trinidad. By now she was used to seeing herself dressed in trousers, collar, and cuffs. A fortnight ago it had been very different. She'd been standing in her suite at the Plaza Hotel in New York dreading the transformation that lay ahead. Lady Ashton and Ursula had checked into adjoining suites the previous day and dined at Sherry's that night. In the morning Ursula had pleaded illness, and Lady Ashton left for a day's shopping at Henri Bendel and Lord & Taylor. Meanwhile Ursula, insisting that her maid leave her alone to sleep, arose from bed and changed quickly.

She laid out a dove gray sack coat and trousers, a starched white shirt and detachable wing collar, a pale gray cravat, and laced calfskin boots. She wound a length of silk cloth around her bare chest to bind her breasts as Miss Tennant had shown her and pulled on the shirt. In her nervousness she fumbled with the gold collar studs and had to redo the cravat twice before it looked even remotely like a four-in-hand knot. Ursula grew more and more frustrated and uncertain as she struggled to do up the gold cuff links on the stiff cuffs of her shirt. Tears pricked her eyes. "Don't lose your nerve!" she said sternly to herself. She then buttoned up the trousers and pulled on her boots. Ursula stared at herself in the mirror, trying to adjust to the "man" she saw before her. She lifted up her hair and turned her head side to side. Now for worst part of all. She grasped a pair of scissors, sat down in front of the mirror on the dresser, and began to hack off her long, dark auburn hair, handful by handful. With each snip she flinched. By the time she finished, however, the cumulative effect was liberating. She tossed her head and laughed. It felt good to be rid of the weight of all that hair. This gave her renewed strength, and she hurriedly slicked it back with a dose of macassar oil. She then shrugged on her coat jacket, straightened herself up, and took one last glance at her transformation. For the final touch, she put on a pair of wire-rimmed glasses containing clear glass. Miss Tennant had been right: With a well-tailored suit and the glasses, she could pass as a young, if slightly effeminate, gentleman.

Ursula repacked the small leather suitcase she had kept locked with all her travel items for Venezuela and took one last look around the room. Her hair lay strewn on the carpeted floor, her trunk with all her clothes remained undone. She hastily tidied up, scrawled a note to Lady Ashton giving her apologies, and placed it on the dresser. She then pulled on a Derby hat, placed a leather wallet containing American and English currency and business cards in her coat pocket, tugged on a pair of gray gloves, and walked out of the suite carrying her suitcase.

At first Ursula was convinced everyone would immediately see though her disguise, but by the time she had walked across the lobby and out onto Fifth Avenue, she realized she was attracting no notice at all. Businessmen hurried past without even an apology if they bumped or jostled her. Ladies in their hobble skirts and fur coats ignored her completely. Ursula strode down the avenue and hailed herself a taxicab to take her to the Chelsea piers. When the driver called out the fare at the end of the trip, tipped his hat once she'd paid him, and said "Thank you, sir," Ursula's confidence had totally rebounded.

That was over two weeks ago, and by now she felt quite comfortable in her own skin. At first she had felt as if she were a stranger in her own body. At one level it helped her create distance between the life she had left behind and the task that lay ahead; on another it only served to make her feel more isolated and alone. The ghosts of England were never far from her. When she closed her eyes at night, she encountered her father, rather like Dante encountering the shades as he crossed the threshold of hell. She would meet her father and hold out her hands to greet him — but he remained forever out of reach. No matter how loudly she called, he could not hear her. No matter how much she gestured, he could never see her. He was nothing more than a dark specter, hollow-eyed and mute.

On board the *Almirante* was a motley assortment of passengers, none of whom seemed particularly interested in a single young man from Surrey with an interest in the botanical sciences. There was Mr. Bertram Fraser, a professor of geology at the University of Edinburgh who had been undertaking a survey of possible petroleum deposits in Maracaibo. There were Señor and Señora Carreño, newlyweds from Caracas visiting family in Ciudad Bolívar. Then there were Mr. Hugh and Miss Cora Buxton, sibling anthropologists who were planning to reenact Humboldt's trek to the upper reaches of the Orinoco in search of the mysterious Yanomami tribe. Ursula naturally gravitated toward these last two at dinner, but as their conversation seemed to revolve entirely around each other's ailments (she suffered from lumbago, he from ague), Ursula's role was limited to that of sympathetic listener. By the time they reached Trinidad, she wondered how on earth they were going to manage, when Hugh spent most of the voyage in his cabin feverish and ill.

Ursula had no problem adapting to the heat. Indeed it felt liberating to be able to sit on deck, eyes closed, feeling the early-morning sun on her face without the constriction of corsets or hairpins. In her wide-legged trousers, Ursula experienced a newfound freedom. She did not need to worry about stockings or heels on her boots. She could lean against the ship's rail, one foot resting on a bar, her hat dangling by her side and enjoy the light touch of the sea breeze in her hair.

When the *Almirante* reached Port of Spain in Trinidad, Ursula spent the day wandering around the botanical gardens and lunching at the Union Club. She arrived back on board as the sun was about to set and the crew were making ready to set sail the following morning. Mr. Fraser left the *Almirante* in Trinidad — he was returning to England on a Holland America ocean liner that had pulled into port the very same day.

Ursula was late, but there was still an empty space at the table with a spare table setting. She sat down and gave each of the other guests a peremptory nod. The captain was seated at the head of the table. A large, burly man with a black beard and thinning hair, he informed them that their final passenger would be joining them shortly. Ursula knew it was him before she even looked up. The *tap-tap-tap* of his shoes on the wooden floor, the rustle of his clothes, his scent. She could have had her eyes closed and known it was him. Lord Wrotham entered the dining room as if he owned the entire shipping fleet. He came and sat down at the empty seat, directly opposite Ursula. The captain welcomed him and asked them all to raise their glasses for the loyal toast. Ursula raised her head, and her eyes met his. Lord Wrotham gave no outward sign of recognition. There was only a barely perceptible widening of the eyes to indicate he had even seen her. She dropped her gaze quickly. The ship's steward handed her a menu, and she busied herself studying it.

"What brings you to Trinidad, Lord Wrotham?" Miss Buxton asked with breathless interest.

"Oh, just business," Lord Wrotham answered with a charming smile.

"And what business would that be, if I may be so bold as to ask?"

"I represent the Royal Botanical Society. I am seeking some rare and beautiful additions to our tropical flora collection." Lord Wrotham's voice was so smooth that no one would even guess it was a lie. Ursula readjusted her wire-rimmed glasses.

"Well, you must speak with our young Mr. Marlow here — he's a botanist, too."

"Indeed."

"Yes," she replied lightly, and then turned to the steward. "I will have the plantain soup and red snapper."

"Whom do you represent, Mr. . . . er . . . Marlow?" Lord Wrotham asked before lifting his glass of wine and taking a sip

"I'm afraid only myself." Ursula lifted her own wineglass to her lips and took a swig.

"Indeed." Lord Wrotham spoke this with such a degree of finality that even Miss Buxton sensed that their conversation was over. He turned and inquired whether the captain expected any rough weather on their journey to Ciudad Bolívar. Ursula inquired whether Miss Buxton was feeling any better.

"My back has been playing up ever since we left San Juan," she confided in Ursula. "I'm not sure how much more I can bear."

Ursula declined to join the gentlemen after dinner for coffee and cigars. She hadn't the stomach for any more of the charade. She felt drained as she left the dining room and headed for the deck. She stood there inhaling the sea air. She knew that her days of freedom were over, but nothing, not even the indomitable Lord Wrotham, could make her waver from her course — she would find Bates. Ursula lit a cigarette and drew on it deeply. She gazed up at Sirius, the Dog Star, bright against the night sky. Out of the corner of her eye, she saw Lord Wrotham approach. They stood for a few moments in silence on the deck.

"Well, I'll say one thing for you," he said at last, tossing his cigar over the side. "At least you chose a decent tailor."

The next morning Ursula encountered Lord Wrotham on deck again. The sleeves of his white shirt were rolled up and his eyes shaded by a panama hat. As she drew closer, she could see his eyes, watchful and guarded, beneath the brim. Ursula tried to maintain at least an appearance of confidence and ease as she sidled up to him in her wide flannel trousers. As usual, she kept her linen jacket buttoned up — she was always wary of being seen in just her shirtsleeves.

"It must be hard in this heat in all that getup," Lord Wrotham said.

"Actually," she retorted, "it's much cooler than what I would otherwise have to wear. At least I'm not tied into a corset and knickers." The words came out before she had time to think.

Lord Wrotham raised his eyebrows, and Ursula found herself flushing.

"One doesn't tend to mention one's undergarments, even if one is pretending to be a man."

Ursula bit her lip. "How did you know I was aboard the *Almirante*?"

"Now, that was sheer coincidence. Serendipity, if you will. As soon as I heard that you had disappeared in New York, I booked passage from London to Trinidad. I originally assumed I would find you in Ciudad Bolívar."

"Really — and what did you hope to do? You won't stop me trying to find him, you know."

"I am well aware of your determination. If you had only had the sense to tell me what you were planning, this charade would have been unnecessary."

"What do you mean?" Ursula asked, her eyes narrowing.

"I would have been able to tell you that my Foreign Office contacts had already located Bates. I could have assured you that the matter was well in hand."

"Oh, yes?" Ursula asked dryly.

"Yes." Lord Wrotham turned and faced her squarely. His blue-gray eyes glinted in the sun. "You didn't really think Anderson and the others would let the matter rest, did you?"

"What are you planning to do?" Ursula asked, and for a brief moment she was terrified that Bates had already been "taken care of" and that she would miss her only opportunity to ascertain the truth of what happened on the Radcliffe expedition.

"Given the trouble you have caused us all," Lord Wrotham said, "you will have to just wait and see." And with that he stalked off leaving Ursula standing on the deck feeling foolish.

EIGHTEEN

Orinoco Delta, Venezuela
January 1911

The *Almirante* sailed out of Trinidad's Port of Spain early the following morning, just as the sun began to catch on the tips of the waves. They sailed along the coastline past Pointe-à-Pierre, before they reached the narrow Gulf of Paria that separated Trinidad from Venezuela. After Trinidad the bright azure water was replaced by a cloudy opaque sea. The muddy waters of the Orinoco delta collided with the ocean in heaving waves that roiled the boat. Ursula stood at the bow of the *Almirante* looking out across the expanse of the delta. Soon though they were navigating their way along the river; beside them the narrow tributaries, or *caños,* beckoned. Somewhere along those dark waterways, where the water lay still and black, was Bates. Ursula felt sure of it. He was there, and he was waiting.

Soon she had to shield her eyes from the green brilliance of the sun hitting the forest. They had entered a primeval labyrinth that seemed to know nothing of the passage of time. It was like looking on the dawn of the world. No sooner would they be bathed in sunlight than they would plunge into the shadows of the tall palms and trees choked with vines.

Anhingas. Moriches. Araguaney. The captain pointed to the jungle as he spoke. The names were meaningless yet resonant. Ursula savored the words. Savored their mystery. A flock of bright red birds rose from the tree canopy in a swirl of color.

The ship prowled along the river. A blue-and-gold macaw flew overhead. Now and then Ursula would catch a glimpse of a hut on stilts, perched on the muddy banks. The river became wider and the sun so relentless it beat down through her jacket and shirt until she was soaked in sweat. Lord Wrotham was standing at the back of the boat, looking every inch the colonial man in his white flannel trousers and panama hat. The forest was now crossed with patches of dry grasses, and there was evidence of rough cultivation in the banana trees and tin-roofed farmers' shacks. Ahead in the waters, a pale pink dolphin raised its head and bobbed. A cayman slid its way off the bank and into the current.

Six hours later they saw the flat-roofed houses of Ciudad Bolívar, the town once know as Angostura. The steamboat pulled in against the gray pier that led to a white stone plaza.

Lord Wrotham booked two suites at the Colonial Hotel just behind the cathedral, and it was here that Ursula made her final transformation. She had brought one dress with her (in case of an emergency), a white short-sleeved day dress. As she made her way downstairs the following morning, she caught sight of her reflection in the mirror at the end of the hallway and was quite startled. Her face was tanned and freckled, her hair wavy and curling about the nape of her neck — she was a stranger to herself. Lord Wrotham made no comment, and though the concierge looked twice at her as they checked out the following afternoon, no one else seemed to notice.

They walked down the hill toward the river and found themselves on Paseo Orinoco, struggling through a dense crowd of traders shouting the prices of their wares. There were cattle being loaded onto a barge, the shrieks of fishermen as they moored alongside the quay, and the unmistakable stench of rubbish lying in the sun. Ursula was soon being jostled and pushed in the crowd. Lord Wrotham held out his hand for her, and, reluctantly, she took it and allowed herself to be led by him. First, Ursula bought herself some much needed clothing and provisions. They then found themselves in a narrow passageway that ran along the back of a row of traders' offices, where they organized their passage back down the Orinoco, into the heart of the delta.

They left Ciudad Bolívar in a rainstorm, huddling beneath an umbrella as it was pelted by the thick droplets, before struggling to get into the shallow-bottomed boat that would take them down the river. There was only a small wheel room, and so they had to content themselves with sitting on deck beneath a tarpaulin made of oiled cloth.

The captain of the boat was one of the canoe people, or Warao, who lived in makeshift piling houses along the banks of the Orinoco River and the smaller *caños.* The boat made its way down the river, the rain lashing at them from all sides. Lord Wrotham gave his jacket to Ursula, who was soaked to the skin through her fine cotton dress, while they sat, arms barely touching, on the bench seat beneath the tarpaulin.

Slowly they wended their way through the labyrinth of tributaries. The jungle pressed in on both sides, dark and dank and dripping. After nearly five hours on board, Ursula caught sight of their destination: an abandoned outpost of the Capuchin order of monks, who had once tried to establish a permanent mission here in the delta to covert the Warao Indians. Only one elderly monk remained, and the mission itself now consisted of no more than the remains of a wooden chapel built on stilts above the riverbank and the living quarters, which were a series of small rooms surrounded by a large wooden veranda that jutted out over the dark, still waters of the river. The monk greeted them from the veranda and, once Ursula was safely up the ladder, provided a brief tour of the rest of the mission. There was a kitchen and dining room, which backed out onto the jungle itself. A parrot hung from the ceiling in a wire cage above the rough-hewn table. Each of the bedrooms consisted of a single wrought-iron bed draped in mosquito netting. A jug and basin were provided in each room, and these rested on a stool placed in the corner, with a chamber pot beneath it. Ursula found it hard to believe these conditions, yet with the sunlight streaming through the slatted windows and the furious noise of birds and monkeys all around, she found herself strangely drawn to this place. It seemed familiar somehow, as if she had seen it in her dreams.

That night she woke to find everything damp around her. The sheets were clammy and soft, her nightdress sticking to her legs and waist. She felt trapped beneath the mosquito net. A terrible smell of mud and decay rose from the river and permeated the entire mission. She dreamed she had been running through a sea of tall grass, a hot sun beating down upon her. She stumbled and fell, the earth beneath her starting to smother and consume her. She was sinking into the earth, suffocating in its darkness. Now all she could hear was the drumming of the rainwater on the tin roof above. Lightning flashed on the horizon, lighting up the room through the chinks in the shutters. Howler monkeys screeched in the trees. The rain started to lash down. She could not return to sleep.

Ursula rose from her bed and dressed quickly. Perhaps some time outside on the veranda overlooking the river would help clear her mind. The fan above her head beat a slow, steady rhythm, but still the heat inside the bedroom was stifling.

Ursula felt like the only person awake in the world. Outside, there was a slight breeze that provided some relief. She stood barefoot on the wooden floor of the veranda, which stretched out over the riverbank on stilts. The storm lanterns flickered in the wind. Beneath her the river advanced and retreated against the muddy shore.

She leaned against the railing, the breeze lifting her white dress so it billowed up and out with a slow, monotonous rhythm. Her arms were bare and seemed to reflect the dying light of the storm. It was passing to the west now, with only an occasional rumble and glow on the horizon. The jungle was once more alive with sound and movement. In the daylight I might well be afraid, she thought. But this night, with darkness as her cover, she felt fearless.

She felt his footsteps through the floor before she heard the distinctive strike of a match. He hadn't seen her as yet, and all she could see was the distinctive blue-orange glow of a cigarette end. As he approached, his tall, dark shape became visible against the shadows.

She turned back to look out over the river.

Her eyes, having adjusted to the darkness, could make out the currents as they swirled along the river. The moon was rising above the clouds.

She heard his footsteps now — heard him stop as he saw her. She didn't turn around. She wanted to wait to see what his next move would be.

He paused, as if deciding whether to approach.

"I remember storms like this in Guyana," he said.

Lord Wrotham remained standing there, his face submerged in shadows. Ursula longed for the moon to appear from behind the clouds. She had only a tentative thread of self-control to hang on to. The night was surreal and strange, the darkness intoxicating. All her senses were heightened. She perceived layers of shadow and shade; it was as if she could peel back the layers of darkness itself. The hairs on her arm felt the soft touch of the breeze. I have to be strong, Ursula thought. I cannot keep showing weakness. It leaves me too exposed.

"Guyana?" She savored the word.

Lord Wrotham inhaled on his cigarette but still made no move to approach. He was like a black cat keeping his distance.

Ursula leaned back against the railing,

stretching out hands to her sides and sliding them back and forth along the polished wood.

"I didn't know you'd ever been to Guyana."

Lord Wrotham came and stood beside her on the veranda. He looked out over the river. Ursula's hand was only an inch away from his.

"I've long wondered about your so-called Foreign Office contacts. Like the revolver I found in your chambers" — Ursula reached over and pulled the Webley revolver out of his jacket pocket — "a mystery."

Lord Wrotham leaned in toward her. "Oh, I'm not sure there are many mysteries to you that are left unsolved."

He caught hold of her hand, took the gun, and slid it back into his pocket. Ursula closed her eyes. His sudden closeness was potent.

"Be careful," she murmured. "You may start to intrigue me."

"I think there's very little danger of that." His voice low and tremulous, like the water beneath them, lapping against the soft edged shore.

"You may be surprised," she answered.

Their fingers touched. His hand closed over hers. Ursula held her breath. Firm, near, his flesh pressed against hers. Slowly she yielded, lifting her fingers lightly and gently till they clasped his. Meanwhile his eyes sought hers. She saw a flash of lightning, far off on the horizon, reflected in his eyes.

"I thought you still suffered from a broken heart," Ursula said, and yet her words seemed so far away, fluttering above her in the night.

"I fear you will be the only woman to truly break my heart."

She expected his kiss to be deep and dark, irresistible and crushing, but instead it was tender, even hesitant at first, and it filled her with yearning. His was a kiss of sadness, like a haunting dream. She felt lost. Adrift. She had these images, all these images, of herself in her mind. Those formed by her dead mother, those instilled in her by her dead father. The dead were ever present. They breathed across the rain forest as the heat of the day, as the rain that fell, as the mist that rose. Always there. She could not quell their voices or silence their breath.

Ursula returned his kiss fiercely. The ghosts of the past receded, the sounds of the jungle retreated, and all she could hear was the beat of blood in her ears.

■ ■ ■ ■

Drowsy, she was being carried back to her own bed. The sheets felt cool against her legs as she was placed down. She saw Lord Wrotham standing silhouetted against the pale moonlight that now filtered into her room through the gauzy netting above her. Then an intense sleep slipped over her, soothing and calm.

As she hugged the pillow to her, curling her knees in tight, she hazily murmured, "Love me again. . . ." more to herself than anyone else.

She felt his warm breath against her cheek, his hand gently moving back the strands of her hair.

He moved nearer and whispered in her ear: "Always."

So dreamlike and strange that when he was gone, when she felt his presence no more beside her, she wondered whether he had said anything at all, or whether imagination had taken hold of her completely.

The morning light broke through the slats of the shutters early. Ursula lay under a cool cotton sheet gazing up thought the mosquito net. She watched the ceiling fan as it whirred and let her hand drift across the bed, tracing the indentation of a dream beside her. The sounds of the jungle were muted, the tree frogs had ceased croaking, the squawk of the macaws had faded into the distance.

She rose and washed herself with water from the jug, opened her trunk, and dressed quietly. The morning air had a calm coolness that was refreshing. She buttoned up her blouse and started to comb her hair, which now reached just above the nape of her neck.

She walked out onto the veranda. Everything was unrecognizable in the day. At night all had been swathed in darkness, the residue of humidity and heat hanging in the air. The morning, with its sharply focused sun and clear sky, had swept aside the night. Everything was new and different.

Ursula found herself standing alone at the long wooden table which had been set for breakfast. A small boy darted in from the rear door.

"*Buenos días,*" he said with a wide white smile.

"*Buenos días,*" Ursula replied, returning his smile. The boy motioned for her to sit, and soon she found herself seated in front of an array of food that still seemed unfamiliar. There was a woven basket full of fruit: bananas, mangoes, and papayas. In another basket there were cornmeal arepas with some kind of cheese, and on a chipped white plate there were fried plantains.

Ursula finished eating quickly, wondering what had become of Lord Wrotham. Only now was she feeling the first tremors of trepidation. The night seemed such a long time ago. She heard the sound of boots on the main jetty leading to the mission. Lord Wrotham was suddenly speaking.

"I told the *comandante* to wait until I contacted him. I made it quite clear that no one was to come here!" Ursula peered around the corner and saw a short, dark-haired man in a double-breasted blue uniform standing beside Lord Wrotham. The elderly monk from the mission was trying to act as intermediary, translating Lord Wrotham's words when his rudimentary Spanish failed him. The man in uniform was talking and gesticulating widely.

"He says that they must act quickly. They are afraid Bates will not stay in the delta long," Ursula heard the monk translate.

"Please tell the *comandante* here that I am quite aware of his concerns, but as I told his superiors, we must wait until Miss Marlow is well away from here before we act."

Lord Wrotham paused, listening to the monk try to explain, before continuing. "Tell him we wait. Miss Marlow leaves tomorrow. Then, tell him, only then do we go and arrest Bates."

The elderly monk looked bemused, but his translation seemed to placate the young commander, who nodded, saluted Lord Wrotham, and turned to make his way down the jetty to the small skiff moored at the edge.

Ursula backed away along the narrow veranda toward her room. She needed a cool place to think, to quell the turbulence of emotions within her. The arrogance of that man! Once again he chose to make decisions behind her back. Was she never to find out the truth for herself? Would Lord Wrotham have Bates arrested before she could speak to him? Ursula was shaking with rage. There was too much at stake for her to be treated like some lovesick schoolgirl. There were too many questions she needed answered. Too many deaths that needed to be avenged.

Ursula felt a tug at her skirt and, looking down, saw the same boy from breakfast with his wide white smile.

"Bates?" the boy asked, and Ursula froze in midstep.

"Bates?" he repeated. "You see Bates?"

Ursula looked ahead to where the boy was pointing. He tugged her skirt more urgently. Ursula nodded unthinkingly and took his hand as he led her to the rear of the mission, to a small gangway and ladder jutting out over the muddy brown waters of the river.

Below, sitting in a dugout canoe, was a man who looked like the Warao Indians she had seen living along the banks. He was squatting at the back of the canoe gesturing for her to come down.

Ursula didn't hesitate; she swung herself over the gangway and onto the ladder (heartily wishing she were still wearing trousers rather than a cumbersome white dress) and awkwardly clambered into the canoe.

Then, without a word, they pulled out from the jetty and the canoe set off down the river to find Bates.

In front of Ursula, the Warao paddled strongly and silently through the narrow tributaries. They made their way slowly down a long canal, skimming over brackish water the color of dark tea. The crooked limbs of submerged roots and branches protruded above the surface now and then, like spectral hands reaching up to clasp the canoe. The Indian stopped for a moment and let the canoe drift as they entered a small lagoon. Above, the sky was luminous, but the water bore no reflection. Ursula gazed across at the banks. The mud was dry and hard on the shore, and she could see the silver flecks of insects skimming above. To her left, though, where the light could not reach, gnarled mangrove roots reared up and the mud was thick and oozing as the water lapped alongside. Deep within, Ursula realized, the sun could no longer penetrate. I would be lost in there, she thought. Lost to the darkness of this place. Forever.

The Indian resumed paddling with strong, swift strokes as he steered the canoe into a narrow channel, almost hidden by vine-choked trees. The brooding heat closing in upon her, Ursula wiped her forehead with her sleeve but could feel no respite. The impatience and anger that had caused her to be here had now dissipated and in their place was a deep and wretched panic. How could she have been so foolish as to have journeyed here alone? She was totally vulnerable now, and the realization of it was like a river swelling within her, threatening to burst the banks. As she tried her best to hide her fear and anxiety, they continued their slow progress, Ursula ducking now and then to avoid the overhanging limbs of trees and vines. As they drifted, she stretched out her hand to see what the black water below would feel like, cool and dripping from her fingers, but the Indian grabbed her arm and stopped her.

"Piranha," he said with a toothless grin.

Ursula began to feel faint. The Indian handed her a leather water canteen, from which she drank gratefully.

Suddenly they were drifting out into a wide waterway, and ahead there was a clearing in the jungle. An island of grass swaying in the sunlight. At the edge there was a hut on stilts, with the skeleton of a wooden boat of some kind rotting on the bank alongside the remnants of old kerosene drums rusting in the sun.

As they pulled up to a small jetty, she presumed she had reached the end of her journey. The Indian helped stabilize the canoe as Ursula gingerly rose to her feet, stepped onto the ladder, and pulled herself up onto the wooden jetty. Before she had even got back on her feet to turn around, he had departed, the canoe leaving as silently as it had come, winding its way back along the curve of the *caños.*

The hut had a corrugated iron roof and an open entrance. It consisted of one large room, and the walls, such as they were, were nothing more than weathered reeds and tree trunks stacked side by side. They were held together on the makeshift frame by vines and rope. It seemed as if they had been hurriedly placed there, for shafts of light were visible between the beams, each of varying width. Like all of the Warao dwellings along the banks, it stood high up on stilts above the mud and water.

Ursula walked carefully along the jetty — the gaps between the slats were wide and precarious. She could see the dark brown mud of the riverbank and the lapping brown water beneath her. Should she call out? she wondered. No doubt someone was already aware of her presence.

She reached the open front of the hut — it was like a massive doorway. Once inside, it was as if the daylight were trying to establish a foothold — fighting through the cracks, asserting itself through the wider gaps, and stabbing through the holes like a spear. It made for a sharp contrast against the darkness of the shadows between and the dark places that hid in the corners of the room. As she called out, she half expected a monstrous figure to spring out from the shadows.

"Hello?" She felt somehow ridiculous.

There was no answer. She steeled herself.

"Is anybody here? . . . Mr. Bates?"

Still no answer, but in the rear of the hut, in a pool of shadow, there seemed to be a movement. A sinewy shape formed and moved toward her. She tried to keep from recoiling.

The shape turned into a woman. Small and slight, with jet-black hair and a neckful of beads. The heavy necklace of color, it turned out, was the only form of clothing she wore. Ursula felt decidedly ridiculous now, in her white English blouse and her long English skirt. She looked, she knew, as if she had walked out one spring morning for a game of tennis or archery. It seemed both incongruous and somehow profane, as if her very Englishness were an affront to the gods of this place. She could sense them everywhere — darkened forms beneath the surface of the leaves and trees. A ripple along the water. A breath on the breeze. The woman stood and watched her.

"I'm Ursula. Bates sent for me." She felt, if it were possible, even more foolish.

The woman showed no sign of any recognition, not even of the fact that Ursula had spoken. She merely stood and watched, like a wary animal waiting for a sign that it was safe to move. Ursula wondered if Bates were somewhere in the darkness and if this woman were waiting for his signal. But there was no sign or sound of movement.

Again Ursula spoke. This time she raised her voice and tried to sound as if she were issuing an order.

"Where is Bates? I must find him. I must meet with him."

The woman gave her a crooked smile.

"Bates gone," she replied.

"Gone?!" Ursula exclaimed, and then immediately checked herself. She must remain calm. This might all be but a game. To display anger or frustration would be imprudent. "Where?" she asked. "Where has Bates gone?"

The woman smiled again but did not reply.

"Will he be back?" Ursula asked.

The gaze meeting hers was wary and appraising.

"Will Bates be back soon?"

The woman merely nodded, and then, after a long pause, she motioned Ursula to follow her inside.

"Can I wait here?" Ursula asked as she followed her into half-light.

No answer.

Ursula decided that the only thing to do was to sit and wait. The woman, whoever she was, was crouching now in a corner, her hands and feet fast at work stripping a large palm frond into a series of strands and setting them aside. A basket lay half woven beside her. As she concentrated on her work, Ursula seemed to fade. She had become nonexistent. Ursula did not know what to do, except remain patient and silent. Her senses were heightened, and again she was struck by the connections — the threads of sights and sounds. A sense of the mystical and the magical. She could believe almost anything here. The most fantastical tale could easily be true.

"It has a hold on you already."

A voice, unclear at first, came upon her. Ursula wasn't sure where it originated, but she rose and turned once around to try to locate the man who owned such a voice. It had a smoky timbre to it — like an open fire.

"Mr. Bates?" Ursula replied, still swallowed up in the gloom of the hut.

"Perhaps," came the answer.

Ursula rose to her feet and walked out of the hut and into the fierce light of day. She had to shield her eyes from its glare, and the man who stood before her was indistinct and blurred as her eyes made the adjustment. She moved her hand away to try to see him clearly, and as she did so, she heard him gasp.

"Isabella?" he asked, in a voice hoarse with emotion.

Bates looked at Ursula as if he had seen a ghost.

NINETEEN

"Isabella?" Bates repeated.

His fair hair was still swept back but was bleached white from sun and age. His face was lined and tanned, his beard gray, and his dark eyes, which had seemed so languid in the photograph, now gazed upon her feverish and wild.

"I am not Isabella," Ursula said. Face-to-face with this man, she found it hard to hide her contempt. "I am her daughter, Ursula."

Bates moved toward her, eyes still fixed upon her as if she were an apparition from a long-ago dream. He reached out and touched her cheek, and Ursula flinched from his touch, a terrifyingly intimate gesture for a man who had tried to orchestrate her death.

"Why did you let me leave?" he asked, addressing her once more as if she were her mother. He seemed out of his wits.

Bates grabbed her chin and tilted her head

up. Ursula had to close her eyes to block out the sun. She fought his grip and shook her head free till they met eye to eye. Bates was transfixed, his eyes betraying an alarming mixture of excitement, incredulity, and shock.

Ursula backed away. "I told you I am not . . ." Her voice faded off. There was now such sadness in his eyes that she was confused.

"No!" Ursula cried out desperately. "No!"

"Oh, dearest one, death comes so easily to me. But you, you have brought me hope!" The mad, feverish glint returned in his eyes.

A terrifying look came over Bates, as if he were possessed by some malevolent spirit. He became agitated. His torso jerked violently. His hands shook. An awful sound, like the howl of a rabid dog, broke from his parted lips, and he fell to the ground shaking.

"Oh, my God!" Ursula shouted. "What is it? What is happening?"

His eyes rolled back in their sockets as the convulsion eased.

The woman emerged from the hut carrying a small glass flask and hurried to Bates's side. She urged him to drink, placed the flask to his lips, and forced him to take a gulp.

The woman then led Bates into the hut and pushed him roughly down onto the floor. She then returned to the corner of the room and resumed her weaving.

Bates lay in the hut for an hour before reviving and walking, unsteadily, back outside.

"I apologize. Sometimes the past comes back to reclaim me." His voice was behind her.

Ursula turned. "Are you speaking of the Radcliffe expedition?"

"Radcliffe!" Bates spat in disgust. "Radcliffe was a fool!"

"But you were once friends, were you not?"

"No. Not friends. They needed me, that was all. They needed a naturalist to help them identify what they sought. Radcliffe was just along to lead the damn thing, as if he were leading military maneuvers in the Sudan. That's how he treated it!"

"And how did *you* treat it?" Ursula asked, her head spinning from the glare and the heat.

"It was my passion," Bates said simply. He now appeared surprisingly lucid and calm. "After my time in Brazil and Guyana, I knew I had to come back to the Americas, and if we had found what we were looking for, we would have been some of the wealthiest men alive."

"What was it that you sought?"

"Plants were what we sought, of course. But we needed the help of the Waraos. It was they who knew the secret."

"The secret?"

Bates eyed her suspiciously, as if he suddenly recalled once more who she was. "Please let us go inside, it isn't good for a white woman to sit in the sun for so long."

Ursula nodded gratefully but followed him cautiously as he led her back into the hut. The woman in the corner continued her work and did not bother to look up. Ursula sat down heavily on a wooden crate.

"This is an unfinished land." Bates started to speak. "One in which we can observe natural selection at work. The constant battle for survival. The need to weather flood or drought. The Waraos know this, they live in harmony with this. To them the world is merely a thin, flat disk, surrounded by water. Beneath that lies the double-headed snake Hahuba that encircles the earth — it is he that causes the tides to ebb and flow. But what we searched for were the Hoanarao or 'people of the black water,' who dwell in the deep reaches of the delta, where the water is brackish and still."

His voice was mesmerizing.

"It was they whose shaman we were told knew of this plant that could control a woman's cycle. Could hold back conception itself. Think of the possibilities. We could have been the very instrument of natural selection."

Ursula shivered. "My father would have had no part in anything so monstrous!"

"Monstrous? When England lay in decay? The bloodlines diminished? He saw only possibility, freedom from poverty, the reinvigoration of the English race!" Bates gave a savage laugh, and Ursula drew back, shaking her head.

"That's why they betrayed me. They wanted all the glory for themselves," Bates scoffed.

"Tell me," Ursula urged quietly.

"He came for me," Bates began. "He came for me before the Indians even started. I heard him coming toward the tent — Radcliffe always was such a clumsy bastard. I thought he was with fever, but when I saw his eyes, I knew, I knew that it was all of them. . . . They had planned it all along. Oh, yes, I had seen the communiqués Radcliffe sent back to them. I saw what he thought of me. A liability. A risk. A traitor. He thought the jungle had taken me already . . . hah!"

Ursula clasped her knees to her chest as Bates continued.

"So Radcliffe comes to me, and I see the knife, I see the flash of the knife, and then it starts. The camp is attacked. There are gunshots, I hear men being thrown into the river. No doubt the piranhas were already feasting. Radcliffe stabs me in the confusion. Oh, the sweet sensation of the blood! He plunges it into my stomach, and then as I fall, he slashes at my chest. I fall and I fall, I hear only the screams . . . but I know that if I lie still, if I keep so very still, they will think me dead already."

Ursula's breath caught in her throat.

"They wanted me dead." His voice was no more than a whisper now.

"They?" Ursula prompted.

"All of them. Anderson. Abbott. Even Dobbs . . . and Marlow, of course, always Marlow. And to think Radcliffe even survived." Bates started to laugh again. This time, though, it was hollow and sobering.

"But you survived, too."

"Barely! The Indians who had attacked were mostly Carib traders. They had heard that we carried many provisions with us — rum, salt, that kind of thing. They were opportunists, and I suspect that if our guides had not been armed, the attack would not have been so deadly. I can only assume Radcliffe surrendered in order to live."

"So how did *you* survive?" Ursula continued to press the issue.

"As I say, I played dead, and once everyone had gone, I struggled to walk. They had taken everything — the canoes, the food, even the water. So I lay down and prepared to die. Do you have any idea what that is like, Ursula? Preparing yourself for death?"

Ursula shivered despite the heat.

"I was saved by the Warao people. They came in their canoes to see what had happened. My memories of that time are hazy, but I spent nearly six months in one of their villages near the mouth of the Río Grande tributary."

"And then?"

Bates cast her a sidelong glance. "I went to Caracas. I was told that my wife and two sons were dead. That they had died of yellow fever in Trinidad. I went mad with anguish. For ten years I waited, and then I found him."

"Who? Who did you find?"

"My eldest son. He had been moved to an orphanage in Caracas during the epidemic on Trinidad. The Hospital of San Stephano, where my wife and other son died, had been looted and burned — all records had been lost. They merely assumed the boy had died alongside his brother. But I found him . . . I raised him . . . until he was grown. Then he went to sea. It wasn't hard to find him an apprenticeship aboard one of Dobbs's ships. That was where he met Dobbs's young son Christopher. It was like a revelation — the means for our deliverance was before us. My own son became the instrument of my revenge."

Ursula's heart nearly stopped beating. The truth now exceeded her wildest comprehension. It wasn't just Bates she was after. From the looks of it, this decrepit creature hadn't left this jungle in years. There was someone else, some lost son doing his bidding.

"Given that you are here," he continued, "I can only assume he has been arrested or is dead." Bates suddenly looked up, a gleam in his eyes. Ursula thought maybe the madness was returning but instead he gave her a sly, cunning look. Like a sandy, bushy haired fox. "No," he said, stroking his beard. "Perhaps he hasn't failed me after all. . . ."

Ursula frowned.

"He wrote to me you know," Bates said, "about them all. Laura Radcliffe. Cecilia Abbott. Even Marlow . . ."

Bates disappeared into the dark recesses

of the hut and emerged carrying a tin box packed with tattered envelopes. "Don't look so surprised. Even here, at the ends of the earth, the Royal Mail Steam Company brings me news from England."

Ursula reached out her hand to take one of the letters but Bates snatched the tin away and shuffled into the back of the hut once more, mumbling and cursing to himself.

"Tell me about my mother," Ursula demanded. The thought that her mother could have ever loved this man was too terrible to ignore. "Tell me about Isabella."

His eyes glinted. "Isabella was an angel. We were so young, you see. She always knew me. She brought out the good within me, and when I was with her, I could forget all else. 'Isabella the angel,' I would call her, and she would have been mine should I have returned and Marlow not. I knew her long before she met Marlow, you see. She was standing at a summer party, her dark hair falling behind her beneath a large white hat. She was all in white, and as she turned, I knew. This one had to be mine."

"Then why did she marry another —"

Bates's eyes narrowed and his body jerked. Ursula drew in a breath, waiting for another attack, but instead his eyes took on a glazed, faraway look, and he spoke in soft, pleading tones.

"Oh, Isabella, do not say it is over. Do not say you must be with that man. When I return — yes, when I return — we can be together again at last. . . . Oh, Isabella . . ." Bates moaned, and his head dropped, and he wept.

Ursula instinctively started to extend a hand to comfort him, but before she could stop herself, Bates reached out and grabbed it.

"You wretch!" he cried before his eyes rolled back and his body convulsed backward, dancing and jerking, the palms of his hands violently smashing up and down against the floor.

Ursula got up quickly and backed away. Now was her chance. She thought, I must escape.

She looked desperately to the river, but there were no canoes and only the forlorn skeleton of a boat on the shore. Behind, in the small clearing, was the other makeshift hut, but beyond that the jungle rose up as a green dark curtain on either side. Ursula yelled for the woman, but she remained hidden in the back corner as if she had disappeared into the very heart of the darkness itself.

Ursula had only one option, and she began running. She got as far as the jetty, and when she gathered up her skirt and began to climb down, her head was violently jerked back by an unseen force.

A voice snarled in her ear, "I will never let you leave me again!"

"No!" Ursula cried out. "No! Let me go! I do not love you! I never did!" She hoped desperately that pretending to be her mother would placate him.

"Do not lie to me!" Bates spat at her. "You know you loved me, and I would have come for you when I returned. That was why your husband wanted to be rid of me!"

Another voice in her ear, and this one sounded quite different from the last. It was silkily warm against her neck. "You don't want to leave, do you, Isabella, my love?"

"I am not Isabella!" Ursula screamed, but Bates was now incapable of listening. He tried to drag her back by her hair, seizing her with a strength that took Ursula by surprise. Bates then forcibly carried her out along the path to the hut in the grass. Ursula's struggles were futile; try as she might, she could not release herself from his grasp.

Bates opened the door to the hut and threw Ursula inside. She hit the ground hard. Winded, she tried to sit up and breathe, but her body seemed rigid with fear. She heard Bates shifting something in front of the hut, and from the sound and the smell of it, it was an old kerosene drum. Ursula nearly fainted with the combination of fumes and heat, for inside, the closeness of the air was stifling. This hut was also wooden, but unlike the ones on the jetty, these planks and slats were firmly affixed to the frame. Barely any light at all entered through the spaces between them. The little that could filter inside did so through the space between the tin roof and the walls. Ursula tried to look about her for some means of escape, but there were no windows or patches of rotten wood. She then searched for some instrument she could use, but there was nothing aside from sacks of flour and maize stacked up in the corner.

"Bates!" she cried. "Let me out!"

There was no reply. If he was still afflicted by whatever madness had overtaken him, Ursula needed to remain calm. Tears pricked her eyes, and she scrubbed them away with her sleeve. She took a deep breath and tried to erase the anguish from her voice.

"Bates, my love. It's Isabella. Please, let me out. How can we be together if you won't let me out?"

Still no reply. Ursula banged her fists against the door, trying to dislodge it, but to no avail. Her knuckles were red and raw.

"Please!" she cried out again. "It's Isabella! Isabella . . ."

Ursula wasn't sure how many hours had passed. She wasn't entirely sure that the day itself had not passed until night came. She watched the crack of light as it faded to gray, and then, as twilight descended, she curled up on one of the sacks, anything to be above the ground when total darkness fell. She wasn't sure what terrified her the most, the thought of what might come in from the outside — the cause of all the scuffling and slithering she heard around her — or whether it was the man himself and the thought that he might enter in the darkness to violate her. Both terrors kept her from sleeping.

Deep into the night, Bates came and stood outside the hut. Ursula heard the rasp of his breath and smelled the distinctive musky odor of rum and sweat.

"Have you come to free me?" she asked, her voice cracked and dry.

Bates laughed. "Ah, Isabella, no . . . Why do you want to be free of me? You never used to. You wanted nothing else but me."

"It's true," she replied. "I want only you now." It was a dangerous game, Ursula thought, but maybe if she could lure him to open the door, she would have some chance of fighting her way free. "I know, I know how hard it has been for you. All these years . . ."

Bates kicked the door and spat again, "You know nothing!"

He descended into a moody silence. Ursula heard him pacing around the hut, his feet crushing the grass. Then there was nothing but the screech of monkeys in the trees and the call of tree frogs, deep-throated in the depths of the jungle.

She struggled against sleep, trying to keep her eyes open, but the night seemed as if it would last forever, and soon the exhaustion was too much. She dreamed of the graveyard in which her father lay buried. She was lying curled up on the wet grass by his grave, inhaling the scent of the earth. She watched, fascinated by the whiteness of her skin on her arm outstretched on the black mound of stone and dirt. A light rain fell and shrouded her in mist. There was the faint pealing of church bells in the distance, followed by a hushed stillness. Ursula rolled over and faced the sky. It was dark and stormy, and as the rain fell harder, the raindrops stung sharp and cold on her face. She looked downward to see the trickle not of water but of blood pouring now from the sky and running off her body into the hard and flinty ground beneath her.

Ursula awoke. She was still in darkness, but the heat had stilled. She thought she heard the sound of an animal padding across the grass, a snarl, then the sound of paws soft on the muddy ground. She drew her knees in close and shut her eyes. The fears in her dreams were more tolerable than the fears that surrounded her when she was awake.

When the light began to return, the heat inside the hut was already intense. The combined smell of fuel and her own sweat made her gag more than once. But when the morning came, she nevertheless started to beat her fists against the door again, crying and screaming to be released.

She ceased all activity as the heat took its toll. She was finding it hard to breathe, and her head swam whenever she tried to raise it. She had not had anything to drink in nearly a day, and her throat felt as though it had been scraped with a knife. Ursula lay slumped in the corner of her cell.

Suddenly there was a crash, and the sound of shouting in a Spanish tongue. Ursula struggled to her feet. There were more shouts and then gunshots. A woman screamed. Ursula fell against the door of the hut, summoning all her strength to yell and plead for help. There was only confusion. Ursula could smell smoke and hear the roar of flames ignited. Abruptly the fuel drum blocking the door came crashing down, and when the door opened, she was pulled outside into the glare of the light. A dark-haired man in a blue and gold uniform spoke to her in urgent Spanish, but she could not understand. She saw only smoke and confusion. Despite this, a strong and determined voice inside her head reminded her what she had to do. Ursula pushed the man away and ran toward Bates's hut. She could think of nothing else but the letters. She struggled inside, as mayhem rained around her. She saw the tin box, grabbed it, and rushed outside.

A blow to the head sent her reeling. Then Bates kicked over another drum, sending kerosene flooding down toward the river. Ursula could see him standing before her, a tower of flames and smoke behind him. He grabbed her and pulled her to the ground. The stench of fuel was unbearable, and then the horrific truth started to sink in: He was going to set her on fire. She could hear the shouting as men tried to maneuver around the flames, and random shots rang out, but Ursula could not tell from which direction they came. Bates stood over her, black against the orange fury of the sky. Her dress was soaked in kerosene, and he needed only to wait for the fire to spread for her to be engulfed.

"If I can't have you, no one else will!" he cried out.

Ursula kicked him in the groin as hard as she could, and he crumpled to his knees in pain. Seizing her chance, she got to her feet, grabbed the tin box, and started to run with the blind energy of fear driving her, toward the jungle. The fire raged behind her. There was a sound of air rushing backward, and a draft hit her in the back. She stumbled and turned to see Bates ablaze and screaming. Horrified, she averted her eyes. The heat of the fire was intense now, the canopy of the jungle caught alight. Ursula looked down at her skirt, stained with kerosene. Time seemed to stop. She watched a line of flame traveling toward her before she instinctively ripped off her skirt, turned, and ran.

She tried to make it through the thick undergrowth, tried to head toward the river, but the thick vines strangled the trees, squeezing the light into tiny chinks, barely visible against the twisted darkness of the jungle canopy. The air was thick with heat. She kept moving ahead out of sheer willpower. She knew that if she stopped, even for a moment, all would be lost. The river was silent — it offered no guidance — but she knew she must find it. The river was her only salvation. She had never felt so alone.

So she now knew the truth. She knew that Bates had been left not for dead but partly alive, yet it was a dead kind of living — darkness had eaten him from within. So this was the truth. Could she really be so sure? In this place all reality seemed unreal. Her dreams made more sense. Her senses deceived her. She heard voices. She saw faces in the shadows. The heat was unbearable. Her clothes were leaden weights. She was drowning even as she placed one foot in front of the other. She stumbled over tree roots and fell deep into the mud. She felt hands upon her, just as a voice inside her started to say, Death would be a relief. You could just stop, catch your breath, let the air enter your lungs one last time. Let your hands stretch out in the darkness. Let the earth consume you.

Just as this voice spoke, another, so calm,

like water flowing over her, made itself heard:

"You can stop running now. You're safe. I have you."

TWENTY

Ursula's eyelids fluttered as she started to wake. The crisp sheets felt cool against her skin. A ceiling fan beat a rhythmic pulse above her. She noticed the brilliant red flowers in a vase on the windowsill, the peeling fresco of the Virgin Mary in an alcove above the sink, and finally the image of Lord Wrotham, bent over that sink, his hands gripping the sides, as water ran down from his face into the basin. He looked up, and she saw the blue of his eyes reflected in the mirror, more vivid than she had ever realized before.

"Ursula!" he exclaimed, and rushed to her side. He took her pale hand in his and clasped it to him. His hair, still wet at the ends, dripped cool beads of water, and like raindrops they trickled down her arm. "It's been nearly a week. I had begun to fear the worst."

"Where am I?" she croaked.

Lord Wrotham propped her head up and put a glass of water to her lips. "Here," he said. "Drink this. Try not to talk. . . ." He then gave a weak smile. "Difficult for you, I know."

Ursula sipped a little water before sinking back onto the pillow. She raised her hand to her head and felt the bandage across her temple.

"You're in a hospital in Ciudad Bolívar. The *comandante* and I brought you here by boat."

"Bates?"

"Dead."

"What about the letters?" Ursula croaked.

Lord Wrotham touched her cheek lightly. "Even now you worry about your friend. Well, you have no need to. I cabled Harrison. The letters contained all the information he'll need."

"So Freddie . . ."

". . . is free." Lord Wrotham dug around in his coat pocket and pulled out a telegram. "I also received word from Harrison this morning that they found a body washed up on the banks of the Thames. The man was carrying papers identifying him as John Henry Bates. Seems he had sought passage aboard a ship bound for India but fell overboard the night before they were due to set sail. The ship's doctor said there were reports of drinking and brawling among the midshipmen."

Ursula stared at Lord Wrotham in disbelief.

"This means that Bates's son is dead," he said.

"Dead?"

Ursula burst into a torrent of tears. The fear she had felt for Winifred, the loss she had felt for her father, seemed lifted, and only now, with this unbearable lightness, did Ursula realize what an immense strain this fear had been. As she sobbed and heaved, Lord Wrotham handed her a handkerchief, and she had to smile. Finally she leaned back on the pillows, sighed with exhaustion, and closed her eyes.

The next thing she knew, she was looking up into the dark eyes of a nurse fussing and tucking in the sheets around her.

"Where's Lord Wrotham?" Ursula asked, sitting up. The nurse gave her a quizzical look and Ursula pointed to Lord Wrotham's panama hat that lay on the bench under the window.

"Ah, sí, sí . . ." the nurse replied, and started speaking quickly in Spanish.

"I'm afraid . . . I'm afraid I don't understand," Ursula interrupted her, and tried to get up.

"*No . . . no . . .*" The nurse pushed her back down and then, with a sign to her to stay put, hurried from the room. Within minutes a tall lady in a long nun's habit came into the room, and Ursula found herself staring into a pair of brilliant blue, good-humored eyes.

"So you've decided to finally grace us with your presence, have you? I was beginning to think his lordship was havin' delusions!" The nun spoke swiftly, with an Irish-tinged accent. "Don't look so surprised. This hospital was established by the Order of Poor Ladies of St. Clare. I've been here three months now — joined the order five years ago in Galway."

"Could you . . . could you tell me where I might find Lord Wrotham?" Ursula tried to sit up again, but the nun stopped her. "No, I cannot," she replied emphatically. "I've ordered him back to the Colonial Hotel to get some rest. He's been here day and night waiting for you to wake again."

Ursula touched her head gingerly.

"Now, you just lie back and be still," the nun ordered her. "You've caused everyone quite enough fuss and bother. Sneaking off on your own to find that madman. . . . You wouldn't read about it in a cheap thrup'ny novel — and there was his lordship dashing back here with Comandante Sarría, demanding this and demanding that. The whole town was in an uproar."

"I'm sorry . . . I don't . . . I don't really remember what happened. Was anyone else hurt?"

"Two of the expeditionary force that accompanied me died." Lord Wrotham's voice cut through the air. Ursula turned her head and saw him standing in the doorway.

"Bates's woman was injured in the crossfire but she escaped into the jungle."

Ursula dimly recalled seeing her flee as Lord Wrotham carried her back to the river's shore. Semiconscious, she could recall little else, except the heat of the sun and an intense thirst that no amount of water could seem to quench.

"What about the Warao man and the boy who led me to Bates?"

"How else do you think I found you? They are talking with the regional authorities, but I'm sure they will be released soon."

"I heard you . . . I heard you speaking to the *comandante,*" Ursula said.

Lord Wrotham walked over to her bed. "Hush, now," he said gently. "It's over."

Ursula let relief wash over her at last. She

watched as the nun left, as the nurse resumed her fussing. Lord Wrotham took a seat by her side.

"I brought you my copy of Tennyson's *Princess;* I always travel with poetry. Thought you could do with something to read."

"I'm surprised you own a copy of Tennyson's poetry."

"I'm not nearly the philistine you believe me to be."

Ursula barely suppressed a yawn. "I doubt I would ever call you that. A fuddy-duddy maybe, but never a philistine. Read something to me."

His presence seemed safe and familiar, and Ursula felt the warmth of his closeness.

He opened the book, flicked through the pages, and started to read.

Ask me no more: thy fate and mine are
    sealed:
I strove against the stream and all in vain;
Let the great river take me to the main:
No more, dear love, for at a touch I yield;
Ask me no more.

Ursula sank back into the pillow. Closing her eyes, she let his words pour over her and within minutes she was asleep.

Twenty-One

The return journey across the Atlantic was expected to last less than five days. Although the RMS *Lusitania* had captured the Blue Riband for her speed once before, anticipation levels were high. There was a certain degree of excitement among all the passengers, for she was a magnificent feat of engineering. Seven hundred eighty-five feet in length and eighty-eight feet broad of beam, her four funnels sent plumes of smoke into the air as her belly churned to reach twenty-six knots in speed. The passengers were for the most part oblivious to the machine beneath them. For them the journey was far removed from the dark, smoking fires below.

Reveling in their luxurious surroundings held no interest for Ursula. Her first-class cabin was certainly fine, and the Georgian-style lounge with its stained-glass barrel-vaulted skylight was undoubtedly impressive, as was the massive domed dining room, but Ursula was ultimately unmoved by it all.

After the initial relief over discovering that Bates's son was dead, Ursula was plagued by doubts. At night, these doubts intruded on her dreams and she found herself reliving those nightmarish days with Bates over and over again. Only in these dreams she could never escape.

She spent most of her days curled up outside on one of the many steamer chairs that lined the open deck. She would lie there for hours, rugged up in a coat, scarf, and muff, simply staring out at the ocean, watching the magnificent sea's many moods ebb and flow. Winifred was free, and her father's murderer was dead. In her mind there was a great relief, and yet her heart remained in turmoil.

The first evening after dinner, Lord Wrotham and Ursula retired to the first-class lounge. Looking around at the faces of those already seated, she became aware of the interest she garnered by traveling with Lord Wrotham unchaperoned. She sighed. No doubt she should be steeling herself for the inevitable scandal when she returned to England, but after everything she'd been through, she could barely muster the strength to care. For his part, Lord Wrotham seemed unconcerned by the pointed stares and whispered comments.

Ursula sank down in the chair and was just about to open her book when Lord Wrotham handed her a folded-up letter, brown at the edges and yellow with age.

"I thought you should have this," he said.

"What is it?" she asked, starting to unfold the paper creases.

"Something Anderson found among your father's possessions. I thought it might shed some light on what really happened to the Radcliffe expedition."

Ursula leaned back in the armchair and spread the paper out in her lap. The handwriting was unkempt, and the creases where it had been folded were beginning to tear. Ursula was careful not to handle the paper too much lest it rip entirely. The date at the top of the letter was July 19, 1888. Ursula briefly looked up, but Lord Wrotham was now standing, gazing moodily out the porthole.

She started to read.

Marlow,

What a damnable business. I've been in this godforsaken hospital for over two months, and they're just now letting me write to you. I can only hope that the British embassy has sent word to Millie and the girls to let them know I am all right. I beg you to check on them for me. I worry lest they hear false reports of the expedition and think the worst of me — you know how malicious those damn reporters can be! I've never been so bloody ill in my life. Worse than the bout of dysentery I got in Malaya. Worse even than the fever that took the lives of three of my men on that Bolivian expedition. I'm getting too damn old for this game. But I guess I should be thankful — I've secured passage on the *Arconian,* due to sail August 1. Thank Dobbs for me. Decent of him to have arranged that for me.

Old friend, we were close — so bloody close I could feel it. Heard word of the tribe from our guide Mario, and we met one of the women elders. Frightening old hag with a neck full of beaded necklaces and skin like a tanned animal hide, but she knew what we were on about. Old witch wouldn't tell us much, though, so I knew we were damn close to discovering it!

So close — and then what do I see but Bates, the yellow bastard, in secret meetings with the Indians. You must have received my earlier communiqués — I warned you what he was like. I knew within days of setting off from Liverpool that this man was not to be trusted. I knew he was going to betray us, and I had no choice but to act. The bastard was conspiring to cheat us all out of what would have rightfully been our discovery.

The jungle plays some damnable tricks on you, but Bates seemed to welcome the madness. Dear God, Marlow, the things he said about your wife I dare not repeat. Obsessed, he was. The abominable lies that fellow told. Insulting to you and Isabella. I struck him more than once, I can tell you, but something dark had taken hold of him. The farther we got into the delta, the worse he became. I could see it in his eyes. Like an animal, he was. He was nothing more than a dog that needed to be put down.

At this point the handwriting began to deteriorate even further.

Then I fell prey to the fever, and I knew he was just waiting for his chance. I could see him watching me. The Indians knew it, too — they were just waiting for the moment to strike. God forgive me for what I had to do — you may have guessed the truth already, but you know I did it for all of us. Not only to secure our discovery but also to silence the bastard. There was too much at stake, you know, and I couldn't risk everything we'd worked so hard to achieve. I only wish I'd acted earlier — maybe I could have prevented the Indian attack.

Please let Isabella know that I tried to protect her good name. She is such an angel. Rest assured, my dear friend, the filth he spoke will never be repeated.

I will write again as soon as I am able, but for now take care of Millie and my girls. Let them know I have written to them and send them my love.

Yours etc. etc.
William Radcliffe

Ursula stopped reading and put the letter down. "So Radcliffe did try to kill Bates."

Lord Wrotham admitted, "It would certainly appear that way."

She chewed her lip thoughtfully. In the back of her mind she wondered if the members of the expedition ever found what they were looking for. "You said Anderson found this in Papa's possessions. Was there nothing else?" she asked.

Lord Wrotham shook his head. "There was no other correspondence about the expedition between Colonel Radcliffe and your father in the files. This letter was found at the back of his desk drawer."

"Do you think my father believed Radcliffe was guilty of murder?"

Lord Wrotham hesitated before responding. "Yes, although he told me he was convinced that Radcliffe was ill, perhaps even delirious, when he wrote this letter. He said Radcliffe was a changed man because of the expedition. He would have these bouts where he was so wretched he would lock himself in his study for days, refusing to eat, refusing to drink. Your father was the only one he would allow in there with him. Your father told Anderson and the others. They all swore to secrecy. Anderson, when he saw it in the drawer, was surprised your father even kept this letter."

"Do you think my father suspected that Bates and my mother —" Ursula started to say, but Lord Wrotham interrupted her quickly.

"I think your father thought Radcliffe was a troubled man — haunted, even — by what occurred, but your father was not to blame.

Rest assured he played no part in the attempt on Bates's life. No matter what Bates may have thought, your father did not order Radcliffe to murder Bates."

"I could never believe that he did," Ursula replied with indignation, but the burden of uncertainty seemed to lift.

Lord Wrotham moved away from the window and came and sat down in the chair. "You need to trust that what your father did was the right thing. He clearly felt that Radcliffe had suffered enough without the indignity of an inquiry into what had happened."

"Maybe he also felt that Radcliffe's actions were justified," Ursula replied stiffly.

Lord Wrotham eyed her thoughtfully. "Maybe," he conceded. "But are we really the ones to judge?"

On the third morning aboard the *Lusitania,* the Atlantic was calm and untroubled. By the afternoon the wind had risen, and the whitecaps gave the sea a tumultuous look, as if something dark and ominous were stirring beneath the waves. The storm, however, did not eventuate, the wind blew itself out, the frenzy died, and the waters became impassive once more. Twilight came, and the sea reminded Ursula of a brooding

341

young man, sullenly waiting for the next opportunity to vent in violent expression.

When Ursula viewed herself that evening in the full-length gilded mirror that adorned the port-side wall of her bedroom suite, she was struck by the reflected gaze that met her own — it was a stranger's gaze. She did not recognize the person standing before her, this person whose clothes hung loosely in folds and drapes of green and silver. She refused the attentions of the lady's maid Lord Wrotham had hired for the journey. "I want nothing further," she said before removing the ornament the maid had so carefully placed in her hair.

Lord Wrotham spent most of the day in the first-class library reading, and that was where Ursula found him before dinner, sitting in a wide leather armchair perusing a copy of the *New York Times.* He was, as always, immaculate in his black tailcoat, white wing collar, tie, and vest.

Ursula sat down on the sofa beside his chair, idly flicking through the magazines laid out on the table between them. She finally selected a copy of the *Ladies' Home Journal.*

Lord Wrotham peered over the top of the paper and, with a smile at what she was reading, said mildly, "I'm surprised at you, reading such material. I thought 'modern women' shunned such things."

Ursula refused to rise to the bait and merely thumbed through the pages idly. "Not wearing your Carlton Club pin, then?" she asked.

Lord Wrotham turned the page loudly. The Carlton Club, in Pall Mall, was the leading Conservative Party club.

Apart from the two of them, the lounge was empty; most people were still in their rooms changing for dinner.

"This reminds me of sitting in the drawing room of Bromley Hall," Ursula commented thoughtfully.

"Yes, but then we'd have my mother," Lord Wrotham said from behind the newspaper.

"Ah, yes, your mother . . . Is she in London now, do you think?"

"I sincerely hope not. I'll be bankrupt if she is."

Ursula lapsed back into silence. Try as she might, she could not be the girl she once was. The idle chatter and teasing in which she'd reveled in the past now seemed both inconsequential and contemptible. She could no longer bear it.

At dinner Ursula and Lord Wrotham sat opposite each other at a long table, trying to ignore the other guests.

"How have you been today?" he asked. "A little better?"

"A little," she replied politely.

"Perhaps you would accompany me for a turn about the deck after dinner?" he said, and Ursula picked up her glass of wine and swallowed a mouthful.

"Perhaps," she replied.

They ate the suprêmes de sole in silence.

Their eyes would occasionally meet across the table, and each time Ursula suspected that Lord Wrotham had been seeking her out. His expression was, however, inscrutable. The steward came around and brought them dessert and coffee.

The conversation farther along the table was animated enough to dispel any discomfort their silence might have caused. Toasts were made, glasses raised, and spirits were high.

Ursula stood to leave, and as Lord Wrotham came around to help move her chair, he bent forward to whisper in her ear. "Americans . . ."

"Undoubtedly," she replied with a rare smile.

The night sky was visible from the promenade deck, and as Ursula gazed upward, Lord Wrotham clasped her arm and steered her toward the railing. They both leaned against it and looked out across the ink-black sea. The wind was picking up and Ursula shivered.

"I noticed you received a cable this morning." It was more of a statement than a question.

"Yes," Ursula replied. "Tom is anxious that we set a date for the wedding."

She looked out forlornly over the great expanse of sea that rolled beneath them. "I agreed we should marry as quickly as possible upon my return to England. In my reply, I suggested the first weekend in March."

Lord Wrotham was silent.

"Does my decision shock you?" she asked.

Her question woke him from his thoughts.

"No," he replied bleakly. "You are a woman of your word."

His lack of emotion galled her. She wanted to smash through his defenses and break him. Break the façade which prevented her from ever truly understanding him.

"You do not have to marry him," Lord Wrotham said quietly.

Ursula looked away. She tried to hold back the tears but they came unbidden. "What choice do I have? I must fulfill my duty to my father. Besides, what does it matter? If not him, who else?"

"You . . . have a sizable fortune, Ursula —" Lord Wrotham reminded her.

Ursula gripped the railing, "So you and Anderson have calculated my net worth and think I could do better? Do you think now that I am alone in the world I can be traded like a piece of property?" Ursula took a deep breath and tried to compose herself.

Lord Wrotham's face had gone white.

"Ursula, I . . ."

She looked at him, searching his face. "How can I possibly marry a man who does not love me?" she asked. "Whose very soul seems so contrary to mine? How can I . . . ?" She was unable to continue.

"Yet despite all of this, you are determined to go through with it?"

There was no use hiding her tears now. They silently trickled down her face.

"What's it to you if I do?"

Lord Wrotham averted his eyes. The wind howled about them, its shrill intensity piercing the silence between them. "Nothing," he finally answered. "Nothing at all."

She could hardly believe the words had been spoken and yet once they had been it was as if she had stabbed a knife into her own breast, the pain was so acute. She looked at him, searching again for the same sign, some way in. There was nothing. She regained herself. The tumult of her own emotions ceased and a terrifying numbness came over her.

"I am tired. It is late. Good night, Lord Wrotham."

She left him leaning over the rails without waiting for any further response.

Inside her suite Ursula undressed slowly. Her reflection in the mirror mocked her again. There can be no normal life after what I have seen, she thought. I am a stranger to everyone.

Ursula unhooked her corset slowly. "You may go," she addressed her lady's maid, whose head had just appeared around the door to the adjoining suite. The maid nodded and disappeared.

Ursula slumped down heavily on the gilt-and-leather chair. A heavy lethargy came over her. She felt sad and alone.

She curled up her knees and gazed at her reflection as she brushed her still-short hair. She had done what she had set out to do. Yet now, where she once felt numb, she felt an ache deep inside her — when she thought of Winifred, when she thought of Lord Wrotham.

The ship's bell clock in the corner chimed midnight, and Ursula realized she had been sitting in the dark for over two hours. She leaned over, turned on one of the lamps beside the chair, and reached behind her for the dressing gown that she had thrown on the back of the chair. She walked over to the dressing table and dabbed some cucumber water beneath her eyes. Then, with a determined gaze at her reflection, she pulled the turquoise silk dressing gown around her and tied it in tight. She slipped her feet into her satin slippers and headed for the door.

The passageway was empty, and Ursula crept outside. Her slippers sounded like a kitten padding along the ornate carpet that ran in a line down the center of the passage. She came to an intersection and tentatively peered around to check no one was about. At this time the first-class deck was quiet, although she could just barely make out the strains of the quartet still playing in the lounge and the occasional scream of laughter, suggesting that one party at least was still going.

Ursula stopped outside suite number seven. She took a deep breath before tapping softly on the door. There was no sound of movement behind the door. She tapped again, this time a little louder. The door opened slowly, and Lord Wrotham stood framed in the doorway. He was still wearing his black evening trousers, his braces, and his white starched evening shirt, now without either collar or tie. His sleeves were rolled up and his hair disheveled.

She stood in the doorway for a moment, suddenly unsure what to do or say. Before she had time to think, he pulled her toward him and closed the door. She stood pinned against the cabin wall, her heart beating wildly. He was leaning in close and she could smell whiskey and cigar smoke on his breath. They stood face to face, his blue-gray eyes dark and watchful. His arms were braced against the wall, his body tilted in toward hers until they were nearly touching. Ursula closed her eyes and breathed him in. The scent of him. The touch of him. It was as though nothing else existed. His kiss was hard and fierce as the windswept sea. She gave herself over to him and the world was all but forgotten.

TWENTY-TWO

London, February 1911

The day after her return to London, Ursula awoke bleary-eyed from lack of sleep. It was a cold, clear late-February morning, but as she opened the curtains to take a glimpse of the world, all she could see was the pale outline of the street below through the damp veil of condensation that had formed on the windowpane overnight.

She heard the grandfather clock in the stairwell chime eight o'clock. The Marlow household, of course, would have been up for hours already. All the coal fires would have been lit, the downstairs rooms swept and dusted, and preparations for breakfast would have started as soon as Julia heard Ursula stir from her bed. Ursula, however, felt ill-prepared to face the day. She was unsettled and tired after the long journey across the Atlantic and confused by the conflicting emotions aroused by Lord

Wrotham. She didn't know what to think or feel anymore. Ursula pressed her forehead against the windowpane, overcome with foreboding. She was engaged to marry a man she did not love and time was running out. The ceremony and small wedding luncheon was scheduled in two weeks' time.

Ursula spent the morning catching up with correspondence and was just finishing a letter to Alistair Fenway requesting a copy of all her father's companies' accounts when Biggs entered the drawing room with an announcement.

"There is a telephone call for you Miss Ursula," he said, the very essence of formality now that she was mistress of the house. "Miss Stanford-Jones, calling from the north, I believe."

Ursula leaped to her feet. The last she had heard (via a cable from Harrison when she was aboard the *Lusitania*), Winifred was recuperating from her time at Broadmoor with her aunt in Yorkshire. Biggs held open the study door and Ursula hastened past and hurried down the hallway. She lifted the telephone receiver with a sudden pang of nostalgia. Now she really did feel she was home.

"Freddie?" she cried.

"Sully, is it really you? Are you finally

returned to us?" Winifred sounded just like her old self and Ursula laughed. "Yes, though it's hard to believe after all that's happened. Where are you?"

"Still in Yorkshire, but I had to call as soon as I heard you were home." They continued chatting until Winifred said, "I heard you set a date . . ." Ursula remained silent. "Are you sure you want to go through with this?" Winifred finally asked.

"I owe it to my father . . ." Ursula sighed, leaving the rest unsaid.

"You know what I think, Sully?" Winifred responded quietly. "I think it's time you weren't in the shadow of any man."

Ursula inhaled sharply. Winifred's words cut her to the bone.

She made up a feeble excuse to end the conversation, put down the receiver, and returned to the study, uneasy. She tried to push Winifred's words aside and immerse herself in her father's business files. There were still boxes and boxes to sort through. Still unsettled but determined to focus on the task at hand, Ursula knelt down on the carpet to separate out what she should keep and what she should discard.

She was surrounded by piles of paper and account books when Biggs interrupted her again.

"Yes?" she lifted her head expectantly as he closed the door and approached her.

"Mr. Tom Cumberland to see you. Should I ask him to wait in the front parlor or do you wish to meet him in here?"

Ursula had been so deep in concentration she hadn't even heard the front door bell ring.

"What? Oh, right . . ."

"And Lord Wrotham telephoned a few minutes ago to see if he could call upon you after supper this evening. If that is convenient, I can telephone him and confirm the appointment."

"Yes. Yes, thank you Biggs. Tell Lord Wrotham to call around eight. And tell Mr. Cumberland . . . tell him, to come in. He needn't wait for me in the front parlor."

"Very good, miss." Biggs bowed his head and Ursula thought she saw a glimmer of the old humor in his eyes.

She got to her feet and smoothed down her skirt. She was wearing one of her suffragette dresses, as her father used to call it. Functional and plain, it was pale lavender with white trim and collar. Hardly her best day wear but apart from her hair, which was growing out and looked a little wild as a result, she deemed herself perfectly presentable enough for Tom.

Tom entered the room waving a bouquet of pink roses in one hand and a cigarette in the other.

"I've taken care of all of the arrangements for us," Tom began. "The vicar at Holy Trinity Church is obviously delighted to be of service. He was very fond of your father, you know."

She closed her eyes to try and calm herself but she felt the claustrophobia of marriage closing in. "I've also taken the liberty of contacting your relations in Scotland."

"You contacted my mother's family?" Ursula exclaimed. She hadn't seen any of them since she was a child, which made Tom's actions all the more inappropriate. "What on earth did they say?" she asked.

"Haven't heard anything back as yet," Tom responded airily. "Oh, and I mustn't forget. Fenway's drawn up a whole lot of papers for you to sign. I brought them with me — thought we may as well get that all sorted."

"What sort of papers?" Ursula asked suspiciously.

"Oh, just some transfers, that sort of thing. It will ensure that you don't have to worry about any business affairs of your father's. After we are married, everything will be placed under my control. It's really just a formality, you understand, my love?"

Ursula was trembling with anger. Winifred's words echoed in her ears.

"I'm afraid signing those papers is quite out of the question," Ursula said with an icy calm. And suddenly she knew what she must do.

Tom eyed her warily. Ursula took a deep breath and continued. "Tom, I cannot marry you. I'm sorry. I know it was my father's wish that we wed, but I simply cannot . . ."

"Cannot marry me?" Tom put his finger under her chin and turned her face toward him. "Nonsense!" Ursula flinched. Tom's mouth tightened, and suddenly, an unmistakable feeling rose up inside her: fear. Detecting her discomfort, Tom relaxed his grip on her and made a visible effort to regain his composure.

"I'm sorry, if I've done anything to —"

"You've done nothing. I simply cannot marry you. I'm not sure I'm ready to marry anyone. Don't you see I need to stand on my own now?"

Tom got to his feet and walked over to the fireplace. "You're making a terrible mistake, of course. How can a woman like you possibly survive on your own? You have been cosseted your whole life. What do you know about being independent?" He suddenly sounded bitter. "What do you know of the world?"

"Tom, I really am sorry —"

"Enough!" Tom snapped. His whole demeanor had changed. Gone was the carefree lover. Instead she saw the real Tom, and he was cold and calculating.

"I have heard quite enough." He almost spat out the words before leaving the room.

Ursula sat at the dinner table glancing now and then at a book propped up against a vase filled with hothouse flowers. After her confrontation with Tom she had little appetite. She pushed the roasted squab idly around her plate with her fork. The room was gloomily quiet with Ursula having only her thoughts for company or comfort. She found it hard to concentrate, as every time she peered hard at the page full of words, her eyes read a sentence before wandering to look at the mantel clock sitting on the mahogany sideboard. It was not even seven o'clock. Finally, with a sigh, she put down her knife and fork, closed the book, and rang for Moira to clear the dishes.

"I'll wait for Lord Wrotham in the front parlor," she told Biggs as she exited the dining room. "You may as well decant the wine and bring it in there."

"Yes, Miss Marlow. Would you like dessert or coffee brought in before then? I believe Cook has made trifle, or there's always her rhubarb pie you're so fond of."

Ursula bit her lip. It wouldn't do for her to fuel any more gossip, given she had left dinner half eaten. "Please tell Cook I'll have a small helping of trifle and then bring some coffee in, as well."

"Of course."

Ursula made her way down the hall and into the front parlor. Already she noticed changes to this room. There was a pile of books and magazines on the flat-topped side table that, when her father was still alive, she would not have dared to leave out. She had also moved some new items of decoration downstairs; a Ruskin pottery vase now stood on the mantelpiece alongside a bronze miniature of the sorceress Circe. On the small coffee table under the stained-glass lamp, Ursula had placed a Cymric silver bowl from Liberty which she filled with rose petals and lavender. Touches, she thought, that made the parlor seem different somehow, more her own.

She picked up the top book, *Collected Works in Verse and Prose of William Butler Yeats,* from the pile on the side table, kicked off her satin shoes, and sat down on the sofa. As she was all alone, she curled up her knees beside her and opened to the front pages. More at ease now, she nearly forgot her determination not to look at the grandfather clock nor concern herself with the time (what was it to her whether Lord Wrotham arrived on time!), and soon found herself successfully immersed in poetry. She didn't even notice Moira enter bearing the tray of dessert and coffee. She tucked her feet in under her and continued reading, content to have her worries subsumed at least for a few minutes in the beauty of Yeats's poems.

"What, no welcoming party?" Lord Wrotham's voice startled her, and she dropped the book in surprise.

"Doesn't anyone knock anymore?" she replied crossly. "I must have words with Biggs. He really should not have allowed you to just barge in here like that."

"Don't take it out on Biggs. I told him not to bother with introductions. I did knock though, you just didn't hear me."

Lord Wrotham crossed the room and picked up the book from the floor. Closing it, he peered down at the title with a smile. "Yeats? Hmm, I would have expected Lord Byron."

"I'm still astonished you can name any poet at all," Ursula replied as she stood up and slipped her feet back into her shoes.

"Your feather is crooked." Lord Wrotham remarked, pointing to her head, and Ursula couldn't help but look over at herself in the mirror that hung above the fireplace. Self-consciously, she tried to straighten the feather band in her hair.

Lord Wrotham walked over and replaced the book on the table. He gazed briefly at the spines of the other books that lay there and smiled again.

"You find my choice in literature amusing?" Ursula asked. When Lord Wrotham did not reply but merely continued to smile, she tossed back her head a little and met his eyes defiantly.

"Not amusing, just surprising," came his reply.

"What brings you at this hour, Lord Wrotham? It's a little late for a social call, isn't it?" Ursula demanded.

"May we first sit down perhaps? Could I even impose on you for some . . . oh, I see you have already requested coffee." He gazed down at the untouched tray, the coffee cold in the pot, and the uneaten trifle. His smile this time was softer but it irritated Ursula all the more.

She rang for Biggs, who entered shortly thereafter.

"Biggs, we would like some refreshment. Perhaps Lord Wrotham would prefer wine to coffee." She turned to look at Lord Wrotham who was just seating himself in the satinwood armchair. "Biggs has decanted a fine Bordeaux, haven't you, Biggs?" Lord Wrotham raised his eyebrows in apparent amusement and Ursula, not so amused, asked Biggs to bring in two glasses. Biggs merely nodded and retreated as Moira hurried in to pick up the tray.

Ursula sat back down on the sofa, crossing her ankles demurely beneath her dress, as she attempted to regain the calmness she wished to portray.

"I came to discuss the question of your allowance," Lord Wrotham coughed. "As trustee of your father's estate, until you are married of course, I find myself in the awkward position of having to ask about your monetary needs."

"You came here to discuss my 'monetary needs,' " Ursula said with a deadpan expression.

"Yes."

"At this hour?"

"Well, what other time was there? I assume you need to purchase spring apparel, and with your, your impending nuptials, I wanted to ensure that you had all the funds you needed for —"

"There aren't going to be any 'impending nuptials,' " Ursula interrupted him sharply.

"I'm sorry, I don't quite understand . . ."

"I told Tom this afternoon that I couldn't go through with it — the marriage I mean. There isn't going be a wedding."

Lord Wrotham opened his mouth but Ursula cut in before he had a chance to speak.

"I decided it was time I asserted my own independence. I plan to take control of my father's business. I'll need your support of course, as trustee of my father's estate, but I've had a long, hard think on it and what would be most satisfying to me, I believe, and honor Papa most greatly would be for me to run them as an independent business-woman."

"I see . . ." Lord Wrotham couldn't keep the note of skepticism out of his voice.

"You think a woman incapable of doing such a thing?"

"You know my politics," was all he replied.

"Your politics hardly serve as an answer to my question. Tell me, do you think I'm incapable of running my father's business because I am a woman?"

"You are also very young," Lord Wrotham commented.

"So was my father."

"That he was, but he had great instincts, and when he was unsure, he was willing to take advice from those he trusted."

"I will accept advice. I may not trust as my father did, but I am not such a fool to think I can run this alone. I will draw upon all my father's advisers. Will *they* accept *me*, though, that is the question? Will *you* accept me?"

"I'm not sure that at the moment you even accept yourself," was his reply.

"Maybe not — but I must face up to my responsibilities."

"What of your plans to be a journalist?"

"I must give them up."

Lord Wrotham sighed. "It seems to me that you give up much to gain possibly nothing. They may never accept a woman. They may never accept you. And your politics . . . How can you reconcile your position —"

"Will you remain as you are?" she asked after a pause.

"As I am?" he queried.

Lord Wrotham got up suddenly and paced across the room. Ursula tried to read his countenance but his expression was inscrutable.

"Yes, as my father's trusted adviser. Will you remain so with me? As trustee of the estate, will you support my decisions? Will you grant me the financial freedom to do what I must for the sake of my father's business interests?"

"I'm not sure I could promise to always agree with your decisions but yes, I will remain as an adviser . . . if that is what you wish me to be."

The question hung in the air and Ursula flushed. The implication was clear. But she wasn't ready to make any commitment, least of all to him. She needed to succeed on her own terms first. If she succumbed now, she feared losing all her newfound independence.

"It is." Her words were quiet, but they seem to echo through the room.

Lord Wrotham stood by the fireplace, his expression still unreadable. Ursula arose and started to approach him. For a moment, as their eyes met, it looked as if he might speak. But he remained silent and Ursula could take little comfort from the manner of his leaving. He merely flipped open his fob watch, commented on the late hour, and then said, with a dismissive shrug of his shoulders, that he had to be going.

"I have to leave for Ireland tomorrow."

"Ireland?" Ursula exclaimed.

"Yes, I am advising counsel on an important trial that begins in Dublin tomorrow." He walked across the room and opened the door.

"But when will you return?" she called out.

"I'm not sure. Hargreaves will let you know when I am back."

And with that he left her standing in the room, wishing he would stay.

TWENTY-THREE

The following morning, Ursula met with Alistair Fenway and Gerard Anderson at the offices of Anderson & Stowe Ltd. in Threadneedle Street. Both men seemed reluctant to accept Ursula's proposal that she involve herself in her father's business affairs. Fenway's suggestion was that Lord Wrotham, as trustee, oversee the sale of her father's mills and factories and invest the proceeds on her behalf. Ursula refused and it took two hours of exhaustive argument before both men came to realize the strength of her resolve. Finally, capitulating to her demands, Anderson drew out a massive account ledger and started to lead Ursula through all the various enterprises that provided the foundation of her father's empire. She ran her finger down the list of Bristish suppliers — all familiar names she'd heard over the years — when a brief notation regarding payment to a German chemical company caught Ursula's eye.

"What's this?" she asked.

Anderson and Fenway exchanged glances.

"I didn't know my father had contacts in Germany. Is it somehow related to the Lambeth factory?"

Anderson rubbed his nose. "Not exactly."

"What is it then?" Ursula demanded.

Anderson turned to Fenway, who, after a hesitation, replied. "Boehrmeyer is a pharmaceutical company. They investigate chemical compounds to see if they have any medicinal use."

"But why should my father be interested in that?"

Anderson sighed. "We were hoping you need never see this. . . ." He pulled out a file from a drawer in his desk. "Read for yourself."

Ursula reached over and took the file. She started to read the correspondence with growing horror. One of the first letters she read was addressed to her father and written in English.

Trials to date indicate that the substance is associated with an 80 percent sterilization rate. The asylum reports, however, that two of the twenty women involved in the trial suffered severe internal hemorrhage and subsequently died. We request your instructions as to whether you wish to proceed with further trials. As we say, the sterilization rate is extremely promising; the question is whether the associated morality rate is sufficiently of concern to halt further commercial development of this substance.

Sufficiently of concern?! Ursula was horrified. So this was the substance discovered on the Radcliffe expedition. Was this what Bates had been talking about all along? It seemed almost impossible to believe that her father had ever considered such an abhorrent plan. She found it hard to reconcile all his contradictions. How could the loving and indulgent father she knew be a man who was responsible for the deaths of two women? Maybe more?

Ursula looked up at Anderson. He refused to meet her eyes and merely gestured for her to continue reading. Fenway got up from his chair and went over to the window. From his profile Ursula could see he was discomfited.

Ursula pored over the remaining correspondence until she found the reply she was looking for. It was in her father's rough handwriting.

Cease all trials immediately. It was my hope that the substance we discovered would provide a means of preventing further degradation of our race but it was *never* intended to be an instrument of death. I cannot in all conscience allow testing to continue.

Ursula hands were trembling as she set the letter down.

"Who else knew of this?" she asked quietly.

Fenway remained by the window.

"We all did. But while Abbott and I agreed with your father, Dobbs wanted to continue further investigations outside Europe — that was the South American enterprise he wanted your father to continue funding."

"Did you or Lord Wrotham know about this?" Ursula directed her question to Fenway. He turned to face her, silhouetted by the light streaming in through the window.

"Neither of us knew anything until your father's death. Obviously, as trustee Lord Wrotham had to be told."

Ursula's mind was awhirl. At least her faith in her father's humanity hadn't been totally destroyed. He certainly wasn't the monster Bates portrayed him to be. Although she had always disagreed with his views on eugenics, she knew his intentions were honorable. He had, after all, been raised in poverty, surrounded by families with too many mouths to feed. But still Ursula's heart sank when she thought of those poor women and the danger posed by such a substance in the hands of unscrupulous men.

"I need some time to absorb all that you have told me," she announced abruptly and rose from her seat. Anderson hastened to grab her coat and hat from the stand in the foyer to his office. Neither he nor Fenway could think of anything to say. They stood by awkwardly as she took her leave.

By the time Samuels had driven Ursula home it was nearly four o'clock. She retired to her room early, sat down at her dressing table, and washed her face with some warm water from the basin. Her reflection in the mirror looked strained and pale. Ursula ran her fingers through her hair. It had grown out a little and now hung in loose curls just below her ears, making her look rather like a medieval pageboy. She reached out and opened the lid of her mother's jewelry box, hoping to find comfort in her mother's memories.

She removed the enamel locket and opened it to look at her father's photograph. In the box she had also placed some of the photographs of her mother she found in the attic and she gazed at each of these, seeking solace in a connection with her mother's past. She carefully replaced these alongside the strand of pearls her father had given her on her fourteenth birthday.

She then lifed out the vermeil rose pendant she had found in the attic, running her fingers along the edge thoughtfully.

There was a knock on the bedroom door which startled her — she dropped the pendant and it slid across the floor, under the bed.

"Come in," she said.

Julia's face appeared in the doorway. "Sorry to disturb you, miss, but Biggs is off visiting his sick mum, and Mrs. Stewart just wondered if you were coming downstairs for dinner. I can bring you up something if you'd rather . . . ?" Julia let the question hang in the air for a moment.

Ursula shook her head. "No need. Tell Mrs. Stewart I'll have dinner in the dining room — but just tea and a little toast will do. I haven't got the appetite at the moment for anything more."

"Right you are, miss."

Julia turned to leave.

"I was thinking I might visit Freddie tomorrow morning," Ursula called after her. "So perhaps you could get my day suit with the fur collar ready."

"Of course, and may I suggest your sable hat and gloves? They will go nicely."

Ursula murmured her assent as she hitched up her skirt and got down on her hands and knees to try to locate her mother's pendant under the bed. It had rolled about halfway under the mattress, just out of reach.

"Oh, miss, please allow me," Julia protested as she rushed to the other side of the bed and knelt down on the floor to retrieve the pendant. She stood up and held it out in her hand. "I didn't know this opened," she said curiously.

"No, nor did I," Ursula said, rushing to her side to find that, to both their surprise, the dainty vermeil pendant had sprung open with the fall, revealing a hidden compartment that contained a photograph.

"Well, you must've — you've a picture of your Mr. Cumberland in there."

"Oh, nonsense," said Ursula as she took the pendant over to the light — and found herself looking at the photograph of a man who was most certainly not Tom Cumberland and not her father, but an incredibly handsome youth, with light-colored hair swept back from his forehead, languid dark eyes, and a mocking smile. Ursula placed the pendant down on the narrow window ledge, her breathing shallow and fast. There was no mistaking it. The man whose photograph had been hidden in her mother's pendant was a much younger, much handsomer Ronald Henry Bates — and without the scars and ruddy beard, he looked exactly like the man who, until yesterday, had been her fiancé.

"Well, if it isn't him, he's the spitting image of Mr. Cumberland, then, ain't he?" said Julia defiantly.

Ursula could barely speak. "It cannot be."

Ursula ran down to her father's study, and rang urgently for Harrison, who was nowhere to be found at this late hour. Lord Wrotham was en route to Ireland and couldn't be reached. And so she sat alone in her father's study, trying to find a sample of Tom's handwriting that she might compare to the tin of letters she'd given to the authorities. She tore through the office files and began laboriously going through the reports and ledgers.

■ ■ ■ ■

The heat from the fire was starting to dissipate, and a cold draft snuck across the room from the window. Ursula reached over and rang the bell. She waited, but there was no response.

"Biggs has one day off and the whole household falls apart," she muttered as she rose to her feet. She shook her head, trying to clear her thoughts, and then made her way out of the study and along the hallway toward the stairs that led to the kitchen.

"Moira!" Ursula called out. "Moira?" But again there was no response.

"Blast!" she said under her breath.

She opened the door to the servants' staircase and called down once more. "Mrs. Stewart!" But still no response. No doubt Mrs. Stewart was asleep in her rocking chair by the stove, a copy of the *Daily Telegraph* in her lap. Cook would probably be sitting up in her bed studying her Methodist Book of Discipline.

The stairwell was gloomy with only the kitchen light to illuminate it. Ursula's stomach rumbled. She had hardly touched her lunch or dinner, and now she was desperate for a nice cup of tea and a slice of

Cook's currant cake.

"Mrs. Stewart?" she called out as she came down the stairs. "Mrs. Stewart?"

The kitchen was deserted. The standard lamp in the corner by the fire cast only a dim light, in which Ursula could see the long table set for tea with Mrs. Stewart's brown teapot, three teacups, and plates, and cake crumbs still scattered on the white lace tablecloth. "Mrs. Stewart?" she called out again.

Ursula could just make out the profile of Mrs. Stewart sitting in her rocking chair beside the fire, her back to her. There was no sign that she had even heard her calling out.

Ursula smiled. Mrs. Stewart really was getting quite deaf these days. She took a couple of steps toward the figure apparently slumbering in her chair before halting. Something was clearly wrong. Ursula suddenly smelled the distinctive pungent scent of his tobacco. It was a scent that was oddly familiar. It took her but a moment to place where she had smelled it before. In Chester Square that night with Winifred. Ursula's skin prickled at the recollection, and she stopped in midstride. She spun around and saw Tom standing in the corner, silent and watchful. Curls of blue-white smoke filtered through the semidarkness.

"I assume you're responsible for this?" Ursula asked, trying to keep her voice calm.

"Don't worry, they are safe. I merely drugged them. It will be a few hours, but Mrs. Stewart here will wake with no recollection of what happened."

"What about everyone else?"

"Julia, Moira, and Bridget are safely asleep in their beds. Your cook unfortunately would not oblige me, so I had to bind and gag her in her room. She was most put out."

Ursula took a slow step backward. Samuels would hear her if she cried out. He normally spent his evenings assembling his stamp collection in his room above the garage behind the main house.

As if reading her mind, Tom said, "I'm afraid the bottle of gin I brought Samuels this evening was a little different — a bit stronger than he is used to. He will have quite a headache in the morning."

Ursula bit her lip.

"I was going to wait until after we were married." He flicked a cake crumb off the table and smiled.

The fire in the grate hissed.

"But then yesterday afternoon, when you informed me we were no longer betrothed, I had to alter my arrangements."

"That is why you killed my father instead of me. You didn't miss when you shot at me — you wanted me alive, you wanted his fortune for yourself. Your father —"

"My father is DEAD!" His dark eyes met hers. "But you knew that already."

Ursula's mind was racing. How could she make it up the stairs and out of the house? How could she raise the alarm?

He was getting close to her now. Ursula stepped back slowly toward the stairwell. She tried to maintain an appearance of calm, all the while trying to plan her escape.

"You'll never get away with it."

"Won't I? They think I'm dead anyway. Found me washed up on the banks of the Thames. Who's to say any different? You? You'll be dead."

"How did you do it?"

"Easy. It's always easy to bribe men who are desperate and don't know any better. The man they found had syphillis and was dying anyway. I merely offered him money and passage to India on the proviso that he pretended to be me. Wasn't too difficult to then stage an accidental drowning."

Ursula's mouth went dry. "But why did you kill them all? Why did you want revenge for your father?"

"You stupid girl. Radcliffe and your father

made fortunes off my father's discoveries and then left him for dead. The substance used to drug Laura was only a fraction of what my father found. And yet they left me and my brother and mother to rot from disease. They destroyed my father's life, and they destroyed mine. The others knew it, too. Abbott. Anderson. Even Dobbs. A conspiracy of silence that has lasted all these years. They should all of them hang for their greed."

Ursula's throat tightened, but she shook her head. "My father would never. . . ." She couldn't finish. She choked and tried to speak again. "Your father was mad. And then he poisoned your mind to think that killing these innocent girls would change everything. He never told you that you'd still be angry — you'll still be alone."

Tom came closer, leaned in, and whispered in her ear. "Your father wanted mine dead, and he gave Radcliffe the order to leave him there."

"No, you're wrong. Your father ruined his own life. He was going to leave you and your mother and your brother. He was in love with my mother. He would have abandoned you no matter what they did."

Tom recoiled, then shook his head as if to rid his brain of all logic.

"It's just as it says in the Bible. As punishment for his sin, his child must die —"

At that moment the telephone rang upstairs. Tom startled as if out of a trance. He stepped away, and Ursula caught sight of the silver edge of a knife blade.

"It will be suspicious if nobody answers that," she said. "You know that."

Tom pointed the knife at her and gestured for her to answer it.

Ursula turned and walked up the stairs. The shrill peal of the telephone continued. She reached the hallway table and picked up the black ceramic receiver. She could feel the point of the knife between her shoulder blades.

"Miss Ursula Marlow's residence," she answered primly.

"Miss Marlow, is that you?" It was Harrison's voice. Ursula was torn between relief and crestfallen that as a policeman he was hardly likely to appreciate the breach in etiquette and realize that something was wrong.

The knife edge nudged sharply in her back.

"Yes," Ursula replied calmly.

"I received a message that you were urgently trying to reach me. . . . What can I help you with?"

Ursula swallowed hard. "Really, it was nothing . . ." She tried to sound unconcerned.

There was a pause before Harrison asked, "Miss Marlow, is everything all right?"

Tom, sensing that Ursula had signaled something was amiss, grabbed the receiver from her grasp and slammed it against the table. It broke into pieces. Ursula held her breath. Tom drew her close to him, his arm curled around her waist, the knife now poised against her throat. "Who was that?" he asked, moving the knife blade closer. A small bead of blood trickled down her neck and onto the collar of her shirt.

"Inspector Harrison," Ursula answered hoarsely.

Tom turned her around to face him. He stroked her cheek with the tip of the knife. "I would have liked to have taken my time."

He drew the knife away, and Ursula seized the opportunity. She gave him a swift knee kick to his groin. Tom doubled over in pain and dropped the knife to the ground. Ursula took her chance and started to run down the hallway toward the front door. Tom flung himself against her from behind, and she stumbled to the floor. The Moorcroft vase on the side table came crashing down. Tom's broad hands were around her throat, his body pinning hers to the floorboards. The weight of his body on Ursula's chest momentarily winded her.

"Shall I strangle you like I did Cecilia?" he whispered in her ear. "She gave no struggle. Like a little bird, she was — one snap to the neck and she was dead."

Ursula struggled against his weight, trying to get free. His grip tightened, and she started to gasp for breath.

"Laura was easy, too. I got great satisfaction from seeing her whore get blamed for it."

"Yes, well, you'll get no satisfaction from me," Ursula spluttered before reaching for a shard of pottery on the floor. She swung it across his face with as much force as she could muster.

Tom screamed out and swore loudly, and his fingers released their grip slightly. Ursula grabbed his hands and tried to pull them away from her throat. As she did so, Tom shifted to regain his grip, and she quickly rolled over, catching him off balance. She scrambled to her feet and hurled herself across the hallway and into her father's study. She tried to close the door quickly, but Tom was close behind her. He leaned in, using his body weight to inch the door open. First he placed his foot in the gap, then his torso. Ursula hadn't the strength to hold him back — the door burst open, and she dashed toward the window. As she did, she caught sight of her father's ivory-handled letter opener still lying on his desk and grabbed it.

They were face-to-face, with only the desk between them. Ursula held the letter opener in her hand. Tom had the knife in his. He smiled before advancing a couple of steps.

"You fight hard," he said. "It is most amusing."

The shrill siren of a Metropolitan Police van could be heard coming closer. Tom's eyes darted to the window. Ursula shoved the desk as hard as she could. It toppled and caught him in the shins. Undeterred, he merely struggled to his feet once more. Just as he was doing so, Ursula seized a leather-bound volume of the King James Bible off the bookshelf and swung it across his face. Tom cried out in surprise before he crumpled to the floor.

Just then the front door burst open, and Harrison and two police constables came running inside.

"Miss Marlow!" Harrison was out of breath and bent over slightly as he stared at her in amazement.

"It seems my previous clashes with the

police taught me a thing or two about defending myself," Ursula commented dryly before her knees gave way and she collapsed to the floor.

TWENTY-FOUR

Ursula awoke to the sound of a delivery van outside her window. She opened her eyes slowly, adjusting to the light. Through the gap between the "golden lily" curtains she could see sunshine streaming in, dappling the parquetry floor in warm pools. A new set of clothes was draped over the Japanese silk screen in the corner of the room and her camel suede shoes laid out under the green upholstered chair. Everything indicated that Julia had been waiting for Ursula to awake.

Ursula sat up slightly in bed before sinking back into the pillows. She felt woozy; her balance was unsteady. She rolled her head to the right and caught sight of a tall brown glass bottle on her bedside table. She reached over gingerly and picked it up. Boots Pure Drug Company Sleeping Draught, read the label. Ursula struggled to sit up. She shook her head to try to clear it.

Her recollections since Inspector Harrison arrived were hazy and insubstantial, no more than ebbs and flows in a diaphanous landscape, washed and pale like a watercolor.

Ursula swung her legs out of bed, sat for a moment to regain her balance, then slowly stood up and pulled on the silk dressing gown that was lying at the foot of the bed. She padded across to the window and, opening the curtains a further inch or so, peered out into Chester Square below. Two men were unloading a wicker hamper from the back of a Fortnum & Mason van. A police constable was standing on the footpath watching. He extinguished his cigarette and called out across the road to a man (who looked suspiciously like Neville Hackett) standing with a notebook in his hand next to a boy in a flat cap setting up a camera and tripod. "Hey! Clear off, the both of you!" the constable yelled, but his words had little discernible impact on either of them.

Clearly the press had got wind of the events of the previous night. Ursula parted the curtains and leaned her head against the windowpane. It felt cool against her forehead. Her silk dressing gown gaped open, revealing the white batiste nightgown beneath. Her dark auburn hair fell across the side of her face. She stood there for a moment not caring if anyone should look up and see her.

"Oh, miss!" Julia's voice rang out from the doorway.

Ursula turned at the reproof in Julia's voice. That was when she saw him. His tall frame filled the doorway. In one hand he carried a green cloth-bound book, in the other a Liberty "Tudric" pewter bowl filled with chestnuts. He stood there stunned, startled as if she had suddenly fallen to earth from the sky. Ursula felt the warm soft light against her shoulders. The chill of the floor beneath her bare feet went unnoticed until she realized, as if awakening, that she was standing before him in nothing but her nightgown, made translucent by the shaft of light from the window. She pulled the silk dressing gown around her self-consciously, a pink flush rising on her cheeks.

"Lord Wrotham." She heard her voice as if from a great distance. "You came back."

The spell was broken.

Julia ushered her quickly back into bed. Lord Wrotham laid the book down on the mantel. "Flowers didn't seem all that appropriate under the circumstances," he said.

"So I brought you my copy of Byron's *Don Juan* and some chestnuts. . . ." He placed the bowl down next to the book. "I'm not sure why, really." He seemed disconcerted.

"Well, what do you give a girl who has just confronted her murderous ex-fiancé?" Ursula replied weakly as Julia fussed around her fluffing the pillows and rearranging the bedcovers.

"Quite."

Lord Wrotham leaned his elbow on the mantel and avoided meeting her eyes. A single lock of dark hair fell across his temple as he bent forward. He frowned and straightened up. In that brief moment, his composure had completely returned.

"How are you feeling?" he asked.

Ursula didn't answer but picked up the glass bottle. "Dr. Bentham, I presume."

"He felt it best to let you sleep."

"How long have I —"

"Two days."

"Two days?!"

"You were not . . . well . . . Dr. Bentham was almost afraid . . ." Lord Wrotham didn't finish. Ursula tried to sit upright.

"What about Tom?"

Julia took the bottle from Ursula and proceeded to mix a small amount in a glass with some water. "Now, miss, Dr. Bentham said you weren't to get agitated. Have another sip. You need to rest. That's what he said."

"Oh, Julia, don't fuss so. . . ." Ursula started to scold, but seeing Julia's look of genuine concern silenced her. She took the proferred glass and gulped the draft down quickly with a shudder.

"I spoke to Harrison this morning," Lord Wrotham answered. "Tom is safely in custody. Now, no more questions! I'm sure Harrison will be around in the next day or so to take your statement."

Ursula sat back and closed her eyes.

Lord Wrotham turned to Julia and asked her to arrange for tea to be sent up. Julia tucked the blankets around Ursula before bustling out of the room (with a dubious glance at Lord Wrotham as she went by).

"How is everyone else — Mrs. Stewart, Moira?" she asked him.

"They have all recovered. I took the liberty of allowing Mrs. Stewart a day off to recuperate with her sister in Hampstead Heath. I'm afraid Moira has left to seek another position, but I managed to convince Bridget to stay, and Julia . . . well, she would not countenance leaving you for a moment."

Ursula smiled weakly. "And Biggs?"

"Returned from his visit to Bournemouth,

and needless to say is mortified. I doubt Biggs will ask for another day off in his life."

Ursula started to laugh, which brought on a coughing fit.

Lord Wrotham started to approach but Ursula waved him off. "Don't worry, I'm not an invalid — I'll be fine. Why don't you bring over that book of yours. Byron, did you say? You're just full of surprises."

Lord Wrotham strode over to the mantel and picked up the book. He hesitated for a moment before turning around and Ursula sensed his mood had altered. He seemed troubled and appealed to her with steady, grave eyes.

"I fear I have let you down," he said in an earnest yet tender manner. "You should not have been left to face Tom alone."

"Well, as you can see I am quite capable of taking care of myself." Ursula realized as soon as she had spoken that her words sounded dismissive, which was not her intention.

Lord Wrotham took a step forward, then recovered himself. His gaze had become guarded and wary.

"I left England," Wrotham continued, his eyes never leaving hers, "not because of any trial in Ireland. I had no business in Dublin at all." He paused. "I left," he resumed slowly, "because I couldn't stand the thought of being in London, of being around you and not . . ."

Ursula's breath quickened. The room seemed to shimmer in the morning light. She felt the color rise in her cheeks.

"Not . . . ?" she prompted him softly.

"Not being anything more to you than the trustee of your father's estate."

He came close to her and knelt by her side, bringing his face level with hers. Like the panther in her dreams, sleek and black, he waited and watched for her response. Ursula raised her chin and met his eyes with the challenge of her own gaze. He reached out and tucked a curl of her hair back off her forehead.

"Love me again?" she asked, in a voice little more than a whisper.

He gripped her arm and replied, with a gaze that mirrored her own.

"Always."

ABOUT THE AUTHOR

Clare Langley-Hawthorne was raised in England and Australia. She was an attorney in Melbourne before moving to the United States, where she began her career as a writer. She lives in Oakland, California, with her family. *Consequences of Sin* is her first novel.

We hope you have enjoyed this Large Print book. Other Thorndike, Wheeler, Kennebec, and Chivers Press Large Print books are available at your library or directly from the publishers.

For information about current and upcoming titles, please call or write, without obligation, to:

Publisher
Thorndike Press
295 Kennedy Memorial Drive
Waterville, ME 04901
Tel. (800) 223-1244

or visit our Web site at:

http://gale.cengage.com/thorndike

OR

Chivers Large Print
published by BBC Audiobooks Ltd
St James House, The Square
Lower Bristol Road
Bath BA2 3SB
England
Tel. +44(0) 800 136919
email: bbcaudiobooks@bbc.co.uk
www.bbcaudiobooks.co.uk

All our Large Print titles are designed for easy reading, and all our books are made to last.